# The Light in Her Window

## Mary Lou Peters Schram

Andrew Benzie Books
Orinda, California

Published by Andrew Benzie Books
www.andrewbenziebooks.com

Printed in the United States of America

First Edition: April 2014

10 9 8 7 6 5 4 3 2 1

ISBN 978-0-9897584-7-5

Cover and book design by Andrew Benzie

*For my friend Richard Brautigan*

*She sleeps this very evening in Greenbrook Castle*
*Without the comfort of a husband*

*And the light in her window is like a wedding ring*
*Shining to the dark and distant woods.*

*from "Rommel Drives On Deep Into Egypt"*
*Richard Brautigan, 1970*

# CHAPTER ONE

When Marian reached the week before her seventieth birthday, she found she was unwilling to turn seventy. Not just unwilling but totally against.

This determination rotated in her consciousness like an airplane propeller gaining speed until it sucked in all the air around it and filled her with a whirling resentment. She had had to put up with a lot in her life. Events had never seemed to turn out as well as she thought they should and many of the goodies that other people seemed to expect in life had not appeared in hers.

She wasn't going to accept this too.

She sat on a slightly rusted $19.99 lounger in her small back patio one sunny morning while she drank cooling coffee and fretted, staring at her one surviving rose bush. Marian had never been much of a gardener; that was Jeb's job.

There was a white rose in her neighbor's yard that seemed to be surviving well enough. Unwilling to ask the neighbor for its name and admit her general ignorance, she had surreptitiously clipped one bloom and taken it to the local rose nursery and bought a bush like it. She had planted it in this sunny corner and sure enough it had ignored her fitful care and prospered right there where she needed it to be. Unlike Jeb's, these small white blooms and graceful branches now spread themselves enthusiastically against the grey wooden fence. All right, one thing had gone right, but she had had to do it herself.

After an hour of drumming her fingers and muttering to herself, Marian got up and went inside for the phone. It was

1

now five years since Jeb's death. The seemingly endless summer of the wine country had only one more month to go. The harvest month, her birthday month, was coming. She wanted to explain all this to her newish friend, Felicia. Felicia, soft-voiced and fluttery, who had never known Jeb, had become the repository of Marian's more difficult feelings.

"I'm not going to do it," Marian said by phone. "I'm not going to turn seventy."

Just because Felicia was willing to listen to new ideas didn't mean she was without opinions. "Well, more power to you, Marian. If you make that work, be sure to tell me how you did it."

Marian sniffed, mumbled a repeat of her words, and retreated to her garden with a new half-cup of coffee, trying to abate her feelings. Maybe she had advanced Felicia to friendship too soon.

"I've never been on a cruise ship," she had complained years ago, not to Jeb but to her sister, Alice, now also dead. "Never stayed in a hotel, just Motel 6 a few times. Never needed a passport."

Of course she and Jeb knew by year two or three that they had made their life harder by marrying when they were only twenty and in their sophomore year at junior college. Nobody had explained then that they were unprepared to earn a living. Jeb's father was dead and his mother lived in a perpetual fog of depression. Marian's parents were constantly at war with each other so their critique was never sought.

Marian couldn't even remember that girl now. The one who had acquiesced to the first man who broke through the careful wall she had built around herself to keep boys away. Jeb had done that by ignoring the wall and coming directly at her, walking her from class to class, talking and smiling endlessly. Once breeched, Marian had had no replacement defenses. Jeb began describing a new life they could share and she was soon hooked.

They grew up in Culver City, home of the first movie

studios, and Jeb's description of their life to be had been a fantasy fueled by Hollywood's version of small town life with comfortable three-bedroom houses on wide streets and a mother who stayed home and cooked in their all-electric kitchen. Their married life didn't turn out like that.

The first baby, Addie, appeared before Jeb had found a way to earn a reasonable income without getting his hands dirty. Marian worked too, as a typist for very little money. In their first five years, they had moved time and again to new apartments which were only marginally better; then the second child, Bro, had been born which meant Marion had to quit and they had no health insurance. Finally they had moved away from Los Angeles and Jeb had gotten into the insurance business and they had acquired their first real house because it came with the job. Then that was taken away. Now. looking back, it had been like an express train with no pause long enough for anyone to get off.

No point in letting all that haunt her now. Just the same it had left Marian with a residue, a cloud of strain and unhappiness floating just above her head.

Finally they had arrived. Jeb was able to retire with a pension and a new house already paid for, after buying his beloved Navigator, a car he had wanted for years. Marian had quit work too. They had paid for, but not yet taken, the cruise to Alaska. For those brief months Jeb had worn an expression of triumph on his face, and he had become rather hard to please, as if he had been the only one who worked all those years. Marian thought he was ignoring her contribution to this achievement. She hadn't found the right moment to say that before his heart seized up and quit.

Maybe that had been his punishment for the sin of pride.

This hard thought opened and then died under the sunshine while the white roses moved gently in the wind, waving their wonderful smell over her. Guilt overcame her. He had worked all those years and he hadn't complained. But... maybe, just maybe, it was Jeb himself who had been the difficulty. If she had chosen someone else, she would surely have had a happier life.

She could hear the doorbell ringing, and stood up suddenly so that her coffee spilled. She had few visitors, especially in a morning. Most likely the garbage man complaining that she had again put her can where the automatic arm on his truck couldn't reach it.

But when she opened the door, it was Felicia, flip-flops on her feet and her fluffy hair barely combed, with an expression of alarm in her wide eyes.

"Don't say things like that so early in the morning. You don't look like you're planning to die."

Marion remembered now that over the years it was friends who had made going on possible. "Don't be silly. Come in. Why do old women have to live alone?"

There was enough left in the coffee pot to pour a cup for Felicia. Marian put the cup in the microwave to heat up.

"You shouldn't take what I say so seriously."

"You sounded pretty serious to me."

They went back out to the patio and Felicia, who seldom sat down the way other people did, perched on a chair opposite Marian.

"It's just that..." Marian started and suddenly that day came back to her.

When it happened, she hardly knew what to do. One moment she was standing staring down at him as his color slowly left. The next she was at the nurse's station signing something, maybe the bill. Almost the very next moment she was standing at the front entrance, outside the double doors that 'whooshed' importantly when anyone entered behind her. She was alone. It had all been so sudden she hadn't had time to call anyone to join her there.

She had driven here, she knew that, but couldn't remember where she had parked the car. After some minutes, she turned and went back inside and asked to use the phone on the Volunteer's desk.

The sign overhead said 'INFORMATION' but that was a misnomer. Even when someone came to the desk with a question, the volunteers, a bevy of pigeons in white hair and pink uniforms, were usually too busy talking to each other to give out any answers.

They hardly looked at Marian. One gestured toward the phone and went back to their twitter.

Marian called Alice, her sister. She apologized because Alice was at work and gave her the news. Alice's voice came over the phone in a screech of alarm.

"Of course, I'll come. But I don't know how soon." She would meet Marian at the house, as soon as she could get someone to relieve her. She couldn't just leave Dr. Felder with no one to help him.

Marian wondered what she was to do till then. She guessed that she was becoming invisible. She went back outside and walked up and down the parking lot till she found her car.

"You know how everything changed when Jeb was gone..." She said now to Felicia.

"I don't know because I didn't know you then."

"Well, they did. It's just as well you didn't know me. The first six months were pure hell. I couldn't do anything that I had been doing for the past forty five-years." There was all the silence she couldn't adjust to. It left her frantic, wore her out. She had tried to explain this to Alice.

Alice had objected. "I didn't notice that Jeb did all that much talking,"

No, he didn't, Marian agreed, but still the absence of his voice dominated her life. Maybe it wasn't the sound of his voice, maybe it was his opinions on everything—they had guided her life all these years.

She found she couldn't fix meals because there was no one to fix them for. When she thought about eating, she would get something out and stand at the sink while she ate it, frequently uncooked.

"Addie came for a weekend several months after Jeb died

and she remarked how my clothes didn't fit me any more. The bathroom scale had been broken for months, maybe since Lilly took a job in Alaska. Anyway Addie coaxed me down to the doctor's office to weigh me and we found I had lost twenty-five pounds. Then Addie took me to Whole Foods and bought some of the ready-cooked food and I found I was ready to eat if I didn't have to cook."

Felicia moved her shoulders in sympathy. "I'm glad I got divorced when I saw everything was going badly. Much easier."

Some time after she had started eating—there was no remembering how much later—maybe a year or two, Marian's friend Bridget, who had never been a close friend, had carried Marian off one night to a book discussion group where they were talking about a book by Alice Munro. Marian hadn't heard anything about Alice Munro because she hadn't been reading book reviews or much of anything else, but after Bridget pressed a copy of the book on her, Marian found it interesting. These stories about life in Western Canada were not at all like Marian's life in Sonoma, California but they had a certain matching bleakness and therefore suited her feelings. By the time she finished that book, she wanted more. That led her to the town library.

Visiting the library also suited her. She had very little money for new pursuits but her days were free and she could drop into the library and pick out a new pile of books on any of the six days the library was open. She remembered now that she had loved reading when she was in college and she had done almost none of it once she began raising children. For a while, books took over her life and began to fill up the silence.

"So that's how you got a new career there?"

Well, it was hard to call it a new career, but yes. Marian frequently queried the library staff on new books and began chatting with them on other subjects and somehow this had led to her working part-time there, and this, although it provided only a little money, gave her an occupation, a focus to her days.

"You look so different," Bridget had said to her one day

when she came into the library and found Marian shelving books.

Marian had touched her hair, which was now short and spiky, and blamed it on Addie. "Every time she comes she tries to do me over."

"And the skirt too. It's very attractive."

The skirt had two layers and the hems were deep zigzags. "Is it? It's so different. All the things Addie likes and buys for me, I can't tell whether they look good on me or not."

Bridget nodded. "You've dropped a whole generation. Good for Addie."

Because this conversation took place only a few feet from the Librarian's office, Marian became embarrassed. "I'm not supposed to get in conversations while I'm working."

But Bridget's approval, because Bridget had disapproved of her thoroughly in the first months after Jeb's death, and now didn't think much of Felicia, had spread warmth in Marian's still aching chest, and released something in her that was nearly like pleasure. It must have been during this period that Marian had started to write down the comments she wasn't supposed to make to customers at the library.

"That's when you started to write?"

"Yes."

Several years before his retirement, Jeb had purchased a computer which they used mostly for checking the weather, or MapQuest, or one-fingered typing to the children. Now Marian took a brush-up course and in the empty evenings, when the current novel she was reading required too much thought, she began to write.

"So that's how you got The Book?" Felicia asked with interest.

"That's it." Marian was not up to describing the whole process that had secured her enough local fame that occasionally near strangers stopped her on the street to tell her how much they enjoyed her book.

She had begun to think that the library might hire her for

more hours and the salary this would give her glimmered ahead of her like a magic lantern. Maybe that was what had brought out the desire to explain things to the library patrons. The library had become her world and it was not a bad world, and endlessly full of voices. Of course she wasn't supposed to give this advice, which was often odd and humorous so she had sat down one silent evening at home and put it all in a short funny book titled "How to Find Things in Your Library." Stu Siskind, the Librarian, had been charmed by it and had Xeroxed copies to give to patrons.

Felicia said: "That's what I thought, that all these things that have been happening to you recently have been good. Then why are you contemplating suicide?"

Marian glared at her. Felicia was not like anyone else Marian knew, which was probably why she was willing to spend time with her. Felicia lived in a way that was incomprehensible to Marian and her friends. Much of every day, Felicia lighted on a chair somewhere and charmed whoever was in the reach of her voice; then at the end of the day she went home to a tumble-down house whose interior she would seldom let anyone see, where the stove and the shower were both usually broken, and the roof badly needed repairing, and wasn't heard from again until she ventured out to some gathering or other and let her gentle voice weave a spell on new people. What little Marian did know about Felicia was that her divorce had cost her almost all her money and she lived on a very small pension left her by an aunt.

"I'm not contemplating suicide. I just want the years to stop for a while now till I feel that I have gotten something back for all the effort I've put out. I don't want to be old till I've done that."

Felicia tilted her head. "Oh? Do we get something back? I'd never thought of that."

"No one else says the things you say!" Marian complained.

With the success of the Xeroxed book, Marian had become something other than 'Jeb's poor widow' and this perception by other people had sunk in. Marian began to think that she might have been capable of doing something like this, only maybe better, twenty or thirty years ago, and had only been prevented by Jeb and the children. Didn't she deserve more time in which to become the person she was meant to be?

Some leaves fell from the maple tree and drifted to the flagstones around them. Yes, many of the vineyards were full of workers already because the grapes were nearly ripe. It was time for leaves to fall.

"I have to hurry. There's lots to do. I have another book in mind. That first book was too simple minded."

Felicia sighed. "But people liked it. Well, forget that. I think you should write another book. But you know, there's no changing your life. Some of those ways—men's lives, women's lives—have been set for thousands of years, maybe more."

"Back to cave men, you mean? Well, I can change my own life, can't I? I don't know how but I deserve it."

Felicia stood up, re-balanced herself and sat again, this time with one leg curled under her. "It was too bad about Jeb. And you didn't even get to take the trip to Alaska. I can't blame you for wanting him back."

"No, I don't want him back. That's all past now. I want something new. I'm not even sure what." Marian threw the cold coffee out on the dirt under the rose bush and stood up, determined to do something critical today, whatever it was.

"I think I'll dye my hair. There's a color I've been thinking about."

Why not? Her hair was exactly the same gray as that of many of her friends. How boring that was, and how clearly it announced her stage of life. There was one color she had only seen once, somewhere in San Francisco months, maybe years ago. It had stayed in her head. An unusual color for hair. A sort of maroon, or purple. If one hairdresser could do that, surely another one could copy it.

Felicia stood up with her. "That's all okay. Start another book, dye your hair. I pronounce you okay for today. I think you'll make it through the week… and to seventy. But call me tomorrow morning."

Marian thought to herself—and then I'm going to give a party, a huge party, everyone I ever knew. All the people I wanted to see again and never got to.

# CHAPTER TWO

Marian had planned that when her hair got to a satisfactory shade halfway between maroon and purple she would turn her attention to the party.

However, this first event hadn't been quite so easy as she had imagined. That was always true, wasn't it? She had had to talk to four different hairdressers to find one that was willing to consider the color she described. This one was in San Rafael. Not terribly far away but she had to take a bus because she didn't trust her old car for that distance. André was not as expected either, a big, frowning man who wore eye make-up and motorcycle boots. But, thankfully, he wasn't hung up on whether or not that color would suit Marian. He looked her over, making Marian aware of the wrinkles around her eyes and the faded, washed-out condition of her clothes, then shrugged and said: "Whatever you want, doll!"

He chopped it off, leaving the remainder so short that Marian wanted to cry but said nothing. Then it took several attempts to get the color to set. By the time she left the shop, she was limp with exhaustion and refused to look in the mirror.

The next morning at home when she did look at it, she was struck with wonder. He had captured a color she had never seen before. She was not up to going outside but spent the day looking in the mirror every ten minutes, getting used to it. It was not till dinnertime that she had to admit that if it was not the color she had asked for—she began to have trouble bringing that color back into her mind—it satisfied all the requirements she had set for it. And, if you got used to it, it was probably all right. It made her skin look pinker—was that good? Her eyes stared back at her, big and dark in her pale face.

Would lipstick help? Should she try to find a lipstick that matched the hair? No. Let it go. Prettiness was gone. That was fine, what she wanted. Prettiness had been gone for several years. The hair made it irrelevant.

By the next morning, she was ready to be seen. She told Felicia this about prettiness being gone by phone.

"I'll come right now."

Was Felicia alarmed or just curious? What if she thought it was terrible, that Marian shouldn't be seen like this? André had said, if she didn't like it, she could put a dark brown rinse on it and take the fiery aspect out. Marian had taken her courage in hand and said: 'Not after I just paid this much for it.'

Felicia stared at her a long time, longer than made Marian happy. "My Lord, is that what you wanted?"

Marian winced. "Exactly. People will forget the gray after this, won't they?"

Felicia considered, twisting a strand of her own straw-colored hair and putting it in her mouth to chew over, while Marian reflected that Felicia was really a very conventional person. "I think you will be known all over town as that woman with the purple hair."

"Good," Marian said. That was what she had wanted. That was a whole lot better than 'old woman' or 'poor little widow', or 'My God, what happened to you.'

"Maybe you should try it with a purple dress."

Marian shrugged. New choices about clothes rested on one's ability to spend money. She had very little and had just spent all she could spare on the hair. She had abandoned the whole idea of spending money after Jeb died.

"I'm almost used to it already. Would you like some coffee? I need to set a date for the party."

Looking at the calendar, she decided on the fifteenth, six weeks away. If she left a couple of weeks to find addresses and get invitations out; then there would be some time for people to make up their minds to come.

"Will you help me with looking up addresses and writing out the invitations?" she asked Felicia.

"Of course," Felicia said, "But I'm on my way to the Farmer's Market." And she looked so uneasy and left so quickly that Marian gathered she would not get much help in that direction.

Marian got out her bike, an old bike which had been left in the garage by one of Lilly's friends, while she thought over the invitation list. She rode the bike up to the Clubhouse to see Elinor, the half-time secretary of Shady Acres.

"I want to rent the Clubhouse on October fifteen. The afternoon and the evening."

Elinor was the first person after Felicia to see the hair. She had trouble turning her narrow, horsy face away from Marian's head. She waited for long minutes for some explanation which didn't come. Marian waited her out. She knew Elinor prided herself on being up on whatever was happening to any of the residents. Any explanation that Marian gave now would be repeated to the next fifty people Elinor talked to. Marian was not going to supply this entertainment.

"What do you want it for? Are you getting married again?"

Marian fixed her with a level-eyed stare that froze the question in the air until it exploded with a small 'pop' like very thin glass and the fragments dissolved like soap bubbles. Elinor needed to realize she wasn't entitled to her air of authority. She was only another Shady Acres homeowner who couldn't live on her social security and had therefore agreed to take on this lowly position, a position which mostly involved listening to the complaints of the other residents and making notes on them.

After a while, Elinor blinked her eyes slowly, and gave up waiting for an answer. "I just wondered. I know it wouldn't be a 50th wedding anniversary or a memorial service either, would it?"

That would be a low blow if Marian wasn't over mourning Jeb, but she was. She ignored this jab and concentrated on her objective. It was well worthwhile. The Clubhouse, a large Gold Rush-era mansion was very handsome and the rental price for residents was quite low. It wasn't often rented, perhaps because the adjoining grounds and swimming pool remained open to all residents. People feared that, after they had paid rent and bought refreshments, this might not keep other residents from popping indoors to join the invited guests and helping themselves to whatever was being served. Which had happened before... the uninvited had stood around gawking at the party while they munched on free goodies and criticized the guests at the same time.

Marian had decided she didn't care about this. She looked over the wide porch shaded with ivy and the lawn which included huge California oaks and 50-year-old rose bushes planted by some early settler who had guessed that this area was Paradise for roses... they went half wild and stayed in bloom eight months a year.

Let the noseys come in and look. She had not given any parties in Shady Acres, even when Jeb was alive, except for a few Thanksgiving dinners for the children. She was not in any House Beautiful or Gourmet competitions. "Just a party."

Elinor couldn't stop herself. "Are you going to have over two hundred? The Fire Department allows two hundred people but only if they aren't all inside."

"Probably not. But if I do, will someone come by and count them?"

"I don't know." Elinor's permed hair was beginning to stand up in odd shapes. She patted her forehead with her balled-up handkerchief.

Marian was pleased at being more difficult than usual. She had to be humble when she was working in the library so it was very pleasant to be on the other side. She knew Elinor was afraid to say what the Association would do because there were six people on the Board and they seldom agreed on anything.

"Tell them two hundred. If more show up, I can just say they weren't invited. Or that I'm so old I have trouble counting."

It was an over-fifty-five community and rife with references to poor memory but Elinor ignored this little joke.

"I'll write down one hundred and fifty. If it's any more than that, I'll say you didn't tell me. What kind of party should I say it is?"

But Marian was not to be flushed out so easily. She stared blankly at Elinor and sailed out after putting down five dollars to hold the reservation. She would pay the rest after she got her pay from the library.

Next she needed to ask a large favor from Bridget.

Most of the houses in Shady Acres had been built at the same time and from the same three plans but, over the years those with slightly bigger lots and better views had been added onto and amplified by various owners until they were worth twice that of the unimproved ones, and looked it. Bridget had one of the most valuable ones. The living room had been doubled in size. The exterior was painted in dark blue with dark red trim, New England colors, selected by a decorator. Probably Bridget was rich, but few people resented this fact because she was generous as well as friendly.

Marian rode her bike past Bridget's house and kept going. She had had an attack of nerves. The bike was ancient—the kickstand was loose and rattled and the bell dinged every so often, making her feel like an impoverished paperboy. She rode around the block and then came back. After Jeb died, Bridget had tried to help Marian with her finances and Marian had behaved badly and only made it up later. She would hate to lose this friendship.

"Is it for Halloween?" Bridget asked, looking at Marian's hair before she had even opened the screen door.

"No. The hair is for me. I needed a change."

Bridget considered this with friendly interest. "It *is* a change. Was it expensive?" Knowing exactly how little money Marian lived on, Bridget worried more about Marian's finances than Marian did.

"No. I suggested he might photograph it, you know, as a

sample for his book in case anyone else wanted to try it, and he agreed. Bridget, would you be willing to furnish the wine for a party? I know you have a winery friend. I thought maybe I could do your typing and filing for several months."

Bridget ushered her in. "What a nice offer. How much wine do you need?"

"Enough for one hundred people."

Bridget couldn't help blinking in surprise. "That's quite a party. "

"I know that's a lot. But many of them will be older women."

"Meaning only half a glass. But some will surely be boozers."

"That's true. I know it's a lot to ask. I will owe you a large favor. Since Jeb died, I haven't even had people to dinner. I need to throw a party."

Bridget nodded in sympathy. It was always hard for her to say no. "I'll ask Augusto what he has too much of. He may be ready to clear out some space with the new harvest coming in. And I'm sure he'll take back whatever isn't opened. What is the party for?"

"My non-birthday."

"Ah." Bridget nodded and waited for more but Marian didn't add anything. She was trying to remember if Bridget was over seventy and would therefore understand or was she younger and wouldn't.

Bridget smiled. "I haven't known you to throw a party before."

Marian launched into a description of the plans so far, and Bridget became charmed. She offered to also borrow from Augusto those plastic stemmed glasses that wineries used when they hosted big parties. Augusto had cases of them but hated using them because he thought they ruined the taste of the wine.

Marian contemplated the plastic stemmed glasses with not much enthusiasm but how could she refuse? "I hope you're going to be in town. You and Norm are number one on my guest list."

"Yes. I'll be here and Norm should be back by then. Would you like for me to bring flowers? I should have a lot of mums left. And maybe there will still be some snowballs."

"That would be wonderful. Thank you so much."

Marian turned her mind next to invitations. Invitations might be something of a financial problem. Marian's email list—people she had corresponded with in the last few years including those who could be found on the library's computer, people who, therefore wouldn't require paper and postage—was not a long list. The big list she had in mind was of people from further back in her life, people she hadn't seen for years, and for them she would need to use the mail. How to pay for this?

When she asked Felicia, Felicia replied: "There's always ESP."

Marian suspected she was being made fun of. She used a little ESP—concentrating on telling Felicia to go home, and sure enough Felicia drifted out. After which Marian felt a little guilty, but not too much.

Which left the problem unsolved. A problem which grew as she lay in bed that night. Now that her plans were forming, names came to her mind every day. She only had to pick a time in her life and names of people she had liked but never seen again blossomed forth without effort.

Faces came first. The further back she went, the more easily she saw the faces or heard the voices, as if all those people had been standing impatiently in the back of her mind waiting to be recalled. Every time she sat down or paused in some task she would select a time or place and the faces and voices would come to her, almost demanding to be put on her list. Soon she had sixty names covering three pages of her lined pad.

A voice or a nickname would be fine if she was using ESP, but for addresses where they could be reached, she needed something more. For this she had the battered dresser in the garage where she kept cleaning supplies and also tossed old address books. It had seemed a little silly when she began keeping them years ago, before she and Jeb even had a house of their own. When someone went out of your life, that was usually it. She moved or they moved to another town and made new friends there and there was never enough time to keep up the old. Or so she had thought, but her heart must have disliked giving them up.

She went to the garage and saw that some boxes left from Lilly's last move were now blocking the dresser including the upper right hand drawer, the one she wanted. Was Lilly ever going to come back and get them? Her youngest child was a mystery to Marian. She was now in the Aleutian Islands, working in a health care clinic.

With some effort, Marian was able to carry the boxes to another corner, getting dust down the front of her white t-shirt. But when the boxes were moved and the upper right hand drawer opened, she was rewarded. The books were all there, back all the way to high school, waiting all along for another chapter in these friendships.

She opened the one from high school first, wondering if she could still reach any of those people. They might be all over the world by now. The first name she saw was Howard Draggett and she felt a sharp wound. Howard would not be coming. Howard had died only a month after they graduated, hit by a car from behind one evening when he was riding his bike home from a summer job at the swimming pool. He had promised to take her to a movie and they had even planned which movie and Marian had been waiting every evening, even that evening, for his call.

After hearing the news of his accident, Marian had shrugged and refused to cry. She was sure Howard's death would make no difference in her life. There were other young men who took her to the movies in those long, warm evenings after his death but that small pain, its distinct spot in her chest, had never gone away. The night he died, because she hadn't heard the news till the next day, she had gone to bed thinking 'maybe tomorrow.'

The surprise of that, the first sudden interruption of Fate telling Marian and her friends that their dreams of the adult life to come might have little relation to real events, had shadowed her next years. Marian had been shaken and only slowly got back her defiance, and even then sometimes it rang hollow to her own ears.

Those were the years of the Draft and a large American army stationed in Germany in case of war with the Soviet Union. The Korean War was over and Vietnam had not yet started so many of the young men in high school welcomed the Draft because they hoped to get the GI Bill. But what if the world could reach its nastier fingers in some way into their sunny Los Angeles life pictured prettily in movie after movie? After Howard's death, the small ordinary details of Marian's life which had seemed so stifling as she waited daydreaming for his call looked like an island of safety.

Now she had lived through all those years of her life till there was the greater shock of Jeb's death, and she was able to wonder—was it sadder or happier for your life to end when you were still hopeful and full of fairytales like Howard, or was it better to stay to the end like Marian was, when all events seemed shaded by sadness?

"This may be harder than I expected," she said later to Felicia, but not because she wanted to talk about Howard... what was the use of it now.

"Tristesse," Felicia said. She had waited, with no particular expression on her face, for Marian who stood before her with a handful of old address books. When Marian didn't respond but continued to look into space, Felicia floated to a window and looked out, gaining a glimpse only of the silvery leaves of Nandina which half covered the window. She sighed loudly, as she had been doing frequently at Marian's recent moodiness.

"What's that?"

"Sadness without any reason."

She seemed about to expand on this subject, but someone else invaded Marian's mind. "Wait."

"What is it?"

Sure enough, someone else had made an appearance. Marian smacked her forehead hard to hold him there. "Billy Whitlock, that's someone I want to see. To find out how he turned out."

"Who's he?"

"He was in my fourth grade class, the class clown, always in trouble but I think I had a crush on him. Scolding never touched him, I loved that. He had the prettiest eyes, with long lashes, and he used to steal looks at me and wink just when he was being accused of all sorts of crimes by the teacher."

Felicia rolled her eyes. "Marian, how are you going to find someone you knew in fourth grade? Did you realize how many years that has been? He could have changed his name. Or be in jail. Or more likely dead."

Marian reached for something to mop her eyes. "Don't say things like that. What if all these people I want to see again are already gone?"

Felicia was immediately sorry. "What is all this? I didn't mean to upset you."

But Marian couldn't answer. She shrugged helplessly. Tears began to trace their way down her cheeks and she had no idea why. What was there about that memory that had triggered tears? "I'm sorry. Don't go. It's just something foolish."

"What did I say? Just that he might be dead. But isn't that true?"

"I don't really know."

"What happened with him? How could it be important when it was the fourth grade?"

"You're right." Gently Marian prodded her memory which did not elicit much more than the first image of Billy and his thick lashes and sideways smile. Was this whole enterprise of finding old friends going to be full of tears? "Not that I can remember."

Felicia was upset as well. "I need to get back and wash my dishes. I'll call you in an hour or so."

Did Felicia have someone she mourned? She had never told

Marian anything like that. "All right. We'll talk then."

After she left, Marian attacked her own kitchen, cleaning off the counters and putting away the butter and jam and the plate on which she had buttered her toast. She remembered the vitamins she was supposed to take and took them for a change. Felicia was right. How could she find Billy? How much chance was there that he was still in Culver City, a dusty city, more a starting point than a destination, steeped in illusion since Harry Culver had opened a real estate office to sell small pieces of empty land he had inherited, and then had invited the Ince Film business to set up a studio. And as a consequence, Harry married a film actress and became a promoter of the new business. What year had that been? Before she was born. Or was that whole account only a story, another publicist's fantasy to give the lives in this backwater more meaning?

As she puttered, an idea returned. She had been trying to think of who could help her find all these old friends and she remembered that Letty, Bro's wife, was out of a job right now and frantic with her lack of something to concentrate on. Or at least she had been when Marian had talked with her on the phone a week or so ago.

Letty was all right, Marian told herself for the hundredth time. Letty reminded Marian of a termite. Once she was set on a task, she kept silently nibbling away until she brought down a house, or at least finished off a wood beam. She had no quarrel with the girl, only found her lacking in sparkle, meaning what? Imagination? Mother-in-law and daughter-in-law was never an easy relationship but Marian had been very glad that someone was willing to take on the responsibility of Bro so that she didn't have to do it anymore.

If Letty was still unemployed, Marian had the perfect job for her; it would involve all the things that Letty was good at— organizing information, making lists and finding out things on the Internet.

She abandoned the kitchen, almost but not quite cleaned up, and took her address books to the desk in the spare bedroom which Jeb had used for paying bills. A short time later Letty answered the phone. Yes, she was still without a job and was therefore fretful. She had been contemplating getting into Ancestry.com but was not all that interested in knowing about her ancestors, only enticed by the prospect of lots of research.

"I can do that," Letty enthused. "Find your friends! You wouldn't believe how many ways there are to look for them. Send me the list with the date and the address where you last saw them and where they went to school or worked. And if they had changed their names once. If they're still alive, I'll find them."

"I'll mail it. Don't spend any money," Marian warned her.

"Oh, they're still alive." But Marian began to wonder. How could she be sure? "Don't spend any money." Letty and Bro were much more free-spending than Marian.

"Don't worry about that." Letty sounded anxious to get off the phone and start the job right now.

After this conversation, which had turned out to be much more agreeable than most of her conversations with Letty, Marian thought she was ready for a glass of wine and a new crossword puzzle. However, it was almost three, and at three she was due in the library for a four hour shift. She would not get dinner and wine till nine o'clock.

Changing her clothes hurriedly and getting out her bike again, she was confronted by the thought that if she was about to turn seventy, most of the people in her past would be about this age. And not everyone made it this far. How many of them would be already gone, maybe like Howard, for many years?

Was this whole task going to be an exercise in futility, a lesson in the shortness of life, a sly way for God to tell Marian her life was nearly over?

September in Sonoma was hot and quiet. Frequently bunches of grapes began not to wait for careful pickers to wield knives against their stems but burst their skins with the happy sigh of a woman pulling off her Full Control panty hose and letting her flesh expand into its real but ugly inches.

This seventieth September, the white rose bush in Marian's patio chose this year to go into a snit and refused to put out any more blooms. When she sat outside with her morning coffee cooling, leaves floated down around her, explaining to her that it had been a dry summer and that while the grapes were ready, autumn was coming on fast and her party-to-end-all-parties could easily be a disaster.

She had paid the rental cost of the Clubhouse and Bridget had secured the promise of the wine but the addresses were still not ready. Letty reported she was working away, turning half-remembered names into living people but her progress was slow. Some days she would boast of an old friend finally located and then within a day, had to report that it was the wrong person. The country was full of like names. Bonnie was one of those still not found.

Maybe by now Bonnie was still the same person she had been those long years ago in New York, Marian had thought, and would finally be willing to venture to the West Coast. That way, Marian could repay the long-ago kindness by showing Bonnie the delights of California and finally their friendship would blossom without needing the two men.

However, this was a name that refused to be found.

Marian could not help communicating this disappointment to Felicia. "I don't know why I want to bother with all these people. They haven't made any effort to see me."

Felicia responded the way a friend should. "They have probably wanted to see you all along and just didn't get to it."

"Well, I wish they'd try." In spite of her own words, Marian was calmed for the day and went back to her address books looking for other names on which she might pin her expectations.

# CHAPTER THREE

The evolution of Marian's writing career in greater detail.

In the first year after Jeb's death, when Bridget, seeking some change in Marian's grief, had first taken Marian to the library and recommended several authors she might like, Marian's evolution from mourner to reader came about slowly. Every day or so, she went into the library and scanned a new shelf waiting for a title or an author to jump out at her. And every day when she went home, there were two or three books bouncing around in her bicycle basket. She had long ago given up crocheting, and she couldn't watch television because Jeb wasn't there to watch it with her.

She buried herself in the books—mostly novels but nonfiction too—whatever she had picked up with curiosity—and she often read a whole book through in a night. It was a strange sensation as the happenings in novels replaced the happenings in her life, and the effect was to make her more cheerful. She did not want to think about Jeb, either his death, or what was worse, the long years she had spent with him. Fictional events were both happier and sadder but were also thronged with people she could like and the wider possibilities of lives other than her own.

She tried Jane Austen because nearly everyone spoke well of her. That was not Marian's reaction. How empty those young women's lives were while they sat around waiting for someone to propose to them! When she said that to Bridget, Bridget told her she might like Charles Dickens better. And she did. Plenty of books to choose from, and all of them full of activity, odd characters, severe hardships—mostly stemming from lack of money. Being poor in Dickens' time was a whole lot worse than being poor in Sonoma where the sun shown a lot of days and there were some helping hands like the Meals on Wheels. But the way people then treated children! It was good that the world had gone on from there.

When she couldn't take any more abandoned or dying children, she tried American fiction instead, picking up books by names that she thought she had heard of, and found life more familiar though not as eventful as Dickens. Hawthorne was not to her taste. Nor was Melville. Strictly men's books. There were lots of newer American novels. She liked writers who had a long list of books to work through. She read Joyce Carol Oates for a while, mesmerized but often chilled by the end of the book. Mark Twain was fun but mostly aimed at men or boys.

When she said this to Jacqueline, another library worker, Jacqueline recommended her favorite reading—romances. Look, there was a whole section of them and they were always optimistic, promising to end happily, leaving the reader feeling good. Marian went through ten of these—being careful to pick different writers so she would be fair.

"Ugh," she said to Jacqueline. "Don't you get bored? They're all alike."

After that, she turned curiously to all the 'fact' books she handled and shelved. Starting with brand new books recommended by the newspaper reviewer, she read about politics and government. Each book had its own reading list. What a lot there was in the world that she had no notion about at all! There was plenty going on in the country. The world too. And of course, some of this was nonsense. What exercised her most was reading at length about how to solve a particular problem, and then when she followed the newspapers, she would find that the problem hadn't been solved by this book or any others, but had changed shape. When she got to this idea, she wanted to bounce some of the things she read off the mind of someone who read more widely than Bridget.

The only one she could think of was Stu Siskind, the Head Librarian. The trouble with this was that by the time she reached this point, he had become her employer.

This had happened easily, without trauma. She was there nearly every day and Siskind noticed her and began to speak to her. One day she complained that it took a long time for a book to get back on the shelf after it was returned.

"We're short of people!" he said tartly.

"That's not a big job. I could do that," she replied.

"Then I'd have to pay you."

Marian had meant she would do it as a volunteer but the next time she was in, Siskind offered her twelve hours a week at minimum wage.

"They won't let me employ a volunteer," he explained.

The difference this small amount of money made in Marian's life was astonishing and therefore made her extremely nervous. Siskind was short and energetic, had short, curly red-blonde hair and wore glasses with very large lenses as if he wanted to make sure he didn't miss anything. When he looked at her, she always thought he was estimating how they could get along without her.

He looked blank at her latest request. "You want something to read? Okay, try this." And he handed her a newish book—*A Short History of Nearly Everything*.

This book took her considerably longer than one night, and afterwards, she began to think that the world was full of interesting ideas. And maybe they only had to be ideas, not factually true. If so, she could pick up nearly any book and find something in it worth learning or else laughing about. Her general level of enjoyment went up after this book. She began to try all sorts of books, becoming an explorer in an enormous universe.

In another six months, she wanted badly to tell other people about the delightful things she was learning. But who would be interested in what she had to say?

"The library is good for all sorts of purposes. Probably you can't find a date for next Saturday night, but you might find how to end the quarrel with your best friend. *The Habits of Successful People* will show you how destructive quarreling is." she wrote one evening on Jeb's computer which had had very little use since he died. Going on in this vein, she soon had more than fifty pages.

Ten times a day she was confronted with her poverty. Could this be solved by selling the book? Rather than asking outright for this, she had taken it all, now sixty pages carefully typed, to Stu Siskind, and asked him if this was a possibility. Instead of laughing at her, he had been at first curious, then interested. He liked that it was a kind of book. After several days of thinking, and without getting into the fraught subject of money, he had the manuscript Xeroxed and offered to library patrons for the sum of 25 cents. Marian had been very nervous about this, sure that people who knew her well, like Bridget for instance, would be scornful at her presumption in writing advice.

Instead Bridget herself who was one of the first patrons to pick up the manuscript and read it, had been delighted and praised Marian for this effort. And then someone from the town newspaper read it also and, wanting an item for her gossip column had recommended it and soon the copies were all gone.

"Why don't you give me a slightly longer version?" the Siskind said and Marian agreed. This time she tried to extend her concept into more books, more areas of interest. More anxious than ever, she found this once-playful occupation harder work.

She included some useful comments that library patrons had made to her, and she added her own sharp-tongued opinions, the kinds of things she said to Felicia which made Felicia laugh, and these she attributed to patrons, without naming them of course. (Quote: "Why is this woman so excited about sailing away with her lover on a pirate ship? I'll bet there are no other women with the pirates and she will end up doing everyone's laundry.")

After months of effort and full of doubt, she left a ninety five-page version on Stu's desk and then fled to the Ladies Room, her hands shaking at her temerity. What if he disliked it, thought it was worthless. Would he fire her?

The next time she saw Siskind, he nodded at her but said nothing. It was Jacqueline who told her that Stu had made some corrections, had her type them in, and then sent this manuscript out to Kinko's to be copied and, this time, bound.

Bound? Marian felt as if she had been struck by lightning. Many of the bits she had written were exactly the kind of comments which made both Addie and Bro scold her as mean-spirited and cruel. Marian had to go home and lie down and try to get back her accustomed place in the world.

It was two days before she could get up the nerve to ask Stu in a wavering voice "Did you like it?"

The Librarian rolled back on the balls of his feet and looked up at Marian who was a foot taller. "Interesting!" he said finally. "We'll have to talk about it one of these days."

This talk had not yet taken place although Marian now saw her manuscript, bound in a cheerful yellow cover, stacked by the desk where books were checked out. They were for sale for a dollar each. Very shortly there were many patrons who had paid the dollar, or who were waiting to pay it because the stack had all been sold and Kinko's was already printing a new batch.

Marian forgot about the promised conversation with Stu and went to bed many nights with a smile because she had been stopped on the street that day by someone she hardly knew, and congratulated on her book.

# CHAPTER FOUR

How had Marian and Jeb happened to marry when they were both so young?

It was spring in Los Angeles. The blossoms and the bulbs had come and gone by the end of March and the flowering bushes were growing at a fiery pace. The question that dogged Marian was—why her life wasn't more like Natalie Wood's. She had the same long, thick dark brown hair, and her long, shapely legs were the equal of Natalie's. But the drama in her own life paled by comparison with Natalie's. Or at least in the parts Natalie played in the movies. If she haunted the streets that were mentioned in the Hollywood gossip columns, would her life begin to resemble Natalie's?

She had been resisting Jeb's advances for some months after she noticed them (they had probably been going on for some months before she became aware of them). When she did begin to notice him, it was mostly irritating and then somewhat amazing. She saw him everywhere at school. Their sophomore year at Santa Monica Junior College was nearly over and moments when he impacted her attention became constant. When they met, their words became brief, brusque, hardly worth the time it took to say them. Nevertheless, these harsh, staccato meeting became the focal point of their days. Before she knew what was happening, Marian had reached that point where her body became something entirely different whenever he came within a few feet of her.

What was he up to? He was waiting for a 'yes' from her without specifying what would follow that word. Marian was so apprehensive that she wondered if she could finish her exams at all. She went to bed at night praying for some alternative that she could assent to.

Then he called her one evening, which was a surprise. They had never talked on the phone before that. He was full of excitement. An old friend of his was now living in New York City and they had just talked by phone. New York was a kick according to Bill. Jeb should see it. Bill offered to put Jeb and Marian up while they got started. They could go to New York and have a honeymoon plus a totally new life.

A honeymoon! They hadn't even talked about getting married yet. Marian's stomach began producing little bubbles. The possibilities of New York burst forth in her mind like the overnight blossoming of a pillowy bush of honeysuckle.

"Go to New York married?"

She had not thought up to this moment if he would even propose an evening out. Marriage hadn't occurred to her, but here it was. Images of weddings from Paramount and MGM filled her vision. The bride was in white satin coming down the aisle in a huge church filled with flowers and beautifully-gowned guests. The line of bridesmaids in pastel ball gowns equaled the line of groomsmen in tuxedos.

And New York besides! She knew suddenly that she was tired of dusty Los Angeles. This town where she had always lived was nothing but endless strip malls, one after another, with the neat neighborhoods of small stucco houses hidden behind them; the only interesting places to go, like the ocean or Griffiths Park, always at least an hour away.

"You mean get married and then go to New York?"

"We can stay with him till we get jobs. Yes, sure, get married!"

"By when?"

His voice quavered as if he was just thinking about marriage for the first time. "School's almost out." His voice strengthened as he got onto subjects he had thought out before. "And I've got enough saved for the bus tickets."

"We're taking a bus all the way across the country?" Some of her delight took a jolt. Only lower class people took the Greyhound.

"Yes. The plane is too expensive and so is the train."

"We could drive."

"Bill says we won't want a car in New York. Besides I'm not sure mine would make it three thousand miles. But this way we'll see the whole country." His voice took on a pleading note. "I've never done that. Have you?"

"No."

There was more along this line as they began to envision this amazing prospect. Marian sat down on the steps with the phone. She thought that she was much more practical than he was. Was he really going to do this? Marriage? Go off together leaving their families behind? If he would do it, she would do it too.

As they got further in to the practicalities, she heard his voice become stiff with shame. One of the few things she knew about him was that the money he earned working after school he gave to his mother to buy food.

"Can you get enough money from your folks to tide us over? Just till I get a job. A couple of hundred would help."

Marian was retreating to the country of doubt. Money was not a comfortable subject at home. The war between Shirley and John, her mother and father, almost always began with the lack of money for something her mother wanted to do. Currently Shirley was complaining that the living room couch was disgraceful and needed replacing. Any mention of this brought on instant scorn from John. How could they spend money on something so unnecessary when he needed new tires on the car? Marian was grateful that Grandpa Frank paid her small fees at Santa Monica City College or there would be quarrels over that too.

"Wouldn't your brother send you something?" she asked Jeb.

"Do you know what privates get paid? Hardly anything."

As soon as the momentous phone call was over, Marian

announced the wedding and that became a Mt. Etna before the subject of New York was even mentioned.

Shirley and John exploded in rare unity. Marian was too young; who was Jeb anyway? Wasn't he Seventh-day Adventist?

"No," Marian said. He wasn't, and she was plenty old enough. Besides she was in love. Wasn't that when people got married? But Shirley waxed into violent negatives and went to bed with a headache, while John stomped out of the house and stayed out till late. Marian was afraid to bring the subject up again but Jeb urged her on. They had to set a date before Bill changed his mind.

Gritting her teeth, she waited several days and raised the subject again in a small voice, which started another quarrel so quickly that Marian was half convinced they would have to go to New York to get married there. She told Jeb this by telephone but he objected. That was not the proper way to start their life. The possibility of not going to New York never occurred to either of them.

Marian's sister Alice agreed to help. Although a year younger, she had had more success in opposing the parents. Actually, she rather liked all the turmoil. She brought a calendar to the dinner table one evening and announced that Marian had to pick a wedding date. Why not the seventeenth, the Saturday right after school ended?

Nervously, Marian opened her mouth and agreed about the date. There were immediate loud objections from both Shirley and John. Arguments broke out between the two and neither Marian nor Alice could get a word in for quite a while. However the date was not being argued about. It looked as if nothing else about the wedding was agreed upon but at least the date was set.

When the day was only two weeks away and Marian was afraid they would have to marry in City Hall, she brought Jeb over one evening, warning him to not be dismayed and with Alice's help the wedding was hastily arranged although quarrels and accusations rained down on all three of the young people.

The minister of the Baptist Church up the street agreed to marry them, at Marian's house rather than in the church since they were not members of his congregation. Shirley and John reluctantly agreed to a simple reception at the house after the ceremony. Alice was energized at this progress and offered to phone invitations to the families and a few friends. Since people would already be there for the wedding, the invitation could include both the wedding and the reception.

When the subject of a wedding dress was raised, objections were so strong that Marian later called her favorite Aunt, Tilda, who offered to buy the wedding dress plus a dress to 'go away' in. Alice went along with Marian to buy the dress and for once the sisters agreed on something.

In all this furor, Marian's own qualms about the marriage were forgotten. It began to seem as if this occasion would come off. They got their blood tests. The minister met with them and lectured them on sex before marriage. Unnecessary, since Marian was still afraid to 'go all the way.' Then John sent his best suit out to be cleaned and Marian began to believe that the wedding might actually come off. She still hadn't asked her parents for money. It occurred to her that it would be easier to ask Grandpa Frank for two hundred dollars than her parents. He came for a family dinner one Sunday and she took him out to the back deck and told him about the trip to New York. Before she could ask, he offered a loan and she agreed.

The day came and Marian's stomach was so upset she was not sure she could get through the ceremony. She carried a small towel with her all day to save her dress in case she vomited. Jeb arrived early and brought his mother, Cecily, whom Marian had met only once.

Cecily was a tall wispy lady who had been depressed ever since Jeb's father died ten years earlier. Originally Cecily had insisted she was too ill to take any part in the affair and was therefore not expected on the wedding day. When Marian first met her, Cecily had been in a threadbare robe and it was in this attire Marian always pictured her, and was therefore just as happy she was not coming.

But Cecily arrived on the day of the wedding in an expensive and but badly-fitting dark green crepe dress and a long string of pearls which might be real and Marian was reminded of the rumor that the family had been well-to-do before Jeb's father's death. A mutual sigh of relief went through Marian and Jeb. Marian greeted her mother-in-law-to-be and was thankful. She put aside the small towel she was carrying and kissed Cecily. The minimal traditions of Los Angeles had been satisfied. This was a good omen for the marriage. Shyly, Cecily kissed Marian back and Marian introduced her to Shirley and John, who gave up their current argument over whether the champagne should be served before or after the service. The three made a few traditional remarks about the weather although it was sunny as usual. They all looked, at least for those minutes, as if they might be the reasonable parents of normal people.

This seemed to usher in a general truce and Marian took a deep breath and stood silently grateful in one corner of the room, thinking that this marriage might be a wonderful new thing in her dull life, something more like the life she saw in the movies.

Alice, in a new dress which had been financed by Shirley and John, stationed herself at the door and greeted people as they arrived, playing hostess while the mother of the bride hid near the door to the kitchen, still fretting over Jeb's unsuitability. Jeb and his soon-to-be father-in-law arranged themselves just past Alice, two awkward gate posts trying to look comfortable while they thought up words to welcome the guests.

Marian was grateful that the armed combat between herself and Alice was stilled for the day. Alice had never gotten over being a second child, and always resented the few perks that Marian asserted. Wedding preparations and the fact that Marian was subject to some disapproval had given Alice new scope. She had plunged into this event as Marian's champion declaring she wanted to make Marian happy. Alice went with John to select the champagne, something neither one knew a thing about. She selected the guests, discussed with Jeb what he should wear, and then, on the day before the wedding, baked a three-layer angel food cake with a sauce of fresh raspberries.

The minister rushed in, twenty minutes late, anxious to start the ceremony. At his instructions, Marian and Jeb, and Alice and Jeb's best friend Orton, who were serving as bridesmaid and best man, gathered in front of the fake fireplace. Marian gritted her teeth, clutched her balled-up Kleenex and told herself—see, there's nothing to it. Orton, to everyone's surprise, came up with the ring from the pocket where he kept his Swiss Army knife. Then with only the barest of formalities, the service was completed before any of the women had a chance to cry.

Afterwards, when borrowed champagne glasses were passed around, Marian watched her friends and Alice's from high school, a scattering of cousins plus friends of Jeb's, without saying anything. She was stunned that all these people had really come and the minister had acted as if this was a normal ceremony. So much anxiety had preceded this day and now it was nearly over. There was nothing else she had to do. Voices began to rise, as her friends gathered around her. They whispered congratulations and giggled. They also felt a sense of accomplishment; it was the first wedding in their group. Some hilarity was released with innuendos about the night to come.

Even Shirley looked happy with the success of this event which she had resisted at every turn. Maybe she liked having one child launched after all. And the much-maligned living room couch looked quite nice with its Hawaiian print cushions only slightly faded. Meeting her mother's eyes on the oversized flowers, Marian realized with surprise she no didn't have to care whether or not it got upholstered. From this day forward she no longer had to worry about the outbreak of a quarrel between her parents. This was the day when her life was changing completely.

Did she look like a bride? She touched her plentiful dark brown hair which was well curled and tied at the back of her neck with a white satin bow. She couldn't remember now how she had looked after she was dressed and curled. The stiff, white satin with its pink cummerbund and her pink leather sandals with low heels had been selected by Alice and Aunt Tilda because Marian was too apprehensive to make decisions, and then put on Tilda's charge card. Once dressed, she had glanced only fleetingly into a mirror to apply some lipstick and rouge.

The eyes of her friends seemed to be approving so it must be all right.

She looked over at Jeb in a pale, green leisure suit—where had he gotten that?—drinking champagne and joking with two friends. He looked like he was having fun. That was the trouble with men. They didn't have all these things to worry about. They could come along for the ride and enjoy themselves. Tonight she would climb into bed with him at the Rodeway Inn and she had no idea what that would be like, except that she would be on the inside of that secret life instead of the outside, and afterwards she would have solidified her position as an adult.

Yes, she was grateful to him for taking her away into a new life.

Suddenly, while Marian mulled over her new husband's behavior, Alice finished her first glass of champagne, set it down and began sobbing.

"She's going away and leaving me!"

Marian was too surprised to say anything. This couldn't be real. She would have sworn that Alice would be delighted to have her out of the way.

Shirley, as if she had been waiting for something like this, rushed to her second daughter and put her arms around her, becoming fully occupied in restoring Alice. Peace returned and conversations continued in a desultory manner. Cake was served and Alice, her eyes wiped by her mother, happily accepted praise for her cake.

"This could be a really good party," she said to Marian and Marian nodded to be agreeable.

Alice then hunted out their cousin Stan and in a few minutes, the two of them had the radio on loud, with Elvis singing 'love me tender, love me true'. John was incensed at this; he moved quickly toward the sound and Elvis went away in the middle of 'tender.'

Foster, Jeb's brother, arrived late in his dress uniform, having gotten leave after all, and put a large package from the May Company on the gift table. He gave Marian, who had never met him, a hug and joked about having planned a Shivaree. Shirley looked alarmed and John indignant so that Foster's grin went away and he retracted. He was only joking—he hadn't had the time or the friends here to set it up.

What's a Shivaree, asked those who were not originally from the Midwest?

Uncle Brady enlightened them. "Mostly it's just a lot of noise trying to scare the bride and groom, but sometimes they grab the bride and kidnap her, I guess like they used to in the Middle Ages. They showed up at my daughter's wedding and took her away to a motel and the groom had a bad time running around half a day trying to find her."

Jeb looked at Marian protectively, as if he would never put up with something like that, and Marian was so gratified she was glad the subject had been raised.

That was most of the activity for this novel day. The cake and the champagne lasted less than half an hour, and when they were gone, people began to leave. It was only mid-afternoon but it was Saturday and most of them had errands still to do in Pasadena or Downey or another of the far-flung towns of Los Angeles County. John and his father, Grandpa Frank had switched from champagne to bourbon and were waxing sentimental.

Marian put on her going-away dress of dark blue shantung and threw her modest bouquet of marguerites at her friends. It was caught by Alice who had positioned herself in the front.

(And sure enough, Marian's unprecedented event would have no equal for two years and then be topped by Alice.)

The day after Marian's wedding, Cousin Bob drove the

newlyweds from the Rodeway Inn to the Greyhound station. Marian was not so sure as she had been the day before that she wanted to go to New York but she said nothing. She had a raging headache from the champagne and was sure she would never drink it again. Also, she was sore from the unaccustomed nighttime acrobatics in the king-size bed. She supposed she would end up liking sex but so far it wasn't much fun. Mostly she hurt.

"Leaving your wedding presents behind?" Cousin Bob asked.

"Just till we get settled," Jeb said, while Marian wondered if she would ever see those things again. It would be very difficult to get Shirley to pack up the gifts and mail them all the way across the country.

"Those are good towels but you can take them back if you have others."

"Thank you," Marian said. "They are lovely."

She wanted nothing as much as to sleep. She had wakened with the thought that she was now chained to Jeb as she had been to her parents. Would she have as little choice about what happened in her life as she had before the marriage? Was that why her mother was always angry?

As soon as the bus started, Marian fell asleep. They were on their way and there was nothing she could do about it. When she woke up it was almost nighttime and they were in the desert with little to look at. Jeb has spread her raincoat over her and was also asleep. Marian wondered if Alice had helped clean up the house after the reception or if she had gone out with Foster which seemed more likely. Then she wondered if her mother and father had had an argument over the cost of the champagne. Also likely, but she didn't want to know about it.

The landscape was dark, unpeopled, with only distant lights. The long nap had left her stiff and thirsty. There was nothing to do except straighten her limbs out, one at a time. She could wake Jeb but then she would have to talk to him and she had nothing to say except complaints. It was better to be on the bus than back at the Rodeway Inn—she was protected from Jeb by the other passengers, and the fact that they were in public.

She decided to blot out as much of the trip as possible. She would sleep most of the way and when she woke up she would be ready for her new life.

Hours and days later, there was a stirring among the passengers. People were searching through their carry-ons and there were irritated murmurs. Finally, the bus went through a long, dark tunnel, horribly noisy, solid with honking cars, the whole mass moving only a few feet at a time. They finally emerged in New York City. Here was their new planet.

Everything looked old and dirty, as if it had all been there for a hundred years. Dark, identical brick buildings six stories high lined the streets on both sides, cheek by jowl, no space in between them, their fronts black with years of soot and crowded with iron fire escapes.

The sidewalks were thronged with people going in all different directions, hardly enough room between them to allow them to pass each other. The streets were so crowded with cars that you couldn't tell the ones parked from the ones moving. The air was greyish, thick with the expelled breath of eight million people. Marian wanted immediately to go back through the tunnel, even though the tunnel had been frightening and she had wanted desperately to get out of it.

"I don't think I'm going to like this."

Jeb laughed. He was excited. "Will you look at that? That's something you'd never see in California."

"What?"

But the 'what' was long out of sight, and Jeb had gone on to laugh about something else.

"How do we find your friend in all this?"

"He wrote me instructions. Don't worry. We'll get there."

The bus terminal was more of the same. People everywhere, directly in the way of wherever you wanted to go. The platform was so crowded Marian wondered how they would be able to get off the bus. Then after they did, she could not see how they would get through all these people and out of the station. Somehow they did.

After three questions to three different New Yorkers who were in too much of a hurry to listen to what he was asking, someone pointed a direction and Jeb led her to a bus stop. After more questions in the louder and louder voice Jeb was using, they were close enough to a bus to think of climbing on. Before they could, numerous people shoved in ahead of them, and Marian was sure she was going to be separated from Jeb. There was no holding of hands because they had three suitcases they were trying to maneuver into the bus.

Just before the driver could close the door in front of them, they got on that bus, Jeb pushing the suitcases forward in spite of people's complaints. Having asked ahead of time, he produced the proper amount of change for their fare and dropped it in the box.

They found a space in which to stack their suitcases and Marian was able to sit down while Jeb stood. The bus ride was long. The city began to change; first it was shinier with big newish buildings and stores, then there were street trees and they were on the Upper West Side, along Broadway. The street had—not houses as they expected—but endless four and five story buildings with small stores and restaurants along the sidewalks and above them offices or apartments that were not quite as old and dark as the ones near the tunnel.

Jeb was nervous about finding the right stop.

The bus driver had agreed to tell them Eighty Ninth Street when they got there, but the first name Marian was able to spot was sixty four. It would be a long way.

"Half the time I can't understand what he's saying," Jeb complained after a while. The driver's words were shouted over all the hubbub of people getting on and off, as well as brakes squealing at traffic lights and honking cars around them. Marian tried to do her part, watching the street signs carefully in case they would not understand the shouted words.

When she did see Eighty Ninth Street, there was too much noise for Jeb to hear her so she pinched him. They got up and struggled up the aisle with their suitcases, going against the tide of passengers headed to the back of the bus, and balanced against the swaying as the bus crossed a lane, moving toward the curb. They couldn't even get off at Eighty Ninth because by the time they reached the driver to tell him to stop, they were past it. They would have to ride two more blocks.

At last they were deposited on a curb, and then shoved aside by people anxious to get on the bus before it left.

"I'll never get on another one." Marian shook herself, trying to shake out the stiff neck which three nights sleeping upright had caused.

She was far more depressed than excited. She thought that when she took off her blue shantung Going-Away dress, she would be covered by purple bruises from these encounters. All she wanted was a long drink of water and then to fall asleep flat on a bed, and after that she would try to deal with New York. There was music in the air here and the people were smaller and darker than she had expected.

It was not so easy walking the several blocks back with their suitcases, and then another long block toward the park, and then up two steep flights of stairs. They were puffing, cross, their shoulders ached and they were worried that it might be the wrong number after all and they would have to walk down again.

A thin young man with a shock of reddish hair opened the door. Obviously the right young man because he and Jeb punched each other and exclaimed: "Hey there."

"You made it."

"No sweat."

"Come on in. We've been debating whether to wait for you or go out to eat. We guessed right."

Jeb looked at Marian uneasily. She registered this: there hadn't been a 'we' when he had talked to Bill a few weeks ago. The 'we' must be the young woman standing behind Bill, dressed all in black, terribly thin with long stringy blonde hair.

This person stepped right up when her name, 'Bonnie', was mentioned, gripped Marian's arm and searched her face. "Glad to meet you," she said energetically.

There was some milling around in the doorway as they tried to sort out greetings and introductions, and then they were all inside, stacking the three suitcases, which had been a chore to drag up the steep flights of stairs, near the door where they dwarfed the nearby table and made a barrier between room and door.

"You look like you're ready for a nap." Bonnie said to Marian, her look kinder than her nasal voice.

"Water will do."

Once settled in, sharing a somewhat battered leather chair with Jeb, and furnished by Bonnie with a glass of water, Marian had a chance to look around. Jeb was offering Bill an abbreviated version of the trip in that simplified language used by young men who didn't want to sound over-educated.

Marian was looking at the room and developed a sinking feeling. Not that there was anything terrible about it, a large room with a wall of windows on the street side. In one corner, there was a raised platform which contained cabinets, sink and stove and a table with two chairs—a whole kitchen nicely designed for one or two people if they were quite small. Along the wall there was a door half open which revealed a bathroom, and a closed one which seemed to be a closet. One room.

Bill hadn't mentioned that fact when he offered to share it with Jeb and Marian. And then sometime in the interim, he had apparently made another offer to Bonnie. Four people in this small space. They would all hear each other breathing all night. Not to mention, rolling over and any other activity they engaged in.

# CHAPTER FIVE

Because Felicia asked. That was why Marian told her the whole story about marrying Jeb and going to New York. And because she had never told anyone else. Even this many years later, she skirted some of the details she remembered as painful. Felicia seemed to know this; at the end of the tale, she made a sympathetic face and waved her hankie in the air as if trying to rid Marian of the memories.

"After all that, was it worth it? Being married? You could have gotten right back on another bus and gone home."

"It was exciting," Marian excused her younger self of years ago. "And it got better. It really did."

Well, it did and it didn't. It was hard. But there was some excitement because it was all new. They stayed with Bill and Bonnie one night, sleeping on the narrow, tilted mattress of the couch. Or not sleeping, to be more accurate. Marian could tell by the breathing, the rolling over, the whispered comments, and restless trips to the bathroom that no one really slept that night.

The next morning she and Jeb were presented with the classified ads and 'Rooms for Rent' was pointed out. Anxious, grateful, embarrassed, they fastened on the first large ad that featured rooms in a hotel that rented by the week. Bill and Bonnie approved the location of this address—downtown, or slightly below midtown, rather than uptown where they lived.

After another long bus ride with their bulky suitcases, Jeb and Marian were relieved to find a respectable hotel with a polite desk clerk. They were taken up in the elevator to see a room with a double bed and a sink. Although small, the room was very clean and reasonably furnished in traditional walnut. There was a door to the bathroom which had a toilet and tub; the only problem being that this was shared with the next bedroom. The sharing was managed by a chain which went from the door of their room to the door to the next room. The clerk showed them that when they used the toilet and tub room, they could hook the two doors together with the chain. That would ensure that the neighbor would be unable to enter the bathroom till they had unhooked and went into their own room. If they were not in the toilet and tub room, they would be unable to chain their neighbor out of the bathroom but could lock their own room door.

"That's weird," Marian protested.

But Jeb, even though he was not in the best humor due to lack of sleep, was charmed by the ingenuity of this. "Far out!" he said.

Gratefully, they plunked down a large portion of their remaining money on a week's rent and fell into bed and slept through the afternoon and night. When Marian woke sometime in the night, she found that their window framed the Chrysler Building just the way they had seen it on a postcard in the lobby. The building must stay lighted all through the night, sending directly to the Californians a beacon and a promise for their adventure.

Charmed, she got up and went to the window to look out. There were lights all up and down the canyons of streets, and many of the office buildings had some lights on every floor. Her eyes were dazzled. This vision promised all the new and exciting events this queen of cities could shower on them, it would replace their innocence with stories to tell their children. She went back to bed and curled against Jeb's warm flesh, satisfied for the moment with the splendor of their future.

"Did it?" Felicia asked but Marian shooed her out.

"Another time."

While Marian happily forgot most of what had happened

over the year and a half she and Jeb spent in New York, the details of their last day there stayed with her.

When she woke up that last morning, their furnished room, which was not nearly as pleasant as Bill's had been, was barely light and incredibly cold. She could hear the steam, shrieking and banging as it started its path through the pipes that wound their way up three floors from the basement, announcing it might reach them eventually. Maybe in an hour or so.

The landlord turned off the heat at six in the evening and didn't turn it back on until six in the morning. Marian wondered resentfully how much money that saved him because the pipes had a struggle to warm up rooms that had been allowed to drop nearly to the outdoor temperature which this morning was down near thirty. That might take nearly all day. But of course, almost no one was concerned with how warm the rooms got during the day; the tenants were all out to work. Warmth would only matter once they got home in the evening.

She had taken to wearing her bathrobe to bed. Even then, it took courage to get out from under the covers, feel for her slippers on the floor, and cross the room. Like Bill's apartment, this one had a tiny kitchen in one corner. Quickly she lighted the oven, closing the door for ten minutes to let the warmth build up, and then opening it to hasten heat to the room. While she waited, she pulled the drapes open and was rewarded by a scene of swirling snow.

"Get up," she said to Jeb whose whole head was under the blankets. "It's almost eight. We have to be at the bus station by ten."

He mumbled something but did not stick his head out. Months of married life had rid Marian of any hesitations about interrupting his sleep. She advanced on him and pulled down the covers.

"You take the first shower," she told the face when it was uncovered, eyes still closed.

"It's too cold. "

"That's why we're leaving. Think about being back in L.A."

Weather was not the only reason they were leaving. There were lots of others.

Since arriving in New York, one or the other of them was always job-hunting, mostly Jeb. That was plenty tiring. Bonnie had sent them first to a temporary agency so that they would get quickly to work. This had succeeded for Marian. She began working almost every day at low-level office jobs—sending out mailings, filing or folding and stuffing. When she finished one job, there was usually another one waiting.

Jeb had a harder time. He didn't type or use a calculator and therefore wasn't eligible for clerical jobs. Many of the kinds of repair jobs he had worked at in California here were under the control of unions. That left stocking jobs in offices, and some warehouse jobs. As he waited days for a job, he became scornful. Though no particular friend of equal employment, he had a Californian's resentment for how rigidly segregated these work groups were.

"No women," he told Marian. "If any women do it, they won't send a man. And no Puerto Ricans. Maybe they think they can't read. Some light-skinned blacks if they've been to college and wear white shirts, and all the rest of the people I'm assigned with are homos. I'm beginning to think the town is half homo."

If that wasn't limiting enough, he was often replaced shortly after he started a new job by someone who was a 'friend of the boss.'

"I wouldn't have to put up with this in L.A.," he said so frequently that Marian began to snap at him each time.

Between Marian's fulltime pay, only slightly above minimum wage, and Jeb's part-time, they could barely make enough to live on. They bought food carefully but Marian was not much of a cook so they were seldom satisfied with their meals and often ended up eating out. Furnished apartments were not cheap. They had the borrowed money to pay back. No matter how carefully they planned, there was seldom enough.

Their evenings were silent because they had no radio or

television or even a telephone. They tried to make their own fun, walking to many of the attractions for which New York was known, and looking in from the outside because they had no money to enter. They swore that they were enjoying the novelty and adventure of all this.

They had come from a place where all the people they had grown up with were nearby. But now they knew no one except Bill and Bonnie and could hardly see them more than once a week so their life was nearly empty of friendly encounters. They called California an amazing number of times.

"Oh yes, we're having a wonderful time!"

Only a short time after they had arrived, spring was over and deep summer brought stifling heat to the canyons of concrete. Unlike L.A., where heat was tempered by breezes from the mountains or the ocean, here buildings and pavements stayed hot day and night. They were not used to seasons; some years, Los Angeles had none at all.

One night when it seemed too hot to even breathe, Jeb talked about that one time in LA when it became too hot to sleep at night and hundreds of people had driven to the beach and slept side by side on the sand. He pooh-poohed Marian's fear and took them to sleep in Central Park under some bushes. But the noises around them in the night were too alarming; Marian was so panicked by them she couldn't sleep and dragged them back to their hot apartment at midnight.

After several quarrels, they changed apartments for one that had no sun. They lost their security deposit on this move, wasting the little amount of money they were ahead. This is not fair, Marian said to herself, afraid to say it to Jeb.

There was a month of respite from heat, and then the cold set in. They had missed the previous winter without thinking about it. Now the constant rains and snow came and the temperatures stayed under thirty. They didn't have the coats or boots they needed. This required a serious outlay of cash even though they shopped at the Salvation Army and the army surplus store.

Again they had to write to Grandpa Frank and explain why they could not return more of his money this month.

"I don't know why everyone thinks this city is so great," Jeb complained.

Marian thought briefly but didn't say: 'I might like it with someone else.' She tried to remember why she had been so eager to marry Jeb. New York required imagination and a quick adaptability to new situations. Jeb had neither of these. Instead, he was easily affronted and quickly resentful.

Although she mulled over this subject while stapling or stuffing or filing, she did not communicate her doubts to him. She remembered her mother too well and thought if she ever sounded like Shirley, she would die of shame. When they cuddled together in their bed in the evening with nothing to read but newspapers full of subjects they knew nothing about, it was still comforting to tell funny stories about their day.

Winter was finally followed by spring. In the warmer rains, they were more hopeful. They sometimes sought out the Museum of Natural History and marveled at the dinosaur. When the temperature encouraged it, they went to a free concert or to Shakespeare in the Park. Forty Second Street movies were cheap. They took the Staten Island ferry and then came back without having set a foot on the island, satisfied because for only pennies they had spent an hour on the water. Summer returned and they now regretted their latest apartment which they had taken for its warmth. They moved again and tried to enjoy the heat, spending several evenings drinking beer with Bill and Bonnie on their soot-encrusted roof.

"You know what's wrong with this town?" Marian said to Jeb. "Nobody welcomes strangers."

It was true. After more than a year in the city, they had made a few acquaintances but no other friends and they looked back with yearning on all their friends in LA, the people they had grown up with who now, at a distance, seemed wonderfully warm and charming.

Marian had an added problem which she didn't mention to

Jeb. She thought the thing she could not get over was being always under assault. Was it just because there were so many people on this tight island or was there really a general feeling of hostility? Strangers ran their hands over her in the subway. Men followed her home from the bus stop and tried to get into the downstairs door before it locked behind her.

Jeb was finally offered a permanent job. He was not joyful but resentful when he told Marian about it. "I have to pay the agency a fee for it. It will come out of my salary for a year and after it's deducted, I'll be getting less every week that whole year than I've been making as a temp."

"What's the job?"

"Just what I've been doing, stocking, doling out supplies, making copies. There's no place to advance to. I could be doing that for ten years. Can you believe it?"

Marian didn't know what to say. She realized she had never thought of what career Jeb might embark on. She thought men simply knew how to do that. She was not unhappy with her work. She was settled into the routine of being a temp. She liked the woman who sent her on jobs which usually shuttled between the same several firms who knew her. She had finally passed a typing test which brought her a bit more money and had found a clothing store where she thought she could buy a new skirt and sweater at the end of the month. Something that would make her look more like a New Yorker and she would begin to fit in.

True, it was tough to live as they had been living, but she had fallen in love with the Metropolitan Museum of Art and thought she could be happy for a year going there every Sunday afternoon and seeing a new department.

She had to say something. "It's because you don't have a degree."

"Well, to hell with them. I know a lot of men who don't have degrees."

Nothing else was said in this direction right then, but when November came with early snow, and they discovered this landlord's habit of no heat at night, Jeb said one evening: "Let's get out of here."

And Marian answered without thinking about it. "Okay."

"Why don't you go first?" Jeb said to Marian's bathroom offer.

"I have to finish packing. I'll make some oatmeal for both of us. There's a little milk left."

So Jeb showered while she finished packing. By the time she got into the bathroom, the air was somewhat warmer and the water was hot. After their hasty breakfast, Jeb cleaned up the kitchen while she dressed. Marian put on her most comfortable jeans and a flannel shirt of Jeb's for the long bus trip, wondering if she would ever feel warm again. They had a small security deposit with this landlord but had decided to give it up as they were leaving without the proper notice.

They had four suitcases now, one more than they had arrived with because they had more winter clothing. It was a heavy, old metal-sided trunk, purchased at the Salvation Army and when packed was too heavy for Marian to pick up. Jeb lined the suitcases up at the door and went carefully through the room and a half to see if they were leaving anything behind.

Marian watched him, too anxious with the details of departure to wonder if this decision was something to be celebrated or mourned. She had given notice on her job yesterday and the agency had agreed to mail her check to her mother's address in Culver City. She had said goodbye to Bonnie two days ago when the two couples met at the rink in Rockefeller Center to watch the ice-skating. It was only then, when Bonnie hugged her, that Marian realized Bonnie was a real friend, the only one she had made in all these months, and they had scarcely had time to get acquainted.

"Come to LA," she urged both Bonnie and Bill, and was surprised at their looks of confusion. Leaving New York and traveling clear across the country was apparently not something they ever contemplated.

Marian and Jeb carried their suitcases up to Broadway and

crossed the street so they would be on the downtown side, stopping every now and then for Marian to catch her breath. Jeb held up his hand and they watched a fleet of full cabs pass them by with passengers on their way to work.

Finally Jeb asked: "How much time do we have? Maybe we'll have to take a bus."

"Not a bus. The subway is faster."

Just then, tires screeched and a cab crossed two lanes of traffic to pull up beside them. The cabbie pulled the lever to open his trunk but didn't get out, leaving Jeb to fit their suitcases in.

The bus station was as crowded as it had been when they arrived. Other travelers complained as Marian and Jeb wedged past them with their suitcases. The rudeness of New Yorkers was in a class by itself.

"Give me the money. You stand here and I'll buy the tickets," Jeb said.

"I don't have the money. You do."

"I do not. I saw you put it in your purse." They looked at each other dismay.

"No. You must have left it on the sink when you were sorting out your change for the cab."

"I did not."

"We'll miss this bus if we have to go back." She was remembering that she had dropped the keys to the apartment into the owner's locked mailbox. She was ready to cry. Maybe this was a sign they should stay.

"We can't get back in."

Jeb looked up at the ticket-buying line and sighed. "This is just the kind of thing that happens in this damned city. I've never been so glad to leave a place. Please, take another look in your purse."

Obediently, knowing it was useless, she opened her purse and found the wide inside pocket was fat with something. Sure enough, the thick stack of bills was there. All their money— enough to buy the tickets and feed them for five days across the country.

She was too relieved to be embarrassed at her mistake. "Okay, I'll buy the tickets."

She bought their tickets while he stood guard over the suitcases. Together they found the number for the bus to Chicago. They would have six hours layover when they got there—time to wash, to walk around, and have something of a meal. They had decided that was worth the extra half day it would add to the trip.

The bus was in place but empty, with its door closed. Marian wiggled her feet in wet shoes. At least they were out of the rain while they waited quietly, first in line.

"If I never see snow again it will be too soon," Jeb said.

When Marian looked around, she saw a line forming behind them. In Los Angles the only line she had ever been in was one at the supermarket. Los Angeles. A wave of hunger for California, for the special look of the streets of low, stucco houses with their yards full of camellias and the incredibly tall, bare palm trees far overhead, overcame her.

"We didn't used to be this glum," she said.

"Not before we got here."

They nearly laughed when, at last, they stepped inside the bus. It might have been the very same one they had come on all those months ago... the dark blue patterned seats, the dirty windows, and tired smell made up of plastic, gasoline and sweat. They already knew where they wanted to sit, half way back on the right-hand side. The views were usually more interesting from there than on the driver's side. Their suitcases had been packed in the bin underneath the bus but they had taken a small knitted throw to the seat with them to keep them warm when sleeping. And two sandwiches for their first lunch.

"Maybe we should have stuck it out a couple weeks more. We didn't go to the Empire State Building or to The Cloisters," Marian said.

Probably they should have also waited till they had saved more money for the trip. Instead they had called Jeb's mother for a loan and the need to pay this back as soon as possible weighed on Marian already.

"No, we shouldn't have. We gave it a try. That was enough." Jeb opened the Esquire Magazine he had bought in the station. He had never bought one of those before. Marian said nothing. She regarded him thoughtfully. It was hard to see what he looked like to others because she saw him every day, but she thought he was still good-looking in spite of a new pinched line between his eyebrows.

She leaned back in her seat and closed her eyes and the whole experience of New York began to flow across her eyes like a personal movie of her life. She had changed a lot since they were last on this bus. The biggest change was not disappointment in the city as much as a change in her opinion of Jeb. He was not the man she had thought she was marrying. Not anything like. Basing her expectations on her father, she had thought that the thing a man would always do first was get on with the task of earning the living without complaint. This was certainly not true of Jeb. Instead he needed constant appreciation for his efforts in this direction. He also seemed to think she was intentionally showing him up when she worked more hours than he did or made extra efforts to make money. Instead, she thought she was helping him out and should be thanked.

She had to admit she was also disappointed in their lovemaking. It had turned into an earnest, doubtful exercise with only occasional hints of pleasure. When afterwards Jeb fell asleep, she would put an arm around him and try to tell him silently that it was all right. They were still together and she really did love him. She knew he was unhappy and didn't know how to make him happier.

The memories of Los Angeles began to replace New York and let contentment in. She had missed the enormous bird-of-paradise plant in her mother's back yard. A plant so unlike anything in New York, she hadn't been able to describe it to Bonnie. The purple jacaranda trees in the next block. The Santa

Monica pier and the wide beach which ended at the rhythmic mesmerizing waves.

"I want to go to the beach the first day," she said, but Jeb was lost in his magazine.

The bus finally started and left the terminal with a roar of grinding gears and edged its way into traffic so thick it looked as if there was no room for one more vehicle. In a short time, they were at the tunnel. The same tunnel, dark, noisy, endless.

And when they exited that, there was sunshine waiting for them as if the sun had come all the way from California just for them.

Would he really be happier in Los Angeles? Would she? Looking back on it, she saw that a sense of the unfairness of their life had overwhelmed her. What made life in LA so much fairer?

# CHAPTER SIX

One problem Marian had found in Sonoma after Jeb's death was that when you got old your friends got old too. And they were usually not as much fun old as they had been when they were young. They got less willing to consider new possibilities. They complained a lot about their ailments, and their politics moved to the right. Not that I'm so liberal, Marian excused herself, but at least I don't always point out how much better things were twenty five years ago.

She was expounding this thought to Bridget who, fortunately, didn't talk like that.

Bridget laughed and said: "Yes, they do complain more but they're a lot less full of foolish ideas like going to Nepal to try hashish."

They had time to debate such ideas because Bridget was driving Marian to Fairfield. Or rather, to a new housing development east of Fairfield, out in what had been farming country only a little while ago. When Marian had confided to Bridget that Letty did not seem to be getting on very quickly with the addresses for the party, Bridget had said: "Do you want me to drive you up there to see her?"

Grateful to be saved the expense of gasoline and the worries about her old car breaking down, Marian had said yes.

On the trip, in Bridget's nearly-new silver Volvo station wagon with its excellent air-conditioning, Marian examined Bridget for signs of aging, wondering again if she was over sixty-five, and if so, would she begin to exhibit the telltale characteristics that so many people developed at seventy? She did not want Bridget to age, to begin to worry about everything and become forgetful and eccentric. She needed for Bridget to continue to be her stable, informative, always-interesting self. And always ready to help out her friends... where would Marian be without that?

Now that she thought about it, Marian recognized signs of aging in herself. Her housekeeping had fallen off: she had people to the house as little as possible and therefore didn't have to clean everything so thoroughly as she had when she still had Jeb looking around with an eagle eye. Well, why not slow down after years of all that work? Who had decried that women should be chained to cleaning and vacuuming forever? Look at Felicia.

People said they wanted to have a long life but look what came with it.

"How are you feeling?" she asked Bridget, remembering there were many other people in Sonoma who depended on Bridget remaining as she was.

Bridget cocked an eyebrow, considering. "I feel fine except that I'm hungry already."

That was all right then. Being hungry was not one of the signs. "If we're lucky, maybe Letty will have baked whole wheat bread. She likes to do that when she's not working. Wait till you see this house."

"If he works in Martinez, why did they buy way up here?"

"The price, of course. It's brand new, four bedrooms and three bathrooms, granite countertops, et cetera, et cetera all for practically half what it would cost closer. I'm anxious to see the landscaping. They were to put it in two weeks ago."

But when they arrived at Bro and Letty's address, the front yard showed only the scarred earth of a building site. The two women looked at each other with the anxiety of mothers everywhere quickly convinced their children are meeting with disaster.

Letty opened the door before they rang. Not a pretty girl at the best of times, she was barefoot, in jeans with the knees out, her dishwater hair in pigtails and her face streaked with tears.

"I was watching out for you," she said, ignoring the dismal picture she presented. "Come in, come in."

Marian's heart fluttered. A disaster of some kind. "Letty, you remember my friend Bridget!"

"Yes, of course. From the wedding. You sent white china. Dansk. Very nice." Letty ushered them into the family room which was on the same level as the entry hall, but painted a dull red-orange, a decorator's color.

"Isn't this nice!" said Bridget, always quick to praise.

Letty mopped her face with a hankie, eager but hopeful. "Do you like it? Bro thinks it's too dark."

The house echoed hollowly around them, a house of many square feet with thin sheetrock and not enough furniture.

"Not at all. It's lovely."

Aside from the paint, the family room was undecorated, furnished only with moving boxes and a small unpainted bookcase full of paperbacks. Across the room, Letty led them up five steps to the kitchen, which was dramatic with dark gray granite countertops and a huge stove which had two ovens and a grilling section. Here she had set out tea cups and a pot for them in blue and white Dansk.

"I didn't know if you would want iced tea or hot. Is hot all right? It seems like the hot weather will never quit but this air-conditioning is too cold." She stood, waiting humbly.

It was indeed cold. Marian let Bridget make the decision while she looked around for signs of improvements since her last visit. She could see into the dining room in one direction and the living room in another. The dining room was empty but a small group of one couch, one table and two chairs clustered in the center of the over-sized living room. She turned back to look at Letty's tears. Tact left her as usual. "What's wrong?"

"No, no, nothing really," their hostess protested.

"You've been crying."

" I'm about to get my period, that's all."

"And Bro, is he happy?"

Letty gave a helpless shrug. "He doesn't like this commuting. It takes him an hour to get to work and longer to get home."

"That must be terrible," Bridget agreed. "I guess the traffic has gotten worse down 80 since they built all these houses up here." She sniffed the air but there was no welcome smell of baked bread and the stove beside them was cold.

"Terrible." Letty let a little sob out and seemed better. She brightened. "But you should come see the rest of the house. I may just stay in all the time, work at home. Wouldn't that be super? Do you want hot tea or cold?"

They opted for hot tea because the kettle was purring softly, sounding eager to please. Then they followed Letty into the living room where the couch and two chairs marooned in a wide expanse of carpet looked to be from Goodwill.

"Oh, look at your yard," Bridget exclaimed because the back wall was all glass.

This was a kindly exaggeration. It was an empty lot, not yet a yard.

"They haven't put the patio in yet." Letty apologized, opening the sliding door, an invitation for them to look out. The two women walked politely over to look at the bare dirt, received a blast of 95-degree heat and declined to step down the long distance to the dirt.

"When will they put it in?"

"Another month maybe."

"Aren't you happy with all this?" Marian said accusingly. "I never had anything like this."

Letty paused from handing out the teacups and mopped her eyes again. "Oh yes. Really I am. It's just hard right now because all our money goes to the mortgage and we can't afford to buy furniture or have the landscaping done right away. We didn't know how much gasoline it was going to take, living way up here. And now it's gone up another dollar. But as soon as my unemployment runs out and I get a job, then we'll fix all this."

The women looked at her silently, so she went on. "We

decided to get a decorator to pick the furniture so we'll be sure to get it right."

Bridget looked at Marian and blinked in empathy. They settled in the chairs, and accepted cups of tea.

"It's lovely the way it is. A really wonderful house." This was Bridget. "You will have great fun picking out furniture. What style do you like?"

Letty declined to respond—perhaps afraid they would disapprove of her choice.

Marian thought anyone might feel lonely here. Through the sliding doors, the bare yard was decorated only by a few weeds that had escaped the earthmover. Twelve feet away, a tall redwood fence stood as a lonely guard against the farmland which had been here first. On the other side of the fence, a plowed field stretched to the horizon ready for winter planting.

"You want to see how much I've done, don't you?" Letty said.

This sudden shift made Marian anxious. "It's wonderful to have you working on my party list. If it's too much for you…" But if it was too much for Letty, who on earth could she find to replace her?

"I got another one yesterday. Emmy Davis. I think. I haven't called yet to make sure." Letty abruptly stood up and motioned them to follow her. They carried their cooling tea in cold hands, and went after her up the staircase to the balcony which was also a hallway for the second floor.

"What a lot of space," Bridget said.

"It is, isn't it?" The girl gave a little sigh which turned into a hiccup. "We wanted four bedrooms so we could have one as an office and two for children. But now I don't know if I'll ever be able to quit working long enough to have a baby."

The desk she led them to consisted of an unpainted plank laid across two filing cabinets. In contrast to the desk, the computer and printer looked new, large, and expensive. On the floor were several open boxes of files and notebooks. Bridget walked over to look out the uncurtained window down the street at the row of nearly identical houses most of which had their landscaping in. The neighborhood seemed to be empty of people, a super-sized suburb of new houses where both husbands and wives were gone all day working to pay for them.

Letty picked up a tray crammed with papers and gave it to Marian. "Here you can see what I've been doing. I'll get another chair."

"Never mind," Bridget said. "I can stand for a while."

Marian looked in surprise at the top page which was headed "Amy Barrow", and the page of sticky notes below the name, "address in high school", "name changed to", "try Alaska", and a list of numbers which had been tried; and false leads, "not in Fairbanks", "try under Starr."

"What a huge amount of work!"

Letty nodded, her face crumpling again. "It is, isn't it? But then just when I think I've got one, I call them up to verify if it is the right person. And mostly I find it's not. That gets so discouraging."

Marian put the tray down helplessly. "You get all the way there and it's the wrong person?" She thought she might quit the search if that happened to her. "What a waste of time."

Letty nodded. "I have to call and talk to the person, otherwise we'd never know for sure if it was the right one."

"How did you get to the wrong person?"

"You wouldn't believe how many people even just in California have the same name. I guess I never knew that before."

And this was only the beginning. Marian had in her purse a whole new list of names. So the project was going to fail. She was going to have to give it up.

One tear ran down Letty's homely face, passed her mouth and then dropped to her unironed shirt. "I'm so sorry, Mother Marian."

Marian was irritated at the word mother. She already had three children, not entirely satisfactory ones, and it had been hard enough to deal with those. Then seeing Letty's unhappy face, she closed her mouth on the words she had been about to say.

Letty was looking hopelessly at her as if awaiting a scolding. "I'm so sorry." She searched her jeans pockets for another hankie.

Something in the girl's humble posture reminded Marian of herself, all the times she had waited silently for her mother's anger, hoping and praying it wouldn't be as severe as it usually was. Her heart, which got little use these recent years, with Jeb and the children all gone, expanded unexpectedly. She hadn't wanted another daughter. If she was going to get another child, she would have liked another boy, one who wasn't so much like his father. But here Letty was, already in the family, needing to be cared for.

"It's my fault. I didn't know it would be this hard. I knew you liked to do research. I thought maybe this would be fun for you." She thought about the useless list in her purse and opened her arms. Sometimes she expected too much of the world. Wasn't that what her mother used to tell her?

Letty came quickly to Marian, and Marian, without knowing she was going to do that, put her arms around her.

Letty, with the side of her face against Marian's cheek, was crying in earnest now, the tears running down Marian's cheek as well as her own. She was releasing all her unhappiness, like a baby who has had to wait too long for comfort. The young body pressed into Marian's arms, was stronger and denser than Marian's own. "You're always so good to me. I wanted to do something in exchange."

Marian was filled with guilt, remembering all the times she had not been good, had complained about Letty as a second wife who didn't seem to make Bro any happier than he had been, which wasn't very happy at all, a new addition to the family who was not distinguished in any way that was noticeable. She patted Letty on the back, enjoying the solidity of her young flesh, unwilling for the moment to disengage and look for a hankie to wipe her cheeks.

Bridget was quiet outside this embrace. After long minutes she spoke. "Maybe we all need some more tea."

"I didn't give you this job to make you unhappy," Marian said. She gave Letty an additional hug before releasing her. She could see her party receding into the past, leaving all those unfound friends at peace without a chance to know the present-day Marian. Had it all been doomed from the beginning?

Letty did not let go right away. Marian backed slowly away.

Bridget tried again. "Letty, let's go downstairs and have some more tea and maybe we can work something out."

Letty sniffed, wiped her tears, and seemed to relax. Downstairs, she made a new pot of tea while Marian rinsed out the cups and poured more cream in the Dansk pitcher, and Bridget studied the empty garden. Tension eased away. They could hear a clock ticking in the house, a friendly sound, and from outside, some pop music; perhaps after all there was someone at home in one of these lonely houses. Or was it a radio left on to discourage burglars?

When they were all settled in the living room again, Bridget asked Letty to tell them about the search... it was so marvelous she had come this far... how many had she found?

"Fourteen." Mostly men, the men were easier, especially those who had stayed in the same town and let themselves be listed. They even liked being called up. It was the women who changed their names, and went to one college after another, and then married a second time, and sounded irritable when asked to identify themselves. And sometime they had elected to have only a cell phone the number of which was never listed but which Letty had obtained from friends, and they became very suspicious about how they had been found.

And how many had she completely given up on?

Not so many, five or six. "I hate to give up. I keep trying a new idea."

Letty grew earnest and energetic in this account. She had embarked on this project with all the enthusiasm of Lewis and Clark, sure she could do it, loving the fact that the search was all new because she loved doing new things, loved proving that she could. The huge empty house seemed to fill up with her fierce desire to make the project work

"There are three people dead. I'm sorry. I didn't want to tell you that."

Marian was afraid to ask who. She would get their names later and adapt to the loss in privacy. She was visited with shame. All this had gone on, on her behalf, while she rode her bike around Sonoma waiting for the miracle to be performed. "You did all that, day after day? "

Letty's face blazed under the magic balm of approval. "I know I can find them. I just get discouraged sometimes."

Marian nodded. "I guess it's harder than I thought because there are many more people in California than there were when I was in school."

"Millions more," Letty agreed. "And some of the old ones have moved to other states."

"Yes, people move more often than they used to."

Letty made a face of disgust. "And change their names. Not just for marriage, sometimes because they want to try a new one. But I can do it."

Marian and Bridget looked at each other. The project had come to life again.

"Maybe I could do some of the calling. When you get discouraged... I could help out."

But Marian was already shrinking from the thought. The wrong numbers! Disturbing people who had forgotten her and asking them to come up to Sonoma! Demanding that they remember her in spite of memories that might have been unimportant to them. "Who would have thought it would take all this to find old friends?"

"Oh no! I'll do it. I promised you. I don't mind doing it. And the call doesn't cost anything on my cell phone, even if it's clear across the country." Letty's tears were gone now. She looked at Marian like a puppy waiting for approval.

"Marian, let her try it a few more days and see how she feels about it. Maybe you could call her every day and find out if there is any place she is stuck where you could help her."

"Yes, I can do that."

Bridget stood up. "We have to get on the road. We don't want to get caught in the commute traffic."

The other two stood up with her. Marian turned and hugged this new-old daughter. "Letty, I'm going to talk to you every day and you tell me if you're discouraged and we'll quit. We can always give up on someone who just refuses to be found. Or I can do some of the calling."

"I can do it. Really I can," Letty said happily. "I'm sorry I got weepy."

Marian kissed this strange child who might not be a beauty but who could put up with Bro and also accomplish a job on which, truthfully, Marian had not had a clue as to how to proceed. "I'm really grateful."

As they went down the wide steps to the entry hall, Letty took Marian's hand and squeezed it. "I'm so glad you came."

"So am I."

"Letty, you've done a wonderful job. And your house is beautiful," Bridget added.

Under all this praise, Letty was transformed, her round cheeks smiling; her pigtails bouncing with enthusiasm. "Don't worry. I won't let you down."

Marian sat in the car, her heart unexpectedly warm. Who would have thought that she could feel this way about a daughter in law who had always seemed a dull adjunct to her dull son!

They had gone from the cold house out into the ninety five degrees and now into a car where the air-conditioning was blasting away, noisy with its efforts. It made both their noses runny and they reached for tissues at the same time. Then Bridget drove swiftly and neatly making their passage down the busy four lane Route 80 smooth as glass.

They were silent until Bridget turned the air-conditioning down so Marian could hear her. "How old is Letty?"

"Thirty-nine."

"Thirty-nine, she seems a lot younger than that. And they are still putting off having a baby?"

Marian nodded even though Bridget was sitting beside her and had her eyes on the road. "She always seemed like a teenager. I don't know why. They've been married six years and they saved all their money for this house. Now that they are in it, they're still afraid to start a baby. I don't know. I try to tell them that the time is coming when they won't be able to... produce one. I had all mine before I was thirty."

Bridget gave her a quick smile and went back to competently passing slower cars. "I had all mine, all four of them, after forty so I guess I understand. She's very sweet. And the marriage seems to be okay, don't you think?"

"Forty!"

"It was a third marriage and we married mostly just to have children," Bridget said by way of an explanation.

Marian confessed. "I've never understood Bro. He's kind of a pain in the neck. He stayed home a long time. Or, rather, he kept coming back home. He couldn't seem to get started in any career he wanted to be in. First he wanted to be a baseball player and he kept playing on the town team and going to tryouts but no one would take him. Then he got married the first time and went to Alaska and worked on the pipeline and got frostbite and came home without the wife. After he got well, he decided he wanted a business degree so he stayed with us while he was getting it. Jeb would get so mad at him I could hardly be in the house with both of them and still Bro wouldn't go out on his own till he met Letty. I never understood why."

"What business is he in now?"

"Plumbing supplies. That sounds unbearable dull to me but he seems to like it well enough. By the time he started going with Letty, I was so anxious to get him out of the house, I would have liked anybody he married. But Letty is okay, don't you think? She seems to think he's wonderful, so that's first step."

"I think she's very sweet. And she likes you."

Marian found she wanted to put the warmth she was feeling into words but was unable to.

"All these years, I didn't know if I liked her. But I'm glad he married her." She turned toward Bridget. "I'm glad you brought me here."

Bridget smiled. "It was a good idea, wasn't it? "

Marian went back to contemplating Letty. Should she call her tonight, or let her alone for now to get adjusted, and call her tomorrow night? And what would she say to this unhappy young woman that would make her feel her day had been worth it?

# CHAPTER SEVEN

Marian woke the next morning with a new feeling of anticipation. As if there was something right in her world instead of the way it had been—with everything wrong for years now.

She sat up, pleased, ready to smile. She should have thought of the party long ago. Did it really take five years to recover from Jeb's death, to think of something for herself, something she might need without knowing what it was? She would call Letty this morning and ask if she had any new names of friends found. And very shortly, she would call a halt to the search and send out the invitations to those people Letty had found.

She put her feet on the floor enjoying the sensation of cool from the tiles. It had been a long time since she had had this feeling of pleasant anticipation about a phone call. She thought of the way new expressions appeared on Letty's face, reshaping her lips and widening her cheeks. But what if Letty had talked Marian's visit over with Bro and he had discouraged her from any cooperation with Marian?

Stop right there. She wasn't going to fall into that trap.

She got out of bed and went to the bathroom, threw water on her face and brushed her teeth. When she came back, she went to her closet and slid the mirrored door which was having trouble staying on its track. Bro. It was amazing how a beloved child could become an albatross.

The trouble with Bro was... what? She had never been able to decide. Jeb had worried over him all his life. Why didn't Bro get better grades in school? Why wasn't he good at sports? Why hadn't he ever made friends who could help him? Why couldn't he make up his mind about what he was going to do to make a living? What if they had lived on the prairie in the 19th century (that was one of Jeb's favorite reference points for no reason that Marian could ever understand) and Bro didn't have the chance to go to college as he had, the freedom to fail at something and then move back home and recover from it as he had. What would he have done then?

Till Marian, even though she also wondered, was forced to stand up for Bro. Not that it didn't describe what Bro had done, but what would Jeb have done under those circumstances? Jeb was forever comparing Bro, the second child, to Addie, the first one, an apple polisher if there ever was one. And a girl besides.

It was not till Bro was twenty-eight, and divorced and recovered from his Alaska adventure of frostbite and illness, and then met Letty and decided to marry, that he had begun to come out of his funk, and finally somewhat satisfy Jeb that he might yet be a rewarding son. Now, remembering Letty's unhappiness and—by report—Bro's, with the new house which they had saved every penny toward for all those years, Marian began to feel sorry for both of them.

Her good cheer began to seep away, as her thoughts found an old track. Why was it that both their girls had seemed to know all along how to start their lives and they had done it the moment they were free of school? They were like Marian's sister Alice in that way. Hadn't Alice, even before she had settled on becoming a nurse, always had that air of certainty, that secretiveness that said she was going somewhere, never mind where, she knew?

Addie had from her early years always admired Alice and then, maybe because that was what Alice did, decided early on to also become a nurse. Addie, like Alice, had not been deterred by arguments, had sniffed indignantly at her father's opinion of nursing. She had pointed out that nursing had a lot of pluses. Because there was a shortage of nurses, she could move anywhere in the country and get a job right away, and there was always the possibility of moving up the ladder as Alice had. She might even marry a doctor and retire to a country-club life.

Probably those arguments had also been learned from Alice.

Behind the wobbly mirrored door, the closet, shorn of Jeb's clothes, was more than half empty. Marian's wardrobe had never been plentiful but since Jeb died and she had no money to buy clothes, and no particular interest in them, what the closet held had become even more limited.

She picked out her second best pair of jeans which she had just hung up the night before. They were close to wearing through on the seat at which time she would need to replace them. It would really help a lot if Stuart would hire her full time.

She went through her drawers looking for a shirt of some kind and, at the bottom, found a tie-dye t-shirt which Bro had given her for Christmas long ago and which she had never worn because it was so ugly. But here it was, newer than anything else in sight.

She put it on in front of the mirror and enjoyed the shock of the colors, orange, bright blue and pink. She added some lipstick, orange because of the tie-dye, and looked curiously in the mirror. What she saw had almost nothing to do with the Marian she was underneath. She laughed. She might beat seventy yet.

She went downstairs and made coffee and fixed some dry cereal for breakfast. Her good mood returned in spite of the fact that there were no more bananas to put on the cereal. For years she had thought of herself as poor but she hadn't known how much poorer it was possible to be. It was an odd way to live. She would really enjoy making a more reasonable income at the library but for the moment the poverty didn't worry her. One advantage to it was that it kept her to-do list simple.

She was ready to sit out back and reached for the back door knob, but as she did that, the front doorbell rang. Probably Felicia.

When she opened it, it wasn't Felicia, it was Bro. Of all people. Bro never came.

"Hi Mom."

"You're looking good." She kissed him. The sun shone around him and on him, so that his pale blue shirt, the flowering pink camellias and the biscuit-colored house across the street all seemed to glow.

He was dressed for work, a sports jacket and a tie. She seldom saw him like this. Bro was a little plump, of course, he always had been. But he looked quite nice. In his forties now.

"Come in. Come in. What a nice surprise."

Maybe it was because she had been looking at retirees all week that he looked very fit, very healthy. His face was tanned, the lower party still pink from shaving. He should be on his way to work in Martinez. He had come quite a bit north of that. Why?

"Would you like some coffee?"

"Sure." He followed her back to the kitchen.

"So what's up?" she asked when she handed him the cup. "I'm sorry I'm out of sugar. I never buy it anymore."

He shrugged—maybe Letty was training him out of sugar— and seated himself at the table in the place that had been Jeb's. She could feel the sides of her mouth turn down in resentment. If she wanted to keep that as Jeb's spot, she had a right to. But she said nothing.

Bro lowered his eyes and started slowly. "I don't have any appointments till eleven so I had some time. Thought I would say hello. How are you doing?'

Marian nodded agreeably, as she used to do with Jeb. "I'm okay. I'm spending a lot of time on this party for my birthday. Only it turns out it's going to be after my birthday. We couldn't get it all put together in time for the actual day."

She hadn't seen him for several months. Had he changed or had she? She had to admit that he had a good profile, his nose a little long but narrow and straight, in fact, he had become a good-looking man now that his face had matured and he had taken to wearing contacts rather than glasses. He must have been spending more time in the sun; his light brown hair was nearly blond.

"I've heard about that." He hesitated.

About what, she wondered.

"That's what I wanted to talk to you about. Your party."

"Of course. Letty has told you about it. "

"That's just the thing."

Marian felt a bump of anxiety at whatever was coming.

"I don't want you taking up Letty's time this way, and getting her all stirred up about whether or not she can find these old friends of yours. As if that was the most important thing in the world!"

He looked quite stern now, taking on the mantle of a man who always has a right to scold his mother. Ponderous as a judge, she thought bristling, making sure that his judgments were always given proper weight.

"But she likes it. She wants to do it."

"She wants to please you, that's all. But that's not what she should be doing. She shouldn't be wasting her time this way. She needs to get out and find a job." His face assumed his stubborn look, a look Marian remembered back through all these years. Bro had always been, starting at two, the most stubborn person she had ever met. By the time he was five, he had had Shirley, or even Frank, beat at that.

"I only did it," she said, trying to hide her resentment. "Because I know she likes that kind of work. She loves doing research on the computer. And she told me just yesterday that she wants to go on doing it."

"Mother, you think that if it's something you want, then the other person is going to want it too. But that's hardly ever true."

Marian's hair bristled. He thought he had the right to interfere between two women because they were only women. "If Letty doesn't want to do it, let her say that to me. I will be happy to okay that."

He finished the remainder of his coffee with dispatch, and wiped his mouth with a good, cloth handkerchief from his pocket since she hadn't given him a napkin. "She said that only because she wants to please you. You've never made her feel welcome. But that's not what she needs to be doing right now. She needs to be out looking for a job."

All that certainty! Marian and Bro had seldom quarreled. When Jeb was alive, he had been the buffer between her and Bro, he had assumed he should deal with his son. But this time Bro was wrong. She wasn't going to give up the warmth she had reached with Letty just because Bro thought he had the right to forbid it.

"She told me she's collecting unemployment."

"That's true, but unemployment is only half pay. If we're ever going to buy any furniture, she has to get a job. And she wants to. She doesn't enjoy staying home there all day with nothing to do."

They were both standing up now, facing each other, gladiators conducting a quarrel toe to toe. For the first time in many months, Marian wanted Jeb in the room. What could she say that would bring him back between the two of them? She had never known how to deal with a son, once he was walking and talking and went off to school, he had become a male.

"Why did you have to buy such a big house?"

"We didn't have to buy it. We wanted it."

"Have whatever kind of house you want. But if Letty wants to quit, have her call me. I'm not going to take your word for it."

"Why is it you always want to ruin whatever I'm doing?"

"Ruin you?" She could feel the tears welling up. She hated to cry in front of him. But she was not going to back down just because Jeb wasn't around to help her out.

"I've always wanted you to succeed. I always took your part with your father. Why is it you want to start a quarrel? I feel sorry for Letty."

He kicked the maple chair with its flowered cushion back away from him, sending it against the wall with a sharp bang. "I might have known it would be impossible to talk to you. And what have you done to your hair?"

Marian laughed through her tears, defensively she had to admit. "What I do with my hair is my own business. And if Letty really wants to help me, that's her business."

"Okay. I don't care what you do with your hair, if you don't care you're making a fool of yourself. But I'm the man in my family and I say 'let Letty alone.'"

He crossed the living room in minutes and went out the front door, almost, but not quite, slamming it before Marian could speak.

She stood inside motionless, and was intensely sorry, mostly because he had gone away. The house was empty again. There was no flow of love and need between human beings. She heard his car start and drive away.

It was several minutes before she could move. Left alone, she began crying. Okay, crying. She hadn't had a fight with any of the children since Jeb died, and she hadn't expected one now. She got a paper towel from over the stove and wiped her eyes. She had to talk to Letty before Bro got home and gave a different version of their meeting. She was not going to let him spoil what had started there.

There was a little coffee left in the pot. She poured it into her cup. It was nearly cold but she drank it anyway. There was time enough to call Letty. Bro was on his way into work and probably would not call his wife from there, leaving this subject till he got home.

As the sense of what had just happened washed over her, the quarrel lost its importance. It had been unexpected, at least by her, erupting between them without warning. Almost like those earthquakes which came on at a time people were fully absorbed in other concerns. Then the concerns dropped away in the enormity of the shaking and what it might mean. Then shortly after the shaking stopped, the news came that the experts had looked at the instruments and downgraded the quake to something like a three-point five, so mild that half the people in the area hadn't even felt it and only a few grocery shelves had spilled piles of canned goods.

She opened the door to the back yard and looked out as she had been about to do before he arrived. The sunlight had that golden look that it acquired in autumn. The leaves that had fallen on the patio were yellow also, their winter look, but the rose bush against the fence had taken on a new life from the brief rain a week ago; it was thick with white buds promising a late blossoming.

What she remembered now was how handsome he looked and how self-confident he sounded. At long last he had reached adulthood and was no longer a child she had to worry over. And he had scolded her about her hair. She smiled a little at that. He had always been incredibly conservative about dress and manners.

# CHAPTER EIGHT

Marian needed to call Letty sometime today, and talk to her about Bro's objections and what Marian had said in response.

Or did Letty know already? Had Bro told her before he left that he was going to end the project? That he forbid them from wasting Letty's time on the party list? Would Letty obey? Then what could the two of them do? Give up the party altogether? The more Marian thought this over, the more discouraged she became. Not only was the party in jeopardy but also Letty would be hurt. Marian had spread her cloak and coaxed Letty inside. She wasn't going to retreat, give up the party and the chance of seeing old friends again, and Letty too. Maybe it would be better to call Bro and try to talk to him. She would try to make him see how important the party was. But of course that wouldn't work. A whole lifetime with Jeb had convinced her of that. Men, or particularly men like Bro and Jeb, were incapable of seeing something like the party as important.

The party was so important because… She couldn't quite say why but it was. After she had seen those people, or as many of them as came, she would we able to go on into the winter, and begin to think about the rest of her life.

She was twisting her hands over this but was afraid to call Letty. She let her mind drift to doing things with Letty in the future. How lovely it would be for Letty to come down to Sonoma and the two of them do something simple like going to the Farmer's Market or to the nursery and buying a few outdoor plants for Letty's back garden.

There were things she could teach her daughter-in-law that

her daughters had never wanted to learn. What fun it would be to give Letty a lesson in bread-making. They would mix it, rest it, take turns kneading it, then punch it down and chat as they waited while it rose, first in the bowl with a wet paper towel over it, and then as loaves in loaf pans in the oven with only the pilot light on. They could look up other recipes and debate them while waiting for the bread to rise and then to bake.

An image of Bro rose up, sharply demanding Marian's attention, almost as if he was in the room and saw her hardening against him. That was the way he had been as a toddler, demanding that she turn away from Addie and give her attention to him.

Me, me, he had said, as always. And whenever she had turned to him, she became caught up in his difficulties. Everything was always so hard for Bro and this had made Marian feel guilty because she wanted to spend more time with Addie. This all came back to her vividly, the times he had struggled with simple things like tying his shoestrings and reading the clock, and demanding that she help. Then his later hurdles with bike riding and arithmetic. Maybe he's really left-handed and you have switched him, one of her friends said. Or maybe he's dyslexic.

When he was struggling, he would send her looks that said: please don't give up on me. After more than forty years these looks still came back to her so that she suffered whenever she was at odds with him. Oh, they knew how to trap you, didn't they? With their baby hands that had trouble gripping a pencil, their skinned knees, and fresh tears.

The day slipped away. She went to bed with the thought that she really would call Letty tomorrow morning. That would be soon enough. Eight o'clock would be a good time to talk to her. Bro would have left for work and they could have a comfortable conversation, solving the problem together.

But at seven-forty five, while Marian was finishing her poached egg and half piece of toast, the phone rang. It was Letty. He must have left early.

"I'm so sorry about Bro," Marian said, startled and anxious, before the girl could speak.

Letty's voice was loud, emphatic. "Mother Marian, you are not to worry about anything."

What did that mean? Marian said: "I don't want you to worry. I will find someone else to hunt up those names."

"You mean you want me to give it up? No way. I said I would do it and I will."

"But Bro?"

"Bro and the furniture will just have to wait. I promised you, and besides I like doing it."

Letty's voice was a hundred times more confident than it had been the day when Marian and Bridget were with her.

"But I don't want to cause any trouble between the two of you."

"Don't worry. As soon as I'm done with this, I'll find a job. I was working before I met Bro and I will work again. At least for a year before we start a baby."

"But wasn't he angry?" Marian voice was low.

"He'll get over it."

Letty sounded so good. But maybe she hadn't told him yet. What would Bro say when he was told no? Even as a child, he could be stubborn and hold a grudge. He reminded her of what Jeb could be like in full anger.

She was too nervous to properly hang up the phone after this call. It fell from her awkward hand, banged against the small table and fell to the floor. When she tried to pick it up, she dropped it again. The memory of old anger had undone her. Ten minutes later, washing her few dishes after she thought she had recovered, she broke a cup by smashing it against the faucet. Looking at the piece left in her hand, she saw her palm was decorated with a spot of blood. She dropped the broken piece into the sink and examined the hand through the soap bubbles. Another spot of blood appeared. She held it under the running water to wash off the soap, and watched the blood bubble up. Water was not stopping the bleeding. When had she ever cut her hand? Not recently enough to know what to do. She got a paper towel and wadded it up and pressed it against the bleeding. It began to hurt. Maybe she had cut it more than she thought.

She turned off the water and abandoned dishwashing. Why didn't she use the dishwasher the way she used to? When there were only a few, it seemed easier to wash them up. But not if she kept breaking them. She went upstairs in search of bandaids. When she found them, she also found it was no use trying to put on a bandaid until the bleeding stopped. She changed the soaked paper towel for a dry washcloth. Then took an aspirin and lay down in bed, her sore hand upright to slow the bleeding. It began to throb.

What a start to the day! Luckily she was not scheduled to work today. Probably she should give up going anywhere on the bicycle. Gripping the handlebar would hurt. She would have to walk to the store for more bread. That would take half an hour and as much time to get back. All this because Bro had upset her.

What was she going to do about Bro? The ringing of the phone startled her. It was only nine o'clock. Who would be calling so early?

Instead it was Addie. Marian sat up happily. If there was anyone she would have called for a smidgeon of sympathy, it was her oldest child. Not that she often asked for sympathy.

"What's happening?" she asked. Addie usually had a reason to call.

"What are you up to?" Addie demanded.

"Nothing much. I'm lying down. I cut my hand."

"Good because I'm coming to see you. In fact, I'm almost there."

"You are? Why?" She hadn't seen Addie since June because Addie had gone to the East Coast for a conference in the summer and then toured New England.

"I have a day off. Orientation." Addie taught nursing at a college in Sacramento. Even though this was only an hour and a half away, she seldom came for a visit.

"That's wonderful. Do you want to go out for lunch?"

After the call, Marian gingerly unwrapped her hand and saw it had stopped bleeding although the cut was a full inch long and still hurt. She put a bandaid over the cut and then thought that was useless. Every time she opened out her hand the bandaid would pull loose. She put a rubber glove on that hand. She would wash herself and dress with the other one. A look through her closet was not very rewarding. She would have to wear the tie-dye shirt to lunch and hope that Addie wouldn't notice it.

The front door banged open before Marian got down stairs.

Addie was getting near to fifty, a few pounds heavier but still handsome. She was not as tall as Bro, had rounded hips and dark brown hair which she wore wound on top her head because she kept it long. After her many years in a nursing uniform, she now wore good-looking suits most of the time. Today's suit was a nubby rust tweed, very expensive-looking.

"You look great," Marian said, kissing her, thinking what a satisfactory child she was.

"Mother! Where did you get that blouse, and what did you do to your hair?"

"I told you I was going to dye it."

"No, you didn't. Is it permanent?"

"Not as permanent as I'd like. I have to have it touched up at the roots at least once a month which is very expensive."

"And the blouse?"

Marian laughed, embarrassed. "Bro gave me this for Christmas years and years ago and I never had the nerve to wear it before now."

"No, he didn't. I did. But I was only ten. I didn't have any taste then. And you've never worn it before, in all these years. Maybe we'd better stop downtown and buy something for you to wear to lunch."

Addie walked into the kitchen and looked everything over, even opening the back door to look out at the patio. Checking things over even though she had left her mother's house thirty years ago and never lived in this house. What was she looking for? She didn't look in the refrigerator. Both Addie and Bro, the first few years after they had left home, anytime they came for a visit, would go immediately to the refrigerator and look in.

Marian was glad the dishes, if not washed, were at least in the sink. "I know, I have to scrub the floor one of these days."

Addie shrugged at that. "Are they ever going to give you more hours at the library?"

"I hope so. He said maybe in the next quarter he'd have more money. Would you like some coffee?"

"No thanks. Did you tell him you really need the money? He may think you are one of these well-off widows."

"Yes," Marian lied. And began to feel ruffled. "I think he really wants me to work more. He's been very nice about the book."

"He should be. You could take that book any number of other places and they would pay you a royalty on all the copies sold."

It was something to have Addie concerned. But also aggravating. Addie had no children to organize and her management skills were of a high order. Given half a chance, she would take over Marian's life and never let go.

"There's a new place to have lunch," Marian suggested. "Bridget says it's very good."

"Whatever. After we buy the blouse."

"They have a good crab salad. Is that all right?"

"Sure. As long as they have salads." But Addie was now looking her mother over carefully, and Marian knew there was another subject that was about to be broached. What could it be? She hadn't mentioned the party to Addie so that wouldn't be that.

They bought a dark brown jersey top which looked all right with Marian's maroon hair and shabby khakis, and then they had lunch in a patio with a fountain and a magnolia tree hanging over them. Addie seemed in a good mood though the unnamed subject that had brought her to Sonoma still hung out there among the trumpet-vines on the nearby wall. She had gotten started talking about hospital policies which needed to be changed, a subject on which Marian had little information and no opinions.

Marian commented in what seemed to be an appropriate way and enjoyed the food, the novelty of being out to lunch, and her successful daughter. After the blouse, she had bought a new lipstick, asking Addie to approve the color. This small luxury made Marian feel festive. She had ordered a glass of red wine to go with the novelty of crab salad, and her hand no longer hurt. The autumn day was warm and mellow.

"Bro called me," Addie said suddenly.

There it was. Marian sighed and said goodbye to her delightful day. Bro must really be upset. The brother and sister seldom communicated. "And what did he say?"

"Mother, I don't understand this. What party is he talking about? And what is it you have Letty doing? This is not like you. I told him he was making the whole thing up."

Marian took a last sip of wine and tried to put her mind in gear. Should she start with being seventy? No, Addie would not understand that. Just start with the party.

"I'm giving myself a birthday party." She explained that had made her think of all the friends she had lost over the years and wanted to see again. That was all. Very simple. But how to find them? Everybody in California moves every year or two. Finding all of them was a challenge. Letty loved looking things up on the Internet. And she was free for a few weeks while she collected unemployment.

Addie skipped over most of that. "Well just because she hasn't got a job now doesn't mean she shouldn't be looking for one!"

Marian threw out her hands. "I don't know anything about that. I never asked her why she wasn't out looking for one. I knew she would like doing this and so I asked her if she would look up a few of these names for me, and she said yes."

"Bro thinks it's some plot you dreamed up to make him lose his house." Addie's tone of voice indicated that she agreed this was absurd.

"You know better than that. Why would I want to injure him? I told her I was grateful for all she had done so far, she didn't have to do any more, but even after he complained she said she still wanted to do it."

"Mother, you get into the most ridiculous situations."

"I don't!" Marian said heatedly. "I never get into ridiculous situations because I never do much of anything. I thought before I die I might try doing some of the things I've never done."

Addie was silent, looking at her mother in mystification. Finally she said, in a low voice: "Is it cancer? A lump in your breast? You're going to be just like Grandma and do nothing till it's too far gone to operate!"

How did you counter something like this? She might as well be communicating from the North Pole. "No. Not at all. Let's go back."

"I want you to see Dr. Dvorak. He's very good. And he's very comforting to talk to."

"Addie, I am not sick. And I don't want you taking charge of me."

Addie looked miffed. She finished her coffee and paid the bill. Through the silence, Marian looked at the lovely patio and the carefully tended plants and the fountain in its carved concrete basin, all of which was so much nicer than her own patio, and thought she might feel better if Addie had never come. The quarrel was going to leave an unpleasant residue.

"Addie, don't be angry," she said in the car.

After a while, Addie replied: "I'm not angry. I don't care if you have a party, and I don't care at all about Letty. Let her do what she wants. But I want you to see a doctor. Okay?"

"Okay," Marian said because it was the only way to get this over with.

By the time they pulled into Marian's driveway, Addie had

changed concerns. "I don't know what to say to Bro. He called and asked for my help, and he never does that so I have to do something."

That was a relief. They sat silently in the car in Marian's driveway while they thought over this dilemma. It was interesting to know, something Marian had never thought about, that Addie wanted to be consulted by Bro and wanted to help him out.

She took a deep breath. When had she ever told any of the children what she thought about the others? Maybe she owed Addie that much for her worried concern. "I think Bro is doing better than he ever has. He looks really good. I think he likes this job and he loves the new house, and Letty is really sweet so he should be glad he has her but he's overstepping by trying to make me do something that has to do with my life. Tell him you talked to me and I said it was Letty's decision but not to worry about it. This is only going to go on for another week or two. If he would just ignore it for a minute, it will all be over and no harm will have been done."

Addie turned to look at her mother reflectively. "You really think he's doing well? I thought he'd never get over Dad dying. And Letty just seems like she does whatever he asks and doesn't add much to the equation."

"Don't sell Letty short. There's a lot more there than we thought."

"Okay. But what do I tell Bro?"

That was a new chapter. Addie agreeing to do what her mother suggested. "Tell him he's invited to my birthday party. You're invited too."

Addie laughed a little unwillingly. "Let me see first what day it is."

"No, really come. You should remember some of these people."

"Okay, I'll see. And I'll talk to Bro and tell him it's nearly over. But you talk to him too."

"All right. I'll try." Marian kissed her. "Thank you for lunch.

And for the blouse. It really makes a nice change for me."

"You make sure that guy gives you a better job," Addie said as she started the car.

Of course, she wouldn't leave without some instruction or other. Just the same, Marian stood waving her goodbye, and was happy with the day. It was something new that Addie had agreed to her mother's solution. A whole new era might be ready to burst out.

Of course, Marian didn't talk to either Stu Siskind or Bro right away. She meant to but was thinking it over… what would she say and what would either of them say, and what would happen after that? What would the consequences be? She really didn't want any more scenes.

While she was still in this stage, she got a call that was even more unexpected. It was from her youngest child, Lilly. When last heard from, which had been last Christmas, Lilly had been in the Aleutian Islands dispensing information about babies and nutrition. The call came at eleven thirty at night, when Marian had been asleep for an hour.

The first thing she said when she heard the familiar voice was: "Are you all right?"

She had a feeling of guilt about Lilly that had lingered all these years.

Lilly was a wispy, pretty blonde who had been elected Prom Queen by the high school football team. From the age of 14, Lilly had had an endless troop of young men following her everywhere.

Marian had tried to defend her. What did it matter if she got married early? That didn't make a difference any more. All the wives ended up working for years and years almost as much as the husbands. Didn't Jeb remember what it had been like trying to find a job without a college degree? Jeb had reacted angrily to that argument and refused to discuss the subject. After college, she came back home less and less. They hardly ever heard from her except when she decided to change continents and dropped by for a day between assignments. It became impossible for Marian to track the thinking of her favorite child, or know the person she was developing into. Lilly had left them all for worlds they knew nothing about, working for Doctors without Borders, or La Leche or Women to Women. When she did come, for a lightning two or three day visit, she was always cheerful, contented, glad enough to see them but had little to say.

"Nothing's the matter," came her daughter's voice over the phone. "What's the matter there?"

"Nothing wrong here," said Marian. "Are you going to come and visit?"

"I might. What's the matter with Bro? Why is he calling me up?"

Marian's surprise came out in a burst of almost-laughter. "He called you? Has he ever called you before?"

"Only when he was getting divorced. Is he getting divorced again?"

"No. He's just upset with me."

"Oh well, that's nothing new. I'm going back to Africa in a few months."

Marian was instantly alert. "Why Africa? When?"

Much as she liked Lilly's independence and thirst for adventure, Marian had been stiff with anxiety the whole time Lilly was there before. The word Africa brought up starvation in Darfur, civil war in Nigeria, gunmen and rape in Zimbabwe, and that terrible virus Ebola.

But Lilly had finished her interest in communication. "I'll let you know." And she hung up.

## CHAPTER NINE

Marian missed Felicia, her sounding board. She dialed Felicia's number but there was no answer. Felicia had not yet evolved to owning an answering machine. She had been away for more than a week now, visiting an old aunt down in Santa Barbara, and had been as vague as usual about her return. She didn't own a car so she was probably waiting for someone to offer her a ride rather than take a bus home.

Marian went off to the library. She was not scheduled to work until tomorrow but she had just finished reading *The Once and Future King* by T.H. White and thought she needed another dose of Arthur and the Round Table.

She hadn't really expected that Stu would be in but there he was in his office, studying something on his computer. Stu was knowledgeable about computers but, just the same, he was frequently at war with them. On impulse Marian walked in.

"Good morning." Her voice was higher than usual.

Stu looked up, frowning. "Good morning, Marian. Are you working today?"

Marian analyzed his tone and thought she had probably made a mistake. He was rather short anyway, but now that she was standing close by and he was seated, she towered over him. He had reared back as if he didn't like that. She looked down on his head and wondered if his grey curls were the result of a permanent. That had been suggested by a patron one day and had stuck in Marian's mind.

She plunged in before she could lose her nerve. "No, not until tomorrow, but I am anxious to find out if you are going to have any more hours for me. My daughter had to buy me a blouse yesterday so that I could go to lunch with her."

Stu's expression which had started out as mild interest now changed to something else. "More hours?"

He touched a key on the computer and watched the pages that appeared. The work schedule. He used arrows to search. There was a pause while he read what he found and then sat back to digest it. Marian felt more awkward than usual. She had thought in the past that he was not entirely comfortable being a boss. She should never have walked in like this and accused him. She was tempted to say something to ease the situation, but didn't.

"You sure you want to work more?"

That was easy. "Yes."

"All right. Gladys is going on vacation next week. I was planning to get a temp in but I can give you half of her hours instead. Can you do another twenty hours next week?"

A mini fireworks display went off in Marian's head. Twenty hours, and she would get paid for it the next week. She could buy food for the party.

"Yes."

"You will have to come in a day before she leaves and train on the front desk. You haven't done that job before. Are you sure you can?"

"Of course." Any ninny could do the front desk. Marian had been taught that drill soon after she started working. When whoever was on the desk had to use the Ladies Room, she had been called on to fill in. Stamp books out, check books in. Didn't Stu notice what went on?

She left the library immediately, without even picking up another book, and went home to bask in success. When she got to her front yard, she found Felicia looking over her bushes.

"Where have you been?" Marian demanded.

"Oh, transporting. You haven't been doing enough watering."

"You mean 'transporting' as in magic carpets? What kept you

so long?" Marian kissed her. She couldn't help it. "You've missed all sorts of happenings. Come in and have some coffee."

Marian recounted her most recent adventure while she made, not coffee, but iced green tea in celebration of Felicia's return. Felicia was not bowled over with Marian's new hours at the library. "I knew all you had to do was ask. But even without that, I knew you would find the money somewhere by the time you needed it. 'Need' calls out for solutions."

What could you do with Felicia? "Well, I'm glad you weren't worried. I was."

Marian went on to tell the story of Letty, Bro and Addie. Felicia lost her flighty air and paid close attention. To her, family affairs were always fraught with anxiety, maybe because she had so little family. "I'm glad you didn't bow down to him. That's what you usually do."

"I don't. Now tell me about your trip."

Felicia sighed. "I'm glad I went. Everyone down there is dying."

"By everyone, you mean…"

"My aunt. Her husband. My cousin."

Marian settled in to listening since that was what was needed. She didn't want to mourn for these people she had never met. She had her own spot of mourning to do and she hadn't done it yet. When she felt she had heard enough, she said: "One of my party guests won't be coming…"

It was Bonnie from New York, almost the first person Marian had thought of when she began to dream of the party. Letty had located Jeb's long-ago friend Bill and Bill had told her that Bonnie had died some years back. Breast cancer. He had a new wife who had come with children which had turned out to be rather fun but meant they had had to decamp from Manhattan and move to Westchester. Letty had invited him to the party without asking Marian but he said he couldn't make a long trip without the whole family.

I don't care about him anyway, Marian thought. But Bonnie… she had very much wanted another chapter to their friendship, a chance for Marian to return all the care that Bonnie had given her. Now that would never be.

Maybe it was too late for the party altogether. She should have done it right after Jeb died. How many of the people she still wanted to see had died in the last year or two?

Only minutes after Felicia left, Marian's phone rang. She was almost too tired to answer.

"What?" she asked indignantly.

It was Addie. If someone hadn't invented the cell phone, Addie would have. She made dozens of calls, day and night.

"Are you going to be home?" she asked her mother.

"Of course. I'm always home."

"Stay right there. We'll be there in ten minutes."

"We?"

"Bro and me."

Marian lay down on the couch and tried to prepare herself for another session with Bro.

Addie might mean this as a kiss-and-make-up meeting, but Bro could be spoiling for another fight. There was no helping it now. No telling them 'do not come'. If she had any gas in her car, she would leave and go up to Jack London Park. She looked at her ceiling and saw spider webs that had returned. There was always something that had to be cleaned, wasn't there? Something complicated and exhausting but didn't make your life any better after it was done. Maybe it was Addie who wanted to fight.

She sat up when she heard the car in the driveway and stood by the door. Minutes later, Addie marched in, taking charge with what was probably her classroom manner. Bro followed, looking tattered and hang-dog.

"I haven't got a lot of time," Addie announced.

"Then you shouldn't be wasting it here," Marian replied.

Both children looked at her in surprise. This was not the same mother they had been expecting to correct, lay down the law to, force her to change her attitude, and manner.

"Mother, don't be like that," Addie pleaded. "You need to

listen to Bro and you never do."

"I do listen to him, and always have."

Prompted, Bro laid out his complaint. "You have no right to interfere in my marriage. That's all. I never interfered in yours."

"You were our child… the question of interference never came up. I told you this was up to Letty. I love having her work on my party but I told her she doesn't have to. You should let her do what she wants. " Marian walked around them to close the front door.

Addie had her own opinion on the matter. "Mother, she wants you to like her. That's why she's doing this. She thinks you never have. Tell her to stop. Tell her you will like her anyway."

"I do like her." Marian found herself ready to spring to the defense of the Letty who was now her friend. "I told both of you that. Addie, why did you go up there and get Bro all excited again?"

"She didn't," he objected.

"Mother, how can you say that? I was trying to make peace. I just called him to tell him you said it would only have to last another week or so." They were all still standing in a rough circle, fortified with sharp words, formalities forgotten.

"It doesn't look like peace. Listen to you. Don't you understand this party is important to me?"

Brother and sister looked at each other and there was a pause. It was long enough for Marian to wonder why she was fighting with her children? She turned away toward the kitchen.

"I'll make some coffee. You might as well sit down."

Instead of sitting where they were, the pair followed her to the kitchen and with formal seriousness took chairs at the kitchen table.

"Mother, I don't understand," Addie said as if Marian was being deliberately difficult. "What party? Why are you giving a party when you don't have any money?"

"But I will have some money. The library is giving me more hours next week."

Addie was confused. New things were not supposed to happen in her mother's life; she was too old for her life to change. "Is he getting ready to fire you?"

"No. I don't think so. I think he wants to give me a bigger schedule."

Bro's expression said he was being forgotten and he didn't like it. He looked at his mother. "You never liked me. Why was that?"

Marian was stung. "That's not true."

"Yes, it is."

Addie was not to be left out. She turned to Bro. "That is true, but you never think of what it was like for me. I was the only child for years and all of a sudden you were there and they both hung over you all the time."

"I never did," Marian said.

"Talk to ME," Bro said.

"Bro, you always had your father. He thought you were wonderful right from the beginning. He was so glad to have a boy. When you were a year old, he went out and bought you work boots just like his, the smallest size they made. They didn't fit you till you were ten."

Marian had dumped out the old coffee and made new. With only the briefest pause to see if the pot was starting to perk, she brought cups and spoons and sugar to the table, and sat down unhappily facing these two who were trying to make her miserable.

Bro turned on Addie accusingly. "Maybe they weren't paying as much attention to you but you always had friends come over to play and all those dolls, a whole roomful of dolls. Every time they had a fight Mom would look at me accusingly, like it was all my fault. Then Dad would leave the house and Mom wouldn't talk to me or play with me. That didn't happen to you."

"I never did that."

"Yes you did. Especially that summer before I started nursery school and you went to work. I kept worrying about what I had done wrong."

Addie spoke up. "I remember that. I was starting kindergarten. Or was it first grade?"

Marian was tired already, her heart hurt. She had to end this. But without any prompting, her mind had flashed back to that time. She remembered that her nipples had begun to hurt at the thought of leaving him when he was still so young. Jeb has lost his job that's why she had to go to work. She could remember the exact day when she first took Bro to daycare so they could both see what it was like. She had been hoping they would take him even though he was still too young, and at the same time was hoping they would refuse. Let Jeb solve his own problems. There weren't so many daycare facilities then; there was only one she could walk to and push Bro in the stroller. In the morning she had banged her finger between his high chair and the breakfast table in a rush to get the meal over and a blood blister had developed immediately, so severe that it hurt when she had to pick Bro up. She had been angry with herself. Why was she always making things worse for herself? She remembered that sea of despair she sank into every time Jeb lost a job.

She poured the coffee into three cups and watched while the two frowned at it, then gave in to the familiar habit and began to drink, pausing to ready new arguments.

"You're right," Marian said to Bro. "I was angry but I was angry with Jeb, not you."

"Why?" Bro asked.

"Because," Marian said firmly what she had never said before. "He had lost his job. He was always losing his job. We would just get our finances straightened out and a few dollars in a savings account, when he would lose his temper and be fired and I would have to go to work."

"I don't remember that."

"Of course you don't."

Now she had their attention. Two pairs of eyes focused on her face. She had been too loyal to Jeb all these years to be honest with them. She might have done better without the loyalty.

Bro was curious, but suspicious, wanting more. "Why was he always losing jobs?"

"I don't really know."

Addie was on another tack. "I thought you liked going to work. You always seemed jazzed about what went on there."

"Not the kind of jobs I always got. Bottom rung, poorest paid, no vacations, no opportunities to get anything better." Marian got out a clean plate and put some bananas on it.

"But why jobs like that?"

"Women didn't get paid much and I was untrained, just a housewife, and I always had to take what I could get in a hurry. By the time I got paid, we would already be behind."

"But there are all kinds of jobs in L.A. Isn't that so?"

Marian sighed. "There weren't so many jobs for women then. Or maybe it was because I didn't expect anything better." That was a new idea that had only come to her in the last year. Maybe she had made some of her troubles herself.

"So why did you take it out on me?" Bro said.

Maybe there was no answer to that. Or maybe it had to do with Jeb. Which was the thought she always tried to bury. "I'm not sure I did. You're nearly fifty. Can't you give up blaming me for everything?"

"But this is my whole life," Bro said with surprising dignity.

Problems like this never had solutions—someone had told her that years ago. "I'll try to talk to Letty. Will that make you happy?"

"Addie?" Bro said.

Addie took on the serious look of one who has to make a judgment.

Marian surrendered. " Let's just have some peace for now, okay." Jeb. The millstone round her neck for nearly her whole life. If she said that, they would be angry with her. And if that was true, why had she stayed with him all those years?

"Okay. We can discuss this another time," Addie agreed.

Bro nodded, frowning agreement temporarily to a truce. Maybe wanting time to think all this over.

Marian stood up and kissed them both goodbye, exhausted, willing them to leave. Did they really have a right, this far from childhood, to come back and accuse her of being a bad mother, or mistreating them when they were young? Was motherhood a lifetime engagement? No mistakes allowed. Hadn't she dragged and coaxed them long ago into rational adulthood in spite of hard circumstances?

Standing by the door, they looked a little sheepish. Kissed her back. Didn't mention the party or Letty. Did she want them to come to the party? If so, she would have to invite them again.

Jeb, why are you still giving me so much trouble five years after you died?

Marian skipped dinner and went immediately to bed with a book she had already read.

When she opened to the first page, she remembered it so thoroughly it could not distract her. She had been very angry with Jeb over a long period of time. And Bro was right. When she was angry with Jeb, she disliked Bro too. Unfair, of course but whoever knew at the time when one was being unfair. Feelings that strong bubbled up and could not be restrained.

# CHAPTER TEN

Letty came to Sonoma three days after Addie and Bro made their unhappy exit. She had called the evening before and announced that she was driving down. If Marian was free. Marian didn't even remember that Letty had a car of her own. Marian, of course, said yes. She didn't ask why. Was Bro still angry? What had he demanded? She pictured Letty as she had been that day with her face wet with tears. The party wasn't worth that. Marian would give it up. Or maybe they had enough guests already.

When Letty walked in, wearing lipstick and a happy smile, she looked like a different person than she had been at home. Her hair was pulled into a neat ponytail and she was wearing a polished beige outfit of shirt and skirt that might have come from Banana Republic.

Marian took one hand and pulled her into the house. She couldn't hide her pleasure in seeing her. "You look so well."

Instead of "hello", Letty said. "I'm done." And handed Marian a sheaf of papers. She stood back and grinned, waiting for a response.

"Done? You did it? Oh, thank God." Marian hugged her.

"Is that enough for your party?"

"I hope Bro's not still angry, is he?"

Letty tossed her ponytail. "He's getting better. I called some job listings yesterday. There's one in Davis, the opposite commute. And one which is work-at-home."

"Wonderful."

They sat down side by side on the couch and looked over the

list of names, addresses, email addresses. Letty had found forty-two, given up on six.

"Letty, you are amazing." The list felt like gold in Marian's hands, won with hard work and perseverance. "I don't know how you did this last group so fast."

"As soon as I have a job, he'll forget all that. But I'm sorry I had to give up on these. I really tried. I even called people with the same last names in different towns hoping to be lucky."

Marian was looking over the list of six. She cycled from delight to disappointment. "I guess I couldn't expect to find everyone after so many years."

Letty went on happily reflecting on success. "People were very good about giving me their email addresses, that isn't always true. That way you can send them an evite and you won't have to buy postage."

"What's an evite?" Marian turned over the longer list. A small errant feel of happiness was starting in her stomach. But something was still wrong. There was someone she was looking for and couldn't find. Who was it? No name jumped out at her.

"I'm going to do that too," Letty said. "It's an invitation where you get a response so you know who's coming. I'm going to design it. I've done them before. Here I brought a sample. What I need is the date and place of the party. And then maybe you want to say something for each one about when and where you knew them, just three or four words."

Marian's eyes had gone back to the short list. No. The name she wanted wasn't on either the found or they unfound list. With effort, she switched her mind to the invitation. "I changed the date of the party, because it was getting so close. It's only fifteen days now. Do you think that's too short a time?"

Letty shrugged. "Most of them are in California. There are only the four in the Midwest, one in Massachusetts, maybe it's too late for her. I told most of them about the party so they're already expecting it. And Patty Plum who is in London. But probably you don't expect her to come anyway."

Marian blinked, thinking first that Patty Plum had always

been difficult, delightful but caught up in her own plans. It made Marian dizzy to think of these people agreeing to come, accepting her desire to see them after all these years. What kind of lives were they living now? That made a difference. What wives or husbands did they have to consider? Those were more people whose lives she was disrupting. She was asking them all to give up a weekend to travel all this way, come to her party simply because she wanted to see them again. What gall!

She was overwhelmed with doubt. Did it help that she was in Sonoma? It was true that people traveled to Sonoma all the time. They came for the wine and because it was known as a pretty town.

"Maybe you should put a drawing of grapes on the invitation, show them something besides my party."

"Okay, but what is the date?"

She told Letty the date. The party was going to be on a Sunday afternoon so people could travel on Saturday, and people who weren't from too far away could still travel home on Sunday evening.

"Those who were flying could come into the Sacramento Airport," Letty said. "We can meet them there, Bro and I."

What would Bro say to that? "I don't know where to tell them to stay overnight," Marian said, thinking of that for the first time, entangled in all these complexities.

Letty was enjoying the planning. "We have those three extra bedrooms. No beds in them but we could always rent beds. I'll put a note in the evite, saying something like 'ask about places to stay'."

Marian quailed at the thought of what Bro would say to this. She had never envisioned worrying about where people would stay. She had only thought about that moment when she walked into the party and there they were.

Now this was a real party. She needed to sit down.

"Well, I could put up two people here," she said doubtfully, thinking that she would have to clean her house more thoroughly than it was now and would she have time to do that?

"Don't you worry about it. I'll go over to the Visitor's Bureau and pick up a list of B and B's and attach it to the evite."

Marian was becoming light-headed. She stood up. Letty had turned a dream party into a real one. Would anyone really come? What if none of them came? What if those who came were too old and she couldn't recognize them? What if the good friendship was what she remembered but they remembered a bad one?

Marian tried to focus again on the minutes when one old friend after another came through the door of the Clubhouse and she could take each hand in turn and bring back all she had lost.

"Letty, you are a marvel." Her voice was weak.

"I'll ask Addie first if she wants to stay with me," Letty said. "Or do you think she will want to stay here?"

How odd. Had Letty wanted all along to know Addie better? "Ask her. I can never predict Addie."

Letty looked pleased at this. She drank half of her sun tea and then gathered up her purse and notebook to hurry home.

"I promised Bro a strawberry pie and I don't even know if there are any strawberries still in the market."

"If you can't find any, make a pumpkin pie from canned pumpkin. That always used to please him."

"Okay," Letty said. "But I don't have a recipe for that."

"There's always a recipe on the can. Or there always used to be."

They kissed goodbye. Marian held the solid young flesh with thankfulness. She felt at sea in this new world where you could find old friends on your computer, where, if you were clever you could really have a dream party. "I'll write one statement for each person about when we knew each other. I'll do it tonight and email them to you tomorrow."

As she opened the door for Letty to exit, she thought that she was in for a long evening. Writing did not come that easily. It might require several cups of coffee. But it would give her practice on the computer which she needed.

"Wait a minute." She hurried back toward the kitchen and picked up a pair of garden snips. "Come next door," she said. "My neighbor is away."

They went next door where Marian unhooked the front gate by reaching inside.

"Where are they?" Letty asked.

"Tahoe. They go to gamble."

Nothing else was said as they threaded their way in the narrow space between the house and a fence, to the back yard which was a small square of overgrown grass surrounded by billowing bushes. Here Marian approached a bush of white roses and began cutting judiciously.

"They let you do this? That's really nice of them."

Marian nodded with satisfaction. "They don't spend a lot of time out back so I keep the bush cut for them. Their drip system works really well, doesn't it? Not many roses still going this late in the year. Mine have quit."

She kept cutting till Letty's arms were full of long branches and white roses. Then they threaded their way back around the house and out the gate where Marian picked up an old copy of the weekly advertiser which no one ever read anyway, and wrapped it around the roses.

"These should be all right till you get home."

Letty dropped the bundle in the back seat and embraced her. "Thank you so much."

"Drive carefully."

When the car pulled out, Marian found her eyes had teared up. Who would have thought that? Turning toward her house, she saw that the fog had swirled in and the house looked lonely.

When she was back inside, she got out the list and went over it. Still his name was not there. Angry with herself, she went to her desk and plowed through several stacks of unfiled papers till she came to her original list. There he was.

Phil Lucas. Her heart gave a little bump. Maybe she had left him off the copy she gave to Letty, intending to put him on later. That was crazy that she had thought of him at all. But she was crazy, wasn't she? Now she was over seventy by a week and looking for a man she had met for only two days forty years ago. Her heart gave a quiver. Never too old for foolishness.

She turned on a lamp. The evening was coming on fast now that it was nearly October. She could just put something in the mail. And hope. She would have to try the old, old address. Should she do it now? She was not hungry enough to start dinner. Maybe if she rode her bike around the neighborhood that would calm her down and then she could look for some notepaper.

The bike rattled and squeaked as she led it out of the garage. Some of her neighbors had their lamps on already. There was no light on her bike. She went back in and put on a white shirt to make herself visible in the dusk. Phil Lucas.

All right. If her letter came back, she would tell Letty he had fallen off the list and ask her to find him. If Letty couldn't find him, that would be that.

# CHAPTER ELEVEN

The good memory of Bonnie's friendship had faded in the difficult days that followed Marian and Jeb's return from New York. After a few weeks of spending evenings with all their L.A. friends that they had been so anxious to see again, evenings where they recounted their New York adventures with increasing embellishments, they grew tired of that and had to admit that their return offered only limited joy.

Jeb's mother Cecily had begged them to come and stay with her. Cecily was lonely. She was living alone in her house since Jeb had left for New York. Foster was far away in the Army and didn't visit much when he did have time. There was no matching request from Marian's parents so they moved into Jeb's old room.

The huge battered, dusty house, which had been built in 1910, closed around the former New Yorkers with welcome silence. It had once been an elegant house. There were ten rooms, with staircases back and front, and numerous closets and pantries which were seldom visited. For days they did nothing but sleep and eat as if they had returned from an Arctic expedition. Luckily the bed was a double and the mattress practically the newest thing in the house so they curled together like spoons and slept better than they ever had in New York. Temperatures were mild. They needed no covers with the window wide open. There was a huge old magnolia shading their side of the house so the room was always dim. Even with its Dodgers posters, the room restored them.

Jeb became comfortable in the house where he had grown

up but after a while Marian was restless. She was partially restored by the peace that had developed between them since they got back and didn't want to complain. The house, so unlike the tract houses in her part of town, made her uneasy. It spoke of the well-to-do life in which Jeb had been born and she had not. That life had died with Jeb's father who had been an officer with the railroad. Marian had hoped for some semblance of that life but now it was clear Cecily was penniless.

Yet they were better off here than across town. Cecily was a world easier to get along with than Marian's mother Shirley was on her best days. Still, besides being nearly as poor as Marian and Jeb, Cecily was set in her ways and those ways were not what Marian had grown up with.

The kitchen was particularly difficult as Marian struggled to prepare meals for all of them. Cecily ate very little. She seldom cooked anything but ate cold canned food standing up at the sink. She was in the habit of using one plate and one cup throughout the day and rinsing them off as needed. Although she tried not to show it, she became alarmed if Marian had too many dishes out or used the stove to cook.

"Mother, would you like for us to get a little hibachi and cook outside? Would that be better?"

Cecily never answered these questions, instead hastily excusing herself, she would flee to her bedroom and not come out for hours. When Marian tried to apologize or ask what she could do to be less alarming, Cecily couldn't or wouldn't answer.

She might have adjusted to Cecily if they were going out to work during the day. They had arrived with only a few dollars left from their New York adventure and this was soon gone with no replacement in sight. Getting jobs was a necessity but there was no easy way to get to any work.

"You mean there's no bus," Marian asked.

"It's over on Central."

Marian tried to count up the blocks but failed. It was a long way and would be a long way walking back at the end of each day. "How do all these people get to work?"

"Everyone has a car. Or someone in the household has a car."

"Aren't we going to have a car?"

"Just wait till I get it fixed," Jeb promised.

Cecily had had Jeb's car for some months after they went to New York, but it had died under her hands and she had made no effort to get it going again. She did her marketing in the corner grocery store or when one of her friends took her to the supermarket.

Jeb started spending every day in the garage working on the old Dodge. "It won't take long."

After a while Marian began to doubt this. Jeb would take his second cup of coffee into the garage every morning, and get out his father's old tools. After lifting the hood of the huge old Dodge, he would thumb through the manual and tinker with various parts. But when Marian went out there an hour or two later to see if there was any good news, she would find the garage door open onto the street, and an assortment of Jeb's old friends gathered there to hear the stories of their New York life. Didn't any of these old friends work?

"Are you getting anything done?" she would ask, sometimes tartly.

"Just be patient. This is not so easy. This buggy's twelve years old."

Cecily was now buying the food that Marian cooked for them. Knowing the woman lived on a small pension, Marian began to feel desperate. She got up one morning determined to do something to move them forward. As soon as Jeb disappeared into the garage, Marian set out to canvas the neighborhood.

She tried asking Cecily for information on her neighbors but Cecily had evidently spent very little time getting to know them. Marian thought if this was her neighborhood, and she had lived there upward of ten years, she would know who was ready to pay for help. Awkwardly, embarrassed, she knocked on every door in the block, introduced herself and asked if they needed any housework or yard work. Some people took the time to politely consider the request but the answer was pretty uniformly no. They weren't unfriendly—that was a help—but most wives were home during the day and did what was necessary.

When she finished both sides of this block, she went down the street and started on the next one. At least she was doing something, not waiting at home for Jeb to make things work.

On her fifth or sixth day of this, she found a couple who needed childcare for their twins while the wife worked. They would be happy to shift from their distant babysitter who only spoke Spanish to Marian watching them in their home. If she gave them a better price of course. The money was not much but Marian was not going to turn it down. She went on knocking for several more blocks until she found one more child. Talking fast, she combined the two jobs in one house and started work the next day.

Cecily shyly smiled her congratulations. Only Jeb was displeased.

"You always do that," he said. "You try to show me up."

She did not want to say—'If I didn't, we might starve,' so she said instead: 'when you get a job I'll quit if you want me to.'

Three two-year-olds was more of a challenge than she had expected. The boy twin, in particular, could not be let out of sight. Speechless but ever cheerful, he could climb over the security gate, or out the window in his room in the blink of an eye. The two girls were more inclined to study things before they moved which gave Marian time to re-direct the action.

The twins had a double stroller which could also take one child standing on the basket in back. Marian promptly tried this; otherwise she would never be able to leave the house. Yes, she could load all three and push them fast to the nearby market and the farther playground. This worked if she put one of the girls standing in back. If she put the boy there he would jump off the moment the stroller paused at the front gate or before crossing a street and she would have to chase him down the street praying that the girls would stay put for a short time.

By evenings when both sets of parents returned, Marian's shoulders ached from picking up children and her head throbbed from anxiety.

In the afternoon hours, when all three children went down for a nap, she would occasionally weep. This is not fair, she said silently to herself, looking out at the sunshine which decorated the yard but offered nothing else for her life. This was not what she had expected married life to be like. What had she done wrong? Shirley and John were begging her to move back home and stay with them till Jeb could furnish her with a place to live. She was afraid of the look that would bring to Jeb's face. Besides, that would tell everyone her marriage had been a failure. She couldn't do that.

Bonnie wrote several letters to Marian in California. Marian wrote back eagerly, remembering the efforts Bonnie had made to see the Californians comfortable in the Big Apple, and wanting again Bonnie's kindness and concern. Marian's letters bloomed and expanded on the prospects for their life in Los Angeles, as she dreamed them up. She also wrote hopefully of Bonnie visiting California or Marian flying to New York for a week.

At the least, these letters were a happier way to spend naptimes than weeping; they left her eyes un-reddened and her heart almost convinced. Dinners cooked for Jeb, and with or without Cecily, prepared with whatever Cecily could find at the corner grocery, and served on the glass-topped table in the patio, became more bearable.

When she got her first week's pay, small though it was, she divided the bills in half. The first half was what she needed for food right now, the second she would save for their next step, whatever that turned out to be. That half she decided to hide in the flowered satin bag where she folded her slips and bras.

With the money in her pocket, she had passed Jeb swiftly on her way into the house, saying only a 'hi'. But when she closed the bureau drawer on the satin bag and turned, he was there in their bedroom doorway.

"Give it to me," he said. "I've got to buy some parts for the car."

"No." She was indignant. When she lived at home, any money she earned as a babysitter was hers to spend.

'Marian, don't be like that. You know we have to have the car fixed."

"No."

He was not used to her disagreeing. He made an angry face and came toward her putting a hand on her arm. "Mare, you know it's necessary. We have to have a car before we can do anything else."

For a minute, she was afraid of him. Was he going to hit her? She pulled away and went to stand on the other side of their bed. "No. I have to buy food."

"Selfish bitch," he said, and turned away and went out of the room and out of the house.

She was shaken. He had never been like this before. He was right. They had to get out of here. She opened the drawer and took out the money she had put away and went out to find him.

After she had given him the money, he looked at her a long time before he said anything. "Don't look like that," she said.

Finally he said: "Okay, I'll see if I can get it fixed for this much. I'm not sure I can. If not, I'll need more."

"I have to buy food with the rest."

He shrugged, willing to let Cecily buy the food.

She followed him back into the house and called one of his friends to come by and pick him up and take him to the parts store. After he was gone, Marian went out to the overgrown back yard trying to calm herself.

It amazed her that in this neighborhood which had mostly been built in the thirties just before the war, the yard looked like the one at her cousin's house in Tennessee which was nearly a hundred years older. There was a chicken coop, now empty, ditto for a rabbit hutch and a small tool shed, all of them weathered gray. There were two Jacaranda trees, both taller than the two-story houses. There were lanky bushes along the back fence, lush untended grass and two wicker chairs so broken they were near to toppling over. Few things in Los Angeles looked old. John and Shirley's back patio was all open so neighbors could admire the built-in barbecue and the striped umbrella inspired by movies.

She felt hidden here and comforted by the age of everything. The neighborhood felt less oppressive. But it was still down at the heels, the front yards not up to those in Shirley and John's neighborhood. Would Jeb ever get them out of here? Or was she right that she needed to do it and not wait for him to.

That evening, after dinner, when Cecily had disappeared and Jeb had gone back to the garage to install the new parts, Marian called her grandfather Frank and asked if she could have lunch with him sometime soon. It had to be on a Saturday because of her childcare job.

He sounded unsurprised which made Marian feel guilty. She probably never asked to meet with him except when she needed money.

Frank McClellan had lost his wife, John's mother, when the children were in high school. Instead of staying with the two teenagers, Frank had handed them off to his sister to raise and gone back to sea, working as a skipper on a freighter until he retired at seventy. By that time, John was grown, established as a salesman to hardware stores, and married with children.

Frank had appeared in this new family's life, and they had welcomed him, though cautiously. What did the man want after all this time? At first, he dropped by only occasionally but he always brought a bottle of whiskey and presents for the girls. Gradually this was expanded to holidays including birthdays. He had bought a little house in West L.A. and an old, but well-kept Cadillac and started a life that was thoroughly unlike his life at sea. He quickly had many friends, took fishing trips in the Gulf of Baja, went gambling in Las Vegas several times a year, and visited the racetrack. .

Shirley watched Frank's new life with interest. "I think he's been planning this all these years," she said.

"So what?" asked John.

Shirley liked the novelty of having Frank visit them. She said that he had lots of money saved and they should work more at getting help from him but John refused to do this. It was Marian who picked up the cue and, when she was having problems getting an agreement with her parents, asked Frank if he could pay her school fees at Santa Monica City College. Shirley and John had a nasty fight because John wanted to refuse his help but Frank agreed to fund her education as long as Marian kept a B average.

Marian found her grandfather not so easy to talk to but she enjoyed being seen with him. Frank dressed, not like a retired seaman but a retired rancher. He had a thick white beard kept short and longish white hair. He wore bolo ties, Western shirts, suede jackets and blue jeans and looked to feel at home wherever he was.

Marian tried to talk to Frank about his life. Once she had offered him sympathy for losing his wife so young and he had stared at her a while and then said she was too young to know what that was like. After that, she kept her curiosity about his life under cover and never said anything that seemed like prying.

Marian admitted to Jeb that she was going to consult Frank for advice.

Jeb was upset. "You don't need to do that. I'll take care of things. The car is almost ready and Bobby thinks the shop will take me back next month."

Marian ignored this. She had lost all certainty that Jeb could arrange anything that would work and she was still angry about the money she had had to give him. Jeb closed the door to the garage before Frank was due to pick Marian up and stayed out of sight. Marian waited in front of the house and climbed into the Cadillac as soon as Frank pulled up. She didn't plan to invite him in to talk to either Cecily or Jeb.

"Hi," she said awkwardly, nervous already about laying out her problems to him.

Frank gave her a long look as he started the car. "I thought we'd go over to the pier at Santa Monica and have lunch there."

Everything suddenly sounded happier. Santa Monica was where Marian and Jeb had both spent two years at the City College and was Marian's favorite beach town. By the time they were on the freeway, she was already feeling better.

"How was New York?" he asked.

She picked among answers. "I liked it. There are always new things to do. Jeb didn't. He couldn't get any work that paid much. And the cold weather was the pits. "

Frank smiled at that. "You should try the Bering Sea!"

"No thanks."

"Too bad about New York. I thought that was a good idea for you two. Away from the family. Trying out new things."

She wasn't going to tell Frank how bad it had been. It was way in the past now. She had almost buried the bits of New York which still came back to her—the heat of summer, the constant stress of finding work and making their money last, the unfriendly landlords and the terrible expense of all the things they couldn't quite afford to do.

Frank parked near the pier and they walked down to look for a restaurant. Once at a table where they could watch the water, Frank ordered a Bloody Mary so Marian had one also, though she seldom drank anything stronger than beer. She watched the sparkle of sunshine on the ocean and the alcohol began to relieve her stress. If nothing else, this was a pleasant change from Jeb's surliness, from the constant worry over the two-year-olds and the difficulties of Cecily's old washing machine.

"What are doing that's interesting right now," she asked.

That seemed to amuse him. "Making back some money I lost at poker."

"Do you lose?" She thought about Shirley's plans for inheriting Frank's money.

He laughed. "Everybody loses now and then. What are you

doing that's interesting?"

"Married life," she offered, thinking that might not be called interesting but certainly all encompassing. And it would signal to Frank that she had been doing something to change her life.

He winked at that and Marian became silent. She ordered a crab salad, delighted to eat almost anything someone else had cooked. Frank had fish and chips.

After some quiet minutes while they ate, Marian said abruptly. "I don't know what to do next."

"How come?"

"I need some practical advice. We need to find jobs and a place to live. We have no money left and we can't get work where we're living. It's like a maze. What should we do first? Mother wants me to come home, at least we could get work from there, but I know Jeb would be miserable there and she would too. "

Frank nodded his agreement. "No. Don't do that. Tell me again what happened in New York."

Marian looked out at the waves and tried. "It was just too tough. Jeb couldn't get any of the kind of jobs he got here. I got work but mostly what he got was minimum wage so we never could make enough money to more than just get by. And he really hated the city. I might have stayed but it wasn't fun enough. Maybe we just expected too much."

"Maybe you took on too big a challenge too soon. Is he really willing to work?"

Marian flushed at this assessment. "I think he is, but it has to be something he likes."

"That's your generation," Frank said with a smile to take the sting out. "We never thought we had to be happy in our work, just get paid."

"Well, things change," she defended, thinking he was really out of touch.

There was silence while he looked at her assessing, and she wondered how she seemed to him. Which she had never thought of before. One didn't with relatives. Why, after all those years he had spent off alone, did he bother with the family and herself?

He finished his fish and chips in short order and lighted a cigarette. "Maybe you should be here, in Santa Monica. Would that work for you? There are buses into Westwood and Beverly Hills. Probably plenty of office jobs here for you. He could probably find something. Can't John help him?"

The sun had come out and sparkled on the ocean. The thought of setting up a household here where she had several friends opened out with the sparkle of the ocean. She had been happy in college here.

"You think you could make things work if you were here?"

She thought of Jeb and how he had seemed a different person when they met here. And the school might have job listings. "But how could we do that?"

Frank's face was stern. "Okay, I'll stake you to a couple of months. You paid back the money I lent you for New York, I know you'll work hard but he has to work too. If he doesn't, I'll give it up."

There was a sting in that. The abruptness of it, the possibility that Jeb might fail further, took her breath away. That she was being judged on her choice of a husband and that she might be losing her own status in Frank's eyes by having chosen wrong. She had married Jeb without thinking how others would see him. Maybe that had been a mistake.

Relief, fueled by the Bloody Mary, flooded her heart. If Jeb couldn't arrange anything that would work, then she would.

"Oh, we will. Both of us. We'll work hard. You're wonderful, Grandpa."

# CHAPTER TWELVE

Back in Santa Monica, Marian reflected on its blessings. She had loved being in college here. It had opened out her world. Not just the ocean at its side. Unlike Long Beach, an industrial port, in Santa Monica the ocean is a playground. There are beaches and beach houses and the pier with its restaurants and gift shops full of photos from the 1920s and ashtrays made of shells. Best of all—the beautiful old merry-go-round with every horse individually carved and carefully restored. To the North and inland are the storied towns of Westwood, Bel Air and Beverly Hills, which lend some of their glamor to that end of the city.

With the old Dodge finally running on money from Grandpa Frank, Marian and Jeb found a one-bedroom apartment near Santa Monica Blvd., in a rather dreary neighborhood of stucco apartment buildings with no yards but which was served by two bus lines.

Marian was nervous because of her promises to Grandpa Frank. She and Jeb both had to find jobs right away, but she was most concerned with hers because she wanted to prove that he had been right to trust her.

She had worked part-time in an office on Wilshire while she was still at City College. After she knew she had a job, she could turn her attention to Jeb, who instead of looking for work, was still waiting for his former employer to come through.

"I'll at least get a good reference because I worked here before," she told Jeb.

He made a face as if bored with her pronouncements but she

ignored this.

Better than a reference, she got her former temp job back, only this time it was fulltime. She would have a small paycheck in only ten days. Maybe everything would start to go well now. Maybe she could begin to think about decorating what was really their first apartment. At the end of her first week of work she couldn't resist taking a bus to the import store.

"Spanish Colonial furniture is in," she reported to Jeb.

"Why is something in and something else out? Don't most people only buy furniture once?"

She looked him over, trying to decide what was wrong with him. He had worked hard on their move, borrowing a truck from his boss and gathering his friends around to carry all their things out of Cecily's house and then up to the second floor to their new apartment. Usually their intimacy at nighttime repaired any small injuries from the day but that night he turned away from her in bed and feigned sleep. Her eyes wet with tears, Marian hadn't the energy to challenge him and insist on some affection.

After that, he seemed mired in depression. Had he really wanted to stay in his mother's dreary home? In defense, she kept up the subject of furniture for several days.

"I don't know. I guess people get bored with what they have. But we don't have anything."

Of course it would be quite a while before they could buy any Spanish Colonial but it was not true that they had nothing. Cecily had given them Jeb's bedroom furniture, plus an old dresser which some grandfather had built himself of cherry wood on a farm in Illinois, and, more surprising, a handsome oak highboy which might have been built in New England and had survived in the family for several generations. Shirley and John had contributed the much-maligned flowered couch which they were finally replacing, and a dull but respectable wool rug they had bought in the first years of their marriage and had never been able to wear out. Secondhand furniture was cheap in the shops on Main Street, good solid furniture which people had brought from Back East when they moved to California, and then discarded when they made more money and looked around for what was fashionable here.

Marian was wishing she could squeeze out enough from Grandpa Frank's money to buy an old pine kitchen table and chairs, but she would have to wait till Jeb was working too.

Away from him all day, she saved up all the things she was used to saying to him, all the small details of her thoughts.

"As soon as we have some money, I'm going to paint the living room dark green and the bedroom rose," she told him one day when she came in after work.

Jeb shrugged and picked up a magazine to read. He had signed up for a subscription to Newsweek and now, with his friends not around to talk to, he read it from cover to cover and the daily newspaper as well.

"I got it," she said at the end of her fourth day as a temp.

"What is it?"

"Just what I've been doing, you know—secretary for the accounting department. But now they want me to stay. I'm going to be a temp for three weeks, then they'll make me permanent for more money."

"How much money?"

She told him, pleased because it was more than she had expected.

Instead of pleased, he was sullen. "You always do that. You try to show me up."

She looked at him in wonder. Was this going to be like New York all over again? She had stopped at the grocery on the way home and bought pork sausage, about the cheapest supper she could make quickly. She put the food in the refrigerator, poured two iced teas although the evening was cool already, and went back into the small, scarcely-furnished living room and sat down beside him on the flowered couch.

"What did you do today?"

"I went back to Dutch's to see if he was going to hire me this week, but he couldn't talk today. Too busy. That's good, they have lots of business. He's going to need me whether he wants me or not."

Marian was not impressed. "Don't you think it would be a good idea if you looked some other places also?"

"I want to see about this first. They already know me there and they like my work. That makes it a lot easier than starting somewhere new."

"True, but if they never get around to offering you the job, we won't have enough money to live on."

He avoided her eyes by looking at the glass he was holding. "They'll hire me. I just have to be patient."

Looking at him she saw that he had gained weight since they got back to Los Angeles. He was inching up from 160 to maybe 20 pounds more. Some belly fat that didn't used to be there bulged above his belt. His face was fuller too. It made him look older, while the pinched skin between his eyes gave his handsome face a cross, uncertain expression.

"I don't think this is a good time to be patient. The whole of West L.A. is full of repair shops. There are lots of jobs listed in the newspaper."

Jeb stood up as if to leave. "You always do this to me. You make everything I do sound dumb. If you don't quit this, I'll give up altogether."

This was worse than New York. Her thoughts scattered in all directions. A crevasse was opening before them. What was wrong with him? She stood up. "I'll get dinner."

"Go ahead. Run away," he taunted.

"We can talk later if you want to."

She took her iced tea into the kitchen with her and made patties of the sausage and set them to fry slowly. She scrubbed potatoes to bake, punched holes in them and turned the oven high. She snapped fresh green beans. She had planned to make an apple pie but when she had the apples sliced into the bowl, they looked too much like pieces of her heart with their cut edges turning brown. Instead, she threw them into another skillet to fry. But now there was a long wait for the potatoes to bake and she had to keep the other things warm on top of the stove.

She got her library book and read it while she waited in the kitchen. When she called Jeb to come to dinner, she found him outside, sitting on the front steps they shared with three other apartments and talking to some men she hadn't met. He took his time coming in while she sat at her mother's card table waiting to serve the food. Did he really want to move back with Cecily and spend his days with his former rum-dum, unemployed friends?

If he did leave her, what would she do? She couldn't afford this apartment alone. How had things gotten so bad so fast when all these months she had thought their times together were getting better as they got to know each other and revealed thoughts that had been hidden?

He came in and sat across the small table from her and ate silently.

"Why did you want to get married?" she asked him when the meal was nearly over.

He looked at her in surprise. "Because I loved you of course. And you wanted to." He said this resentfully as if it was all her fault. "Why did you want to get married?"

"I wanted to start a new life together, a grown-up life."

He blinked. "What's a grown-up life? You mean like our parents?"

"Somewhat. But better. I don't think they're very happy, yours or mine."

He took this as criticism. "Well, my dad died years ago, so my mother hasn't been happy since. What could she do about that? Nothing. I've never gotten to know your parents except a couple of times before we got married. They don't like me."

Marian didn't want to get into that subject. All the things wrong with Shirley and John. Things she knew too well and intended to avoid in her own life.

"Didn't you think you would have to work?"

"Yes, of course. I'm not afraid of working. But I didn't think

I'd have to go back to having my hands black all the time. And I don't like you always showing me up, making me look bad." Resentment flowed out of him.

It occurred to Marian that there was a huge gap between what she saw in the world and what he saw. How would they ever get across that? Her head was beginning to hurt and her chest too… probably her heart. She examined her husband of nearly two years, unable to see him as she had seen him when they were in school and she had thought he had a silent maturity the other boys didn't have. Maybe that had just been unhappiness.

"I'm not trying to show you up. I'm trying to help you, encourage you. I guess I don't show that. I want us to do this together." Her eyes were full of tears but she refused to let them fall.

"All I hear is what's wrong with me. This is like New York all over. There aren't any jobs for me because I don't have a degree. Dutch is the only guy out here who ever hired me. What else can I do except wait for him?"

"Didn't your brother ever look for work?"

"Mom wouldn't let him take a low level job. As soon as he graduated he went into the army because they would send him to school."

Marian thought she would be sobbing any minute now and she didn't want to show that. Okay, if this was the end, then she would deal with it somehow but she would give a great deal not to have to go further into this terrible subject right this moment. If she didn't look at him, then maybe he wouldn't say anymore.

"I'm tired. I'm going to go to bed." She stood up. "You've got the newspaper. Why don't you see if there are jobs in there!"

Of course, before she could go to bed she would have to wash the dishes, otherwise she would have ants by morning. Then a bath because she had to work tomorrow. Then that narrow bed which always woke one up when the other one rolled over. She took plates to the kitchen too tired for any of this.

When she got out of the bath, Jeb said, "I'll sleep on the couch."

She nodded, grateful to have the bed to herself.

Marian woke to the alarm at 6:30 because she had to be at work at 8:00. She had had a good night's sleep but not so good that she was ready to face the end of her marriage. She put it out of her mind and concentrated on getting ready for work.

To her surprise, Jeb got up soon after she did. She could hear the creak of springs from the living room, and a few minutes later, he dropped a shoe. She met him in the kitchen where he was making coffee.

"Good morning."

"Good morning. I'm going down to the corner to get the paper. I'll take a look at the job listings and see what's happening."

She was silent with surprise, but decided it was better not to talk about it. "Good. Do you want oatmeal?"

"You go on to work and I'll make my own when I get back."

Jeb never told her what he found in the newspaper but two days later, he reported that Dutch had hired him back, fulltime, at another fifty cents an hour. His resentful look was replaced by a one of triumph. Marian congratulated him happily.

In celebration, they went out to a movie that Friday night and made love when they got home, the first time in a week.

At the end of Jeb's first week back in the auto repair shop, she mourned with him as the black under his nails became impossible to get out.

"You could wear rubber gloves," she suggested.

"Oh yeah, and have the guys laugh at me."

It had been months since both of them were working. Somehow this was harder than New York. They seemed always to be on the run. One reason—in New York, the work day usually started at nine. Here in Los Angeles, it started at eight, and went on eight full hours plus the lunch hour. Getting to and

from work consumed more time. And they had other tasks—
the Dodge required frequent attention from Jeb while Marian
spent more time shopping for food and cooking than she had
ever done in New York. She was trying to spend less money
and produce better meals.

On Saturday mornings, drinking coffee and sitting side by
side on the Hawaiian print couch which Shirley had grown to
hate and which was still the only piece of furniture in their front
room, the subject of decorating came up again and this time it
was Jeb who pursued it.

"Should we have drapes?" he suggested.

They were on the top floor on a two-story building and the
space which downstairs was taken up by the staircase was here
added to their living room making it a generous size with two
wide windows that looked South and West.

Marian thought over drapes and the fact that to make them
she would have to go back and borrow her mother's sewing
machine. "No one is close enough to look in. Let's do without."

"Okay, but we need some lamps." There was a ceiling light
which did for necessary nighttime seeing but was unpleasant for
reading or even conversation.

"Two lamps. In opposite corners," she agreed.

"And an easy chair plus a table to put a can of beer on."

"Or a coffee cup, or a book. We need a bookshelf too. I
want to take another course in the Fall."

"Why don't we just start with a lamp? Let's go to the import
store."

"Okay. It's your paycheck," Marian said, carefully because it
was Jeb's first paycheck that was supplying the easy hopefulness
to this conversation.

He nodded. "Okay. After the rent, there should be enough
for one lamp."

They went that morning to the import store which had
modern-looking black iron or brass lamps, all more expensive
than they expected. The cheaper ones were the table lamps.
Maybe they should buy the table first. While they were there,

they toured the adjoining section for chairs and small tables. Then they went out to sit in the Dodge and discuss their findings.

"We should try the secondhand stores," Marian said, remembering New York.

They did that and were heartened by the prices. There were a number of floor lamps sturdier than the new ones and also cheaper, but Marian did not care for the styles.

"These are the kind that my parents threw out years ago." Then she wondered if she had hurt his feelings because Cecily hadn't thrown this style out but still used them.

They went back home to have tomato soup for lunch and looked in discouragement at the living room which was unchanged in spite of the visions they had had of it.

"You know," Jeb said. "I could take one of those paper lanterns and hang it on a light socket with a cord and fasten the cord to the ceiling, maybe through a ring, and then staple it down the wall to the plug. There's a light socket and a cord at home in the garage so all we'd have to buy would be the lantern. We could have a lamp any place we decided we wanted it."

"Would that work?"

After lunch they set out on a round trip, first to Cecily's house to find the socket and light cord and then to the import store for the lantern. By evening the lantern was up, hanging over one end of the couch supplying a soft light to their room. That evening, they drank a glass of wine there, setting the glasses on the floor while they admired the living room with its new light and beyond the lantern, the brilliant Western sunset which took hours to dip into the ocean.

"I didn't know you could do that," she said to Jeb.

"Just watch me."

"I'd like to have my parents to dinner one of these days."

Jeb turned nervous. "Wait a little while... till we get something for them to sit on."

After this success with the lantern, a transformation took place. Slowly of course, because Jeb talked out all the parameters of each addition and tried out variations of it before he settled on what would work, but then he would concentrate silently and produce it.

He built a new counter in the kitchen with tools and wood scraps from Cecily's garage creating more space for Marian to work on. They could even eat there till they bought the pine table and chairs that Marian was saving money for.

Marian complained one day that Jeb's new *Newsweek* was on the porch floor because it wouldn't fit in their small mailbox. Jeb went down to look at the box and was quiet when he got back. Marian went on with her Saturday morning cleaning and forgot about the subject but two days later, Jeb presented her with a massive, brand new mailbox built of 1" by 6" boards. He had added a name plate and a lock, and painted it bright green. As mailboxes go, it was a little over the top.

"What do you think?"

"This is wonderful," Marian said, trying not to laugh. "Our neighbors will be jealous."

Jeb grinned with pleasure at her praise. "Now the postman will probably give us all the junk mail he can't get in other people's boxes. But at least we'll get our magazines."

The next month he bought an old library table with a broken leg from the junk store and cut down the height and made it into a coffee table. He looked at this a while, then he stripped the varnish off and stained it walnut till it was quite their most elegant piece of furniture. That evening they walked back into the living room just to marvel at this.

"This time you really did it!" she said.

A few weeks after that was done, one of his friends with a pick-up truck took Jeb to a lumberyard and he came home with some long boards.

"What's that?" Marian asked, but he refused to answer.

He went into their bedroom and she decided it was better to leave him alone in there. A great deal of hammering and sawing could be heard for a while. When she went in to look, at his invitation, she saw he had built a huge box.

"I still have to stain and varnish it."

"What is it?"

It was a double bed frame for a foam mattress so they could finally give up their single bed.

"You are a wonder," Marian said to him, and this time, meant it. "I didn't know you could do all this."

"My dad used to do these things. Otherwise I wouldn't have thought to try." He was reflective. "All his tools are still there in the tool shed, and even some drawings he did. It's like getting to know him.

"I was only eleven."

When his father died in an auto accident, Marian thought. She waited for more but no more came. Instead, Jeb turned and went down the stairs.

"Why don't you talk?" she said loudly to the sound of his footsteps going down the stairs. In her family, feelings were almost always expressed. There were none of these long silences when nothing happened. Maybe she had been unconsciously looking for that, wanting to get away from the constant arguments that went on at home between Shirley and John or between Alice and herself. Maybe she had admired Jeb's wordlessness. But it was too much sometimes, way too much.

Having thought this instead of saying it, when he returned she started in on the subject of the dining room table and chairs. She had saved almost enough money. Could they go and look at them this afternoon?

It was very tempting to buy a television on time payments but they decided no. It was too expensive, would take all their spare money for months, while this building activity was more fun. Instead of watching television, on most evenings after dinner they took a walk. On the weekends, when they weren't exploring secondhand stores, they went to high school football and basketball games, or walked on the pier.

Marian joined the library and began to look at books rather than magazines. Probably she should take another course. She hadn't even taken "American Authors" which everyone she knew had liked. But to give up two evenings a week for that seemed too much for just the chance to find out which books to read. She could find them on her own.

Summer came and went with barely a blip of change to make itself known. The winds were higher for a while but Santa Monica remained sunny during the day and cooled by breezes at night. They took picnics to the beach and some of their friends from high school came over to the shore for a day of sunning and volleyball. In the evening they returned to Marian and Jeb's apartment to drink beer and talk about the different worlds they were exploring.

Why had they tried New York, and having tried it and found it wanting, had stayed all that time?

"It's not a bad life, is it?" she asked one evening over dinner when she and Jeb were alone together.

"Pretty good," he admitted. "Pretty good. We're doing way better."

Marian didn't respond to this because a little more expressiveness would have been even better!

Marian woke up one morning knowing that something was wrong. What was it? She searched the evening before. They were not at odds. Subjects had been more or less as usual. No quarrels. Their usual walk. Some difference as to who would take a bath in the evening and who in the morning. She rubbed Jeb's sleeping shoulder for comfort without intending to wake him. So what was wrong? Her nose for one. Something smelled different. And tasted. She concentrated on her mouth trying to search out the oddity. She was not used to thinking about her body very much. As long as everything she needed to use worked, she could ignore it. Her tummy too was off. As if she had eaten something half spoiled.

After her bath, she woke Jeb and dressed hurriedly. He had more time in the morning than she did because he drove to work while she had to catch a bus into Westwood. When Jeb came into the kitchen table where his bowl of cereal was waiting, he found her sitting without eating, in her usual place, her face taut with worry.

"I don't feel good." It was smelling the milk when she poured it. It had smelled all wrong.

Jeb sat down and picked up his spoon but kept his eyes on her face. "That so? What is it?"

"I don't know what it is. Do you suppose I caught polio at the game the other night?"

He regarded her thoughtfully, eating his cereal in a workmanlike way. Finally, when he was finished and put down his spoon, and looked around for coffee, he said: "Did you have your period this month?"

Marian gasped, choked, threw down her napkin. "You have the wildest imagination!"

She jumped up to take her dish to the sink. Jeb was silent. She came back to the table and took his cereal bowl away from him even though he wasn't finished yet. To make up for it, she poured him a cup of coffee and gave it to him.

After a while he said: "Well, did you?"

"No."

## CHAPTER THIRTEEN

Marian was unable to think of any reason other than cancer for the strange way she felt, so she asked sister Alice for the name of an obstetrician. Alice was now in nursing school and therefore should have a lot of names.

"Aren't you using a diaphragm?"

"No. I haven't gotten pregnant in two years so I thought it couldn't happen. Maybe until I was older."

Alice looked skyward for help with this idiocy. "You should hear the stories I hear. Fourteen is old enough. Even thirteen. I never go to a party without a diaphragm."

It was Marian's turn to be shocked. "You mean every time you go to a party, you have sex? "

"Well, not every time, but how do I know when a real dishy guy is going to be there?"

Marian looked her younger sister over. Alice was still a little plump but pretty and thoroughly flirtatious. She wore her curly dark hair down to her shoulders, except at the hospital when she had to pin it up under her cap. Her skin was very white and she always had dark mascara on her long lashes. Her most frequent expression was of profound innocence.

"Does Mother know this?"

"Of course not. And don't tell her. I need to live at home for at least two more years, till I can finish my training and get a job."

"I won't tell… if you get me a doctor. Someone who is good. And as for you, you'd better be careful. You don't know what kind of men there are out there."

Alice tossed her long hair. "I'm not the one who got pregnant. What does Jeb say about this? Or haven't you told him?"

"He's waiting to see if it's true. I always heard this about nurses. That they're very promiscuous."

"Don't believe everything you hear. After I've worked for a couple of years, I'm going to go to medical school. I can't do that if I'm pregnant."

Marian was impressed in spite of herself. Who would have thought the gossipy, socially-minded Alice yearned to be a doctor!

The doctor provided by Alice was young, just having opened an office in West L.A. with barely enough furniture and a half-time secretary.

"Oh, very definitely yes." He grinned with pleasure. "How old are you? The younger the better."

"Why?" Marian asked while she struggled with the certainty that her life was over.

"The younger the mother, the healthier the baby. I don't know why we can't get that into women's minds. They should get married and have babies the minute they finish high school."

Marian didn't want it in her mind either. "When?" she asked, thinking that there was a lot to adjust to before a baby arrived and her real life ended.

"Well, you tell me when you last had a period."

Marian couldn't remember that. Since coming back from New York their life had been too chaotic. And there were neither seasons nor school semesters to mark the passing of time. Finally, she and the doctor agreed that she must be nearly four months. The baby would probably be born in July.

Marian went home in a state of shock. Forget why she didn't wear a diaphragm! Forget why she couldn't remember when she had last had a period but Jeb could. The item to worry about was what they were going to do for money when she could no longer work. It would be a lot better if it was Jeb having the baby. She was making more money than he was.

She had taken the afternoon off to see the doctor. Now she could go straight home. But once there, she lay down on the bed and let her mind go blank. She wasn't used to having free time in the middle of the day. Or of being alone in the apartment. She stared at the cracks in the ceiling and the marks where the painter had switched from rolling up and down to sideways. Her body had betrayed her. From now on, she couldn't trust it at all. After a short while, having nothing else to do she fell asleep.

When she woke up, she raised her head to look at the room. Was there space to put a crib in here?

She was sitting at the kitchen table drinking iced tea when Jeb came in. He studied her face for a minute. "It was true, wasn't it?"

"Yes."

His face broke into a grin. "How about that? Maybe it's a boy!"

"Jeb!"

"Aren't you happy?"

"How can I be happy? What are we going to do?" She found she was close to tears.

"We'll work it out."

"How? What can we do to make up my salary? I don't even know how long they will let me keep working. A lot of places they make you quit as soon as you begin to show." A sob broke through and crumpled her reserve.

"We can always move back with my mother."

That brought tears running down her face in earnest. "That would be even worse."

He moved to put his arms around her but Marian leaned away from him. "Your hands!'

Usually, when he first came home, he spent twenty minutes or more at the kitchen sink scrubbing the dirt and oil from under his fingernails.

"I washed them at work."

"They don't look clean."

He shrugged. "I always wash them at the shop just before I leave. They've got special soap."

"But you always wash them here again." She had picked up the dishtowel to mop the tears from her face.

"Yes. Well, I'm trying to get the nails really clean for you. I might as well give that up. I'm never going to get them clean enough."

"What do you mean by that?"

"That now I'm never going to get out of this job. I might as well give up even trying."

With that he left the kitchen and Marian had to start dinner while she tried to understand what he meant. She settled on the simplest meal she could think of. Tuna salad with a hard boiled egg in it, and sliced tomatoes. Jeb had been outside for half an hour by the time she went looking for him. She found him sitting on the front steps as usual talking to his friend from next door. When she studied him, she saw he still had the remains of pleasure on his face.

"You're happy about this!" she accused when they got inside.

"It will be fun, won't it? I remember when my cousin Tom got a baby, he talked about it all the time. How it changed every day. How he would tease it till he got a smile."

Marian tried to think about that but could find nothing happy in it.

"I guess you can show that Alice a thing or two now."

Marian almost smiled over that. "She hasn't even gotten engaged yet. She's thrilled with this nursing business. She can't wait till she gets a cap. I told her I would never be able to handle the bedpans but she says that's nothing compared to the blood and vomit."

"What does she like about that? Why did she want to be a nurse in the first place?"

"Because she's on the inside of something. She can talk about all the things she knows and we don't. Do you really like the idea of a baby?" It had never occurred to her that he would.

His boyish look left. "I'd like to be a Dad. Mine died so long ago. Wait till I tell Mom. Now we'll have our own little family and they will all see what we can do."

By Saturday, Marian had grown accustomed to the weird sensations of her body; it overpowered her sense of self, and stilled her with the knowledge that the baby was growing without any help from her; she merely had to wait till it was done, and she could get back to her real life. She obediently bought the recommended vitamins and, at suppertimes, they began to talk, disconnectedly, about where they could possibly put a crib.

Grandpa Frank was in Vegas and Marian was just as glad. She didn't want to have to tell him there would now be a longer delay in returning his money. What they would do when she had to quit working still eluded them.

Marian thought she should break the news to Shirley and John in person.

"Can we come to dinner?" she asked her mother by phone.

Shirley was immediately suspicious. "What's up?"

"Nothing is up. We just haven't seen you two for a while. We've been doing all sorts of stuff to our apartment."

"We were planning to go to the movies on Saturday. I guess you could come on Sunday. Is there a problem?"

"No problem." Marian mentally crossed her fingers.

When Shirley opened the door, she looked carefully at her daughter. "You've gained weight!"

"No, I haven't. Is Alice going to be here for dinner?"

"Not a chance. We don't see her much now that she has half her days in college and half working at the hospital. They certainly work those girls hard. "

Jeb handed Shirley a bottle of wine selected by Marian, and Shirley looked at it suspiciously. Her eyes darted over her son-in-law in a careful examination. Marian wondered when her mother would finally begin accepting Jeb, if ever.

"What's all this?"

John came in from the back yard and shook hands with Jeb.

"Just open the wine, Shirley, and don't look a gift horse in the mouth."

He kissed Marian, and it occurred to her that maybe he missed having her around. They all stood in an awkward circle while Shirley held the bottle of wine and waited for more of an explanation.

Marian and Jeb were silent so Shirley shrugged and announced: "I've made pot roast." This was a concession because she hated to cook and usually thought pot roast took more time than it was worth.

It was Jeb who finally broke the news. "We're pregnant," he said proudly.

Shirley nodded her head. "I knew it. Didn't I say that?"

"Well," John blinked and then said heartily. "We'll have to drink to that." He ignored the bottle of wine Shirley was still holding and went to the cupboard where he kept his Kentucky bourbon.

"How do you feel? Are you sick yet?" Shirley put the wine down on the table and moved close enough to peer at Marian's face.

"No." Marian said, although she had been earlier in the day when she first got up.

Glasses of bourbon and water were poured and passed all around.

"You have to be careful now and not gain a lot of weight."

"Mother! The baby has to weigh something."

"Let her alone, Shirley. Come to the living room. Let's sit down a minute and adjust to this."

John, of all people, who had refused to aid the two with money for their new apartment, quickly began to worry over their expenses to come. How would they cope with Marian not bringing in a paycheck?

"We're working on that," said Jeb who seemed more confident than he had ever been with her parents.

Shirley, against all Marian's expectation, began to think with some excitement at the prospect of a grandchild. "Wait till I write to my mother! She will start knitting right away."

"Remind her that Los Angeles is not as cold as Tennessee," said Marian. "I wore Granny's sweaters for years, sweating the whole time," she told Jeb.

The whiskey began to work on them and all their voices rose, particularly Marian's because she found she wanted her parents' approval more than she ever had. It didn't matter much anymore what they thought of Jeb, but she wanted them to love this child. Why was that, she wondered as she listened to the others.

Because, it came to her, the child was already curing some part of her marriage months before it was born, maybe it would also cure her relationship with her parents. A vision rose above the familiar walls and the new flowered couch, and superimposed itself on the spurious painting of a Paris street scene that was her mother's prize possession. The vision was a picture of a loving family sitting together delighted with each other. Would that ever really come about?

Before they could finish their whiskey, Shirley shooed them all to the dining room. The roast was getting cold.

They had the wine with dinner, and they all shortly fell into free-associating over the coming child and on children in general, all of them talking pretty much at once without bothering very often to listen to each other.

"I hope it doesn't get to looking like Grandpa Frank," Shirley said.

"What's wrong with Frank?" John asked indignantly. Then remembered: "His dad, my Grandpa, always looked at a new baby right away to decide if it would be a good worker. Claimed he could tell from the beginning."

"Mother, what's the thing about blue eyes? I'd like for it to have blue eyes like Jeb."

"Chances are against it."

"Marian, you were a very fussy baby. I thought we'd never get a night's sleep."

Finally, late in the evening, full of roast beef and slightly glazed with alcohol and chocolate pie, they left for Santa Monica. Shirley and John both kissed Marian goodbye, a rarity.

"That was nice," Marian said about the evening. Maybe it was coming true.

"Only time he's ever talked directly to me."

That baby was Adele, forever afterwards Addie, slightly late and slightly under-sized but otherwise healthy. She had dark hair like Marian's and Jeb's blue eyes. She was a cranky baby, rather small and opinionated. The nurse or doctor who put mercury in her eyes right at birth to prevent an eye disease splashed a grey line across the top of her nose which gave her a chipmunk look for the first three months, until it faded. After that she became very cute, sometimes even pretty.

Marian was frightened by the fact that Addie did nothing at the ages specified in the baby book. She talked early but walked late.

"It must be the fault of your genes," she said to Jeb. "My mother said we all did just what we were supposed to."

When Addie's first tooth came six months before it was supposed to, Marian threw the baby book away, and decided to rely on a new mother's group she had joined.

Marian found herself changing with this new life. She read parents' magazines and found some satisfactory exercises that pulled her stretched stomach back in. She fussed less about Jeb's shortcomings and more about how Addie measured up to other babies. She spent weekdays on the beach so that Addie could get sunshine and Marian could read magazines and daydream.

The financial problems worked their way out as they have a habit of doing. Jeb's boss recommended him for a six-week training program on GM cars so that a few months later, Jeb got a substantial raise in pay. When Addie was almost a year old, they found a two bedroom apartment farther from the beach for the same price they had been paying for one bedroom. Alice got Marian a Saturday job as a ward clerk at the hospital and Jeb took care of Addie on those days, driving her around to all his friends' houses to show her off.

There was peace in the household and in not too long it seemed as if Addie had always been in their lives. Sex became a pleasure again though Marian was very careful with the new diaphragm.

For several years in their new apartment, they were absorbed in decorating it. They repainted the walls pale gray and Marian bought a secondhand sewing machine and sewed drapes and bedspreads and covered pillows. They stripped down furniture from the Salvation Army or junk stores and re-finished it. They found pictures they liked, sometimes posters or prints from artists' shows on the Boardwalk or from galleries which would have sales. They learned how to buy old frames and strip them, cut mats and glass and frame their art themselves. They bought patterns and painted flowers on Addie's wall and stars on her ceiling. Then after a couple of years of this involvement, they found the apartment was full—there was only so much you could do with four rooms.

Marian thought Jeb was rather bored too but he wouldn't admit it. He wanted them to get a dog but Marian was against it. She didn't need something else to worry about. It was in the middle of this hiatus, that she opened a can of varnish one Saturday in preparation for putting a new coat on the coffee table which was getting scuffed and she immediately had that sensation again. There was no mistaking it. Somehow her diaphragm had stopped working.

She closed the varnish back up and sat down to deal with this news. How could anyone manage two children? What could she do with Addie in those early months when you had to feed a baby six times a day and then burp it and then get up in the night for indigestion. She had a hard enough time now finding any spare moments for herself—getting her hair cut, or working on a tan. With two children, that time would disappear entirely.

Jeb was out at a car auction. Just to look, he had promised, not to buy. We're going to have to replace this car one of these days.

Marian went to check on Addie, who turned out to be playing quietly with her dolls in her room. Marian went back to the kitchen, made a cup of coffee and sat down, trying to adjust. She was now working five afternoons a week; she would have to quit again. That was not all bad. She was ready to leave that job. It was a small real estate office with ten salesmen, each of whom tried to treat her as a private secretary. Every day found her racing to keep as many of them happy as possible. The one time she had complained to the manager, he had told her that was part of her job, she would have to learn how to handle the men.

All right, she would quit her job, wait until she began to show, maybe the sixth month if she was lucky. Then what would they do to make up the money? And how much was a new baby going to cost them? And where would they put it?

Jeb came in while she was still sitting there. He was anxious to talk about a Mustang he had seen, a sweet little car, dark green with a white top. One look at her face told him something more momentous was coming.

"What happened?"

"I'm pregnant."

"Oh, yeah?" He sat down across from her, stared at her, not sure how he should react.

Marian wished that he would kiss her, hold her, tell her it would all be all right. Finally, instead, he blinked and grinned. "Hey, maybe it will be a boy this time!"

That was Bro, nicknamed by Addie with a name that stuck all through high school. When Marian tried to remember details about Bro's early years, she found all the memories she could bring back were of Addie because Addie had gotten there first and changed their lives so completely.

Bro, christened Howard Abbot, was born five years after Addie. In contrast to Addie, he was a plump baby with hair almost blond, who slept through the night at three months.

Marian admitted to Jeb that she found Bro rather dull. Jeb, on the other hand, thought having a son put them in a newer and better orbit. Perhaps the problem with Marian was that this was all a repeat of the earlier babyhood. Nothing that Bro did was amazing. It had all been gone through already. He was slightly late to walk and talk and seemed easily contented.

Before Bro reached a year, Marian started a new job working thirty hours a week. She told Jeb it was because she had found a babysitter who needed the work, and to make sure Marian kept her skills. The real reason was that two children at home was more work than working. She had had enough of dirty diapers, falls from the crib and lost pacifiers. Besides it was all boring.

After a year and a half of working three-quarter time, Marian found that she was bored at work also. What was wrong with her?

# CHAPTER FOURTEEN

When Marian and Jeb's fortunes began to change, Jeb finished junior college in night classes and embarked on a six-month training period for insurance sales. After a number of false starts, he was finally able to escape from car repair and start in the insurance business.

However, before they could raise their heads and contemplate a better future, something happened that darkened all dreams of the future.

It had been a sunny September; then the skies turned gray in October. Marian was at work at her three-quarter job in a funding company when Morrie, the comptroller, announced over the loudspeaker that he had gotten a call from his wife. Why, the staff wondered in low voices, should they care?

Not that they had anything against his wife. Morrie was a bent, thin, anxious-looking man who wore expensive suits too big for his slight body and took off or put on his glasses several times an hour. If one didn't know that he owned fifty five percent of this successful business, one would think that nothing went well in his life. Until you met his wife who dropped into the office a couple of times a week; then you were likely to re-assess. She was quite pretty, expensively dressed, and drove a white Jaguar. Her tinkling, self-confident voice filled the offices when she was there, but she was so friendly, it was hard to dislike her.

Morrie's voice crackled over the loudspeaker: "She says President Kennedy is going to make an important announcement at two o'clock and everyone should listen."

Odd! They were mostly Republicans. But this was Beverly Hills, anything could happen here.

"If Morrie's wife said he should commit hari-kari, he'd do it," the front desk girl whispered to Marian.

This invitation gave the whole office a chance to take a break; they ambled obediently down the hall. Marian was just learning how to set up a spreadsheet on the IBM typewriter which had an extra-long carriage and she was grateful for the interruption. Morrie herded them nervously into his palatial domain. His wife was coming to join them; her high heels could be heard clattering in a rush down the hallway.

The lower level clerks were especially pleased at the novelty of being in the boss's office, and only pretended irritation at this interruption to their day. They examined the shrine of pictures of Morrie with various major names on the nightclub scene while he tuned the radio in to a news station.

The announcer said: "The President of the United States."

Then the high voice with its unmistakable Boston accent, familiar to all of them even those who hadn't voted for him, came on.

"My fellow Americans… the urgent transformation of Cuba into an important strategic base by the presence of large, long range, and clearly offensive weapons of mass destruction…" The President spent long paragraphs introducing a subject which they couldn't grasp at first.

"What did he say?" the front desk girl asked.

No one answered her for minutes. Perhaps it was because this subject was so far from their normal life.

"Usual bullshit," someone said. Marian thought it was the office manager, a tall dramatic woman with piled-up hair who reportedly had first come to California as a showgirl.

Morrie turned off the radio, and still no one moved.

"You can go back now," he said gently.

After a while they shuffled out without anyone answering the front desk girl.

"What is it?" Marian asked the head salesman in a whisper. "I didn't understand."

"War. Missiles. The Cubans are going to bomb Miami if we don't bomb them first."

Now that the words had been repeated, Marian realized she had heard them, it was only that her mind had refused them.

"Atomic bombs," the head salesman went on loudly. "I knew he'd never be able to handle this job."

Back in their own offices, no one was able to start working again. Marian sat looking out a window and saw, not Beverly Hills but the newsreels from her childhood—the landscapes of Europe in 1945, scorched earth, town after town of buildings that were only shells. Nagasaki.

Addie was about to die. She didn't die right away, how could she survive in a world that was nearly obliterated? She wanted to talk to Jeb but was afraid to call him. She needed to go home and see her child and hold her. She looked down at her pink cotton dress, saw it but felt as if it had already been burned away... she felt naked, exposed to the bombs that were coming.

The almost two weeks that followed were like nothing else in her life. She clung to Jeb but could barely speak to him and went about her duties like a robot. When she touched Addie, she saw her no longer alive, but a naked burnt skeleton curled toward the earth. When she looked at the undistinguished stretch of Santa Monica Blvd. where they lived, its palm trees and three story apartment houses, she saw instead acres of shattered earth with the smoke of destruction still rising slowly toward the sky.

With great effort she adapted to the point where she could go to her job, come home and talk to Addie and bathe her and put her to bed. She could cook enough to feed them all but she could not read or even sit and rest. If she had no activity, she would stand in the middle of a room and look at nothing. Jeb seemed scarcely much better. He called his mother twice a day, afraid for her but saying little.

Then the crisis was over. The missiles had been removed from Cuba and the President announced the country was safe for the moment. Comedians joked that it was safe for the week, maybe. Terror subsided slowly while the exhausted citizens tried to forget it. The first weekend it was over, Marian spent a full day at home weeping soundlessly on her bed trying to get back to her accustomed world.

John, Shirley, Alice, Grandpa Frank, even Cecily seemed to forget this time of terror, but Marian was aware that the time had changed her and there was no changing back. She had hardly ever been fearful before. Now she woke at night and couldn't go back to sleep as she saw perils multiplying in all parts of their life. If everything was due to collapse in a few years surely she and Jeb deserved some slice of the good life... after all these years of penny-pinching and doing without, shouldn't they get to live like other young families?

They should have a house of their own.

In his new career, Jeb sold auto insurance for a company in West L.A. The money was slightly less than the repair shop but he was finally able to get the black from under his nails. Marian added a few more hours to her own schedule to make up the money and watched Jeb in silence, wondering if this career would last. When he had been at it for six months and the paychecks continued to come, she began reading the employment ads in the Los Angeles Times.

"There's an insurance job in Fresno," she said carefully one day.

Neither of them had ever been to Fresno even though it was only a few hours north.

"It's hot up there!" Jeb demurred, having learned disparagement in the insurance business.

"It says they'll help us buy a house."

"Do you really want a house?" he asked, making it sound as if that was as frivolous as wanting a trip to the South Seas.

They had been over this subject before. Marian felt the ground squishy under her feet. She did. She badly wanted a house. The desire had been growing slowly in her consciousness ever since Addie's birth but Jeb had followed her in this only very, very slowly.

A house would give them privacy and respectability. Hadn't they both grown up in that sense of security in a single family home?

Yes, but not everyone did. Besides, they couldn't afford it.

Here Marian would bring out her savings account book to show him that she was nearly up to one of the small mortgages new tracts now asked for. Then she got them on a family outing east of the city where developers were building housing tracts further and further into the dessert and pricing them so cheaply almost everyone could afford one.

But those houses were too far away from their jobs.

At least they could keep trying and something would succeed.

After this statement, his reasoning got less rational and more emotional and Marian realized that he was mostly afraid, afraid he would never be able to accomplish what she wanted.

After the Fresno discussion, silence had ticked on for a while as house hunger gripped her and she said abruptly. "Get your resume out and update it."

"It probably won't work," Jeb said. "I still don't have a BA."

To their surprise, the company responded by setting a day for an interview. Jeb borrowed an almost-new Mustang from a fellow agent who was single, and drove up to Fresno. Marian called in sick, too nervous to work that day while he was gone. She bought a decorating magazine and took Addie and Bro to the beach for the day. Addie was instructed to watch Bro while Marian sat under an umbrella, looked at the magazine and let the sun brown her legs.

Addie was full of complaints. Bro kept crawling into the waves, and she had to haul him out. Then he cried. Every time she hauled him back to Marian, Marian gave them bananas and crackers and urged Addie to wear him out so he would take a long nap this afternoon.

"All he does is complain. You take him for a while."

"Come on, Addie. Cooperate for another hour. I'm having a

day off."

"I want a day off."

Marian had to laugh at that, and finally took the sandy baby into her lap while she read about all-white kitchens from Milan and white leather couches. Would she ever be able to keep children off a white couch?

Bro settled down and played with his scoop in the sand but Addie went off a little way and settled into a snit which she refused to give up. What was there about children, Marian thought, that determined them to do just the opposite of what their mother needed? At lunchtime, she gave up and gathered up her umbrella and the toys, the blanket and snacks and led them to their car to drive home.

Jeb returned triumphant at six o'clock, parking the borrowed Mustang in front of the house after beeping loudly. As he came up the stairs, she could see that he was pink from a day in the sun of the Valley. He gave Marian a joyful hug at the door.

"I got it." He had done exceptionally well in the course which was designed just for this purpose, to find new agents. They also liked that he was fluent in Spanish though not Hispanic.

"Already?"

"That's right. They liked me. Listen to the pay."

At the amount, Marian opened her mouth but didn't know what to say.

"That's the base salary. I get a percentage of what I sell so some months I might make double that."

Was it possible they would have enough money for extras, for a dishwasher, new clothes, a week in Mazatlan? Did that ever happen?

"Isn't there some trouble up there with the workers trying to start a union?"

"That's the grape-pickers. Not in Fresno. Let them start a union—they deserve it. And guess what else! They have a house all ready for us to buy. Someone who just left the company. Wait till you see it. It has three bedrooms and two bathrooms, tile floors and a fireplace."

"I don't believe it."

"It's true."

A week later, the four of them drove to Fresno on a Saturday and Marian saw the house. The neighborhood was nicer than the one in Culver City where she had grown up. The lots were wider and there were street trees. The front of their house charmed her immediately. They parked in front and the kids jumped out of the car, eager for freedom.

"Stay on the sidewalk!"

A pinkish stucco house, hidden behind abundant bushes of scarlet bougainvillea which also clambered over the garage and the high fence to one side. The brilliant flowers embraced the narrow porch so that it was left in shadows. There was more bush than house across the span of the front. The cascades of blossoms promised s charmed life inside.

"Look, they let the lawn die."

Another car had pulled up. It was the secretary from Jeb's new company who had been assigned to show them the house. "They never got the sprinklers put in," she said. "Maybe you could put bark down over the dead grass and you wouldn't have to water it."

She was having trouble making the key work in the front door lock.

"I knew it," Marian said out loud when they got in. True. It was not entirely clean, also a little scuffed up. They found two stains on the carpet, a cracked window, the garage door off its track, and an aureola of grease spatters around the stove in the kitchen.

"See that," Marian said.

"It's a lot better than our last apartment was, isn't it?"

He was right. There was nothing they hadn't dealt with before or that couldn't be fixed in short order.

In the garage there was—miracle of miracles—a washer and dryer. A warm feeling began to spread through Marian's chest. Cutting out trips to the Laundromat would free up four or more hours a week for her.

Jeb was jubilant. He jiggled her elbow to say 'not bad, huh' but he could get no response.

"It's nice, isn't it?" the secretary said. "Wait till you see the..."

Jeb put a hand on her shoulder and silenced her. "Wait," he said and the two women were silent as directed.

After they toured the bedrooms and bathrooms, the secretary said: "The Morenos really liked it."

"What happened to him?" Jeb asked.

The secretary hesitated. "There was a disagreement. But they wanted to go back to L.A. All their family was there."

"Wait till you see!" Jeb whispered.

"You'd better make this job work," Marian whispered back. But she knew what was coming next.

The house was a typical ranch style. It had the usual kitchen at the front, and living room at the back with sun-faded drapes over the window wall and sliding door to the back yard. There were three bedrooms, two quite small, and two and a half baths. The floors in the hallways were made of cork which wasn't wearing well. Marian had no comments. She would take this house no matter what flaws it had.

"Go ahead," Jeb said to the secretary. "Show her."

Grinning, the woman, whose name was Debbie, pulled the living room drapes open and revealed the back yard which was more swimming pool than yard.

The pool, just as Jeb had promised. Instead of saying anything, Marian pushed open the sliding door and walked out. The water in the pool was low and the rest of the yard was mostly concrete. It was a real pool, oblong, not rounded, large enough to require swimming across. There was a concrete walkway around the lip of blue tiles, no diving board but a handrail at one corner where there were steps down into the water. She thought of getting up in the night and going outside and slipping into the pool and floating on her back in the dark while she looked up at the stars.

"You knew this!" she accused Jeb when she could talk.

He tried to quell his grin. "Think maybe you can stand this?"

Debbie was grinning too. "The Morenos put it in, and then they only got to stay a year. That's why the company took over the mortgage."

"What did he do wrong?" Marian thought, but didn't ask.

Did they even look at the stove and refrigerator? She couldn't remember much of anything after that. A swimming pool. They would have a swimming pool. They could have their friends from Santa Monica up for a day of swimming.

"I told you so," Jeb grinned, when Debbie had left.

"Yes, but I didn't believe you, or I thought it might be one of those above-ground pools." She was thinking that it would take an earthquake or a war to get her out of this house.

She felt faint. From the patio, they could look across the hazy valley to the ridge of mountains. This was the Big Valley which stretched throughout most of the state, the place where California's amazing wealth grew under the hot sun. There was a feeling of bounteous space and possibility here. While they stood near a lemon tree, she plucked a tiny green fruit and brought it to her nose for the pungent citrus odor. A feeling of thankfulness descended on her. They had made it, were about to make it, into a life that had always been promised but had seemed out of reach for years.

"You sure you've got the job?" While they stood in the open doorway looking out at the pool, she touched him so he would know this was not a criticism, only a need for reassurance.

He was not resentful. He was expanding, changing already. He breathed good humor along with confidence. "It really is real. They gave me a start date. We have to sign a contract for the house. They own it so they will take payments out of my check. Which is a good thing, isn't it?"

"Yes." All her certainties about Jeb began to fade. He was capable of moving them into the kind of life she had always wanted but which had seemed out of reach. How had he done this? With her gratitude came a longing to be in bed with him, to stroke him and rub her breasts against his chest.

"Mother," Addie yelled. "Get Bro."

Both parents turned swiftly. Bro had crawled to the edge of the swimming pool and was leaning over the edge, gazing, fascinated, into the sky-reflecting water. Jeb was across the patio in only a few bounds, grabbing Bro just as he tipped over the edge, scooping up the baby with a loud 'No'.

It was minutes before Marian could move toward them. The exhilaration was gone. A pool was craziness. Addie couldn't swim yet either and Marian wasn't very good at it. Either one of the children could die before they could save them. What could they do? Locked doors? Hourly threats? Have the pool drained?

She needed to turn down this house right now.

She faced Jeb as he came toward her carrying Bro who was crying because he had been on the verge of this new joy. One look at Jeb's face, and she was unable to say what she wanted to say. She couldn't spoil his look of happiness.

They rented a truck to move. Jeb would drive the truck; Marian would drive the car with the children in it. Jeb's friends offered to come around and help load the truck. Not a small matter because everything had to be carried down from the second floor and they seemed to have acquired three times as many belongings as they had moved in with five years earlier. It would not be a long trip. Maybe they would have to stop once or twice because one of the children was crying or for a restroom, but even then, they would have plenty of time to unload the truck on the same day.

Suddenly they were in a flurry of leave-taking. Marian had to give notice on her job and count up the money she would receive for leaving the Christmas Club behind. She had to close out her savings account because the money would probably be needed right away in the new house. Jeb had to give notice on his job and repair the old car for possible breakdowns on the trip. Instead he sold the car and agreed to payments on a secondhand convertible to celebrate.

They had several farewell parties to attend. There was a leave-taking dinner with Shirley and John. John was on a leave of absence from work for stress. He took golf lessons on the public course, had acquired a tan, and claimed that he had never been happier. Shirley, on the other hand, seemed more highly stressed than John. She worried constantly whether they would have enough money for their retirement.

On the night they went to Culver City, Grandpa Frank came over for the evening bringing a bottle of bourbon. Since Jeb had begun to pile up college credits in night school, Frank had become a big supporter. As he reminded them occasionally, Grandpa Frank had come out from Tennessee during the Depression when having or not having a job could be a matter of life and death. Under the shining light of Jeb's new success, the three men became convivial, and sampled the bourbon so thoroughly they all woke up the next day with hangovers.

"Aren't they having a farmworkers strike up there?" Frank asked.

Jeb shook his head sharply: "No. Just a bunch of crazies."

There had also been a 'going-away' dinner with Cecily and her new boyfriend. Yes, Cecily had a boyfriend—a tall taciturn man, very good-looking, who was a stagehand at a film studio. Cecily looked ten years younger and bubbled with plans for their life together. Jeb disliked the boyfriend intensely which required Marian to reassure Cecily several times during the evening that Jeb would get over this eventually, and the two men would learn to get along.

"In about a thousand years," Jeb declared angrily on the way home.

They threw a party for their Santa Monica friends and Alice came to Marian's house for a long day at the beach. During this day Alice cried several times over remembered stories from their childhood. Alice was already an emergency nurse at Santa Monica Hospital and was married for the second time; the first marriage having lasted only a year.

The other person who cried over their leaving was Addie's

best friend, Rachel, aged eight, who lived next door and resisted all attempts at comfort, insisting she would never find another friend like Addie.

Marian remarked that their leave-taking had developed some echoes of their leave-taking for New York all those years ago.

"Oh, don't say that." Jeb was distressed at that, and Marian realized the connotations were not good. Well, she couldn't help if it was a negative thought. So much had happened in the years since, there was no chance the move would turn out the same.

One thing was clearly different. She was sad already about leaving Santa Monica. Things had gone well for them here and she would miss the ocean. All these years she had been going to the beach at least once a week. It was like the house of a friend, a place she could go for comfort, distraction, empathy. She could walk in the wet sand just a few feet above the waves while all sounds except the cries of the gulls and the pound of the surf would be blotted out and she could let her mind drift until whatever worries and regrets she carried evaporated in the mist.

How would she do that in the hot farmed land around Fresno?

# CHAPTER FIFTEEN

They planned to spend their first day in Fresno painting the kitchen so that on Monday when Jeb had to go to work, Marian could unpack the kitchen boxes and put everything away. But nothing as complicated as a move to a new town is ever that simple. With only one car, they would have to buy paint today, and they didn't know where there was a paint store. The telephone was not in yet and they found no phone book left in the house.

Marian had packed the coffee and canned milk in her overnight bag, and she had bought sweet rolls when they had stopped on the highway so they could have that much breakfast the first morning. However, as she searched through kitchen boxes for napkins and sugar, she realized she was still tired from yesterday's trip.

"I don't think I'm up to a day of painting."

Jeb was opening kitchen cupboards. "Look at this. We can't paint over this."

The shelves were covered with red contact paper. Dirty, greasy contact paper.

"That's horrible."

Jeb agreed, sighing. "It's going to have to come up and then we'll have to get the sticky part off the shelves. That will take a couple of days."

They relaxed into the morning. With the doors to the back yard locked so the kids couldn't get to the pool, they ate breakfast at the built-in breakfast table in the kitchen. Bro got a bottle and Addie got an orange. Bro was pushing a stuffed bear around on the floor and making sounds like a fire engine because his fire engine was packed somewhere.

While Jeb flexed his stiff shoulders, Addie said for the fifth time, "When can we go in the pool?"

"Not soon."

"What's the use of having a pool?"

Her parents ignored her while they debated their plan of action. "You could call that Debbie, the secretary, about a paint store," Marian proposed.

Jeb sounded reluctant to start moving. "I don't want to bother her on a Sunday. I think they go to church. If we just drive downtown, we should see a paint store. There's probably a Sears."

"All right, if we go downtown, we can look for life jackets for the kids."

"I doubt if we'll find any. There's no ocean here. And we need a bank so I can deposit my paycheck but I can't do that on a Sunday. I'll have to do it tomorrow at lunchtime."

"Why don't you take the kids with you and get the paint, and I will wash down the outside of the cupboards. I'd like to get some of the kitchen put away."

"We can't get it scrubbed and painted and the paint dry soon enough for you to put everything away."

"Why didn't we think this all out sooner?"

"And I can't carry Bro into a store when I'm buying paint. And I have no idea where to find life jackets."

Marian felt a headache coming on. "Well, I can't have him here unless I watch him fulltime and then I won't get anything done."

She picked up the coffee pot impatiently and tried to pour more into her empty cup but she did it too suddenly and knocked the cup to the floor where it broke in several pieces. "Damn. I have no idea where I packed a sponge or the cleanser."

"In the car," Jeb said, jumping up. In this move, he accidentally bumped into Bro who was trying to climb up Jeb's chair. Bro fell back to the floor and began to cry.

"What are you doing to him?" Addie asked indignantly.

Marian began to laugh. She put down the coffee pot and picked up Bro. She reminded herself that she had all week to get the kitchen put away. She didn't have to go to work anytime soon, if ever. "Let's all go downtown, see Fresno, enjoy the sunshine and look for Sears together."

It was a fruitful trip. They found Sears Roebuck and selected new paint colors, a pale grey-green for the living room and hallways, plus yellow for the kitchen. They also bought padlocks for the kids' doors, and in a sporting goods department, to their surprise, found life jackets. They bought Big Macs and took them home to eat in their own backyard with the kids already encased in orange life jackets. Marian and Jeb sat at the picnic table while Addie brought out her favorite doll to eat with her.

The sunshine was brilliant, working up to hot but not there yet. This was going to be like going to the ocean, only closer.

Bro would not sit down but accepted bits of hamburger to chew on while he explored the yard.

"This is pretty nice, isn't it?" Jeb asked, grinning. "You were worrying too much."

They had that five minutes of peace, a time during which they contemplated their good fortune, along with half of their Big Macs, and then it was over.

Marian looked up and was confused by a flash of clothing passing her. Jeb had jumped up and was dashing to the water where he executed a long dive across the pool with his clothes and shoes still on. She heard the splash only after it was over. Bro had gone under. When she saw him, his rear end was up but his head was still under water. A minute later his blonde head came up in Jeb's arm, squirming and yelling. The life jacket was too large for him and had slipped sideways.

"What have you done?" Marian screamed at her husband as she knelt at the nearest edge of the pool to pull the baby out of his arms.

They were at the shallow end and Jeb stood upright in the

water, breathing hard, trying to catch his breath, as he surrendered his burden. "Why are you mad at me?"

It took some minutes for Marian to get a good hold on the heavy, wriggling child and stand up with him protesting in her arms. Jeb waded awkwardly to the end of the pool and climbed out, his clothes streaming water around him. He reached for Bro.

"Here, I'll take him."

"No." She carried the wet, red-faced child into the house, ignoring the trail of water they were leaving on the carpet, and sat down with him in her lap. "Shh, shh. It's all right."

Jeb pulled his shoes and socks off before he followed her. He sat on the nearest chair, still breathing hard, his clothes dripping. Bro continued kicking his legs in remembered panic, crying while rubbing his face against Marian's shoulder.

"Shh, it's okay," she said over and over until he had exhausted himself and his head lay against her neck, fingers finding his mouth.

Addie had followed them in and stood in the doorway, her eyes wide with shock.

Jeb reached out and patted her head. "He's all right."

"He walked right in," Addie said indignantly.

"He'll learn. I've got to get out of these clothes."

When he stood up, Marian could see the wet circle he had left on the chair they had upholstered together.

"He's not learning," she said angrily, but of course it was not Jeb's fault. She couldn't even relax her tense posture, afraid Bro would panic again if she moved.

Addie came to stand beside her and patted Bro's damp head. Finally the baby's breathing slowed, and his eyes began to close. His red face and blonde curls were already dry while her arm was becoming numb with the strain of his weight.

Marian's stomach was cramping around her half a sandwich. The violence of her fear had exhausted her. When she put the baby down in his crib and covered him with a sheet, he curled up willingly, his fingers fell away from his mouth as his eyelashes brushed his still wet cheeks. Jeb had put on a new padlock before they ate. Now he locked it after she came out of Bro's room.

"He'll never learn." She went into their bedroom, and lay down on the bed and let the tears come.

Jeb took Addie with him to put away things in her room while Marian tried to recover.

They had walked directly into disaster and now it waited for them just a few feet outside the patio door. There was no escape.

That week, while they slowly got unpacked and their house straightened out, there were two news stories about children in Los Angeles County who had fallen into their family pools and drowned. The pool came to dominate their every thought as well as every conversation. They quarreled. Marian thought they should drain it, just do without. Jeb found this ridiculous.

"Then he falls in and breaks open his head on the concrete."

"Why don't we build a fence around it?"

"We'll look like idiots, like people who don't know what to do with a pool. I'll ask some of the men at work."

While Jeb researched their possibilities, the doors to the back yard remained locked and Addie was instructed never to open them. As a big sister, she was mad at Bro for all this fuss.

"Why doesn't he just learn to swim?"

"Addie, you don't know how to swim either."

"But I'm not falling in."

Mariam wasn't convinced of Addie's safety either. For the time being, both children wore life jackets all day and were padlocked in their rooms at night.

The man from the telephone company came to install their phone on Wednesday. On Thursday, Marian got a call from a woman named Caroline, the wife of Bob, one of Jeb's co-workers, inviting her to lunch with a group of 'the girls'. Marian was flustered. Maybe this was a test of Jeb. In a new town she had no friends to consult, no job that showed her value; the confidence she had had in Santa Monica was gone. She used Bro and Addie as a defense.

"Oh, I can fix that," Caroline said. "I'll get you my housekeeper's sister who's in eighth grade and is completely reliable. She'll do it."

Marian was trapped. When Esperanza appeared at her door, she was no taller than Addie but had an air of competence that outdid Marian's. Marian explained that the pool was a problem and Esperanza nodded her understanding and said she would walk the children to a school playground which was close by. Addie and Bro, when introduced, were tired of life jackets and padlocks and eager for something new.

Shortly after those three were off down the street, Caroline arrived in a green Dodge convertible. Watching her come across the lawn, Marian saw that the blouse and skirt she had decided to wear because they looked good at work in Beverly Hills was all wrong. Caroline clearly outdid her—fashionably thin, with a cloud of crinkly blonde hair and wearing a white linen sundress and a big hat. She sparkled with good cheer.

"Well, this is fun," She said, kissing Marian a few inches away from her nose.

As they walked toward her car, Caroline excused the Dodge convertible by saying that she always got the car during the day by taking Bob to work every morning and picking him up at the end of the day.

She also had dozens of questions about Marian and Jeb's past history. "We've been anxious to get to know you but we wanted to give you time to get settled."

"We both grew up in L.A." Marian started explaining. But before she could impart much more, and while she was trying to think if she should also drive Jeb to work every day, they arrived at the restaurant.

Two women who matched Caroline in hats and sundresses were standing under the tented roof to the entrance, out of the sun, waiting for them.

"Peg and Lala," Caroline announced as she honked, pulled

the car to the curb and yanked the keys out of the ignition all in one motion.

The two women eagerly patted Marian and air-kissed her with enthusiasm.

"We're so glad to get someone new," the one named Lala said. She was a small, tidy bleached blonde with a snub nose and a tan way darker than her hair. ""Not much goes on in Fresno you'll find."

"You have to excuse Fresno. There's not a lot to do here and not a lot of people to talk to." Caroline.

"And we already know everything about each other," Peg said. "We've been lunching together for five years."

"Caroline invented the whole idea of lunching."

"I did not."

Marian was carried into the restaurant on this subject, thinking that the only lunching she had ever done with other women in Santa Monica had been the one-hour break they got from work. For that, she had usually carried a sandwich. On any days she didn't happen to work, there were the children. Moreover, she had never been sure she had the right to spend money on a meal which Jeb did not share. When she said this last sentence, the other three laughed their disagreement in a friendly way. None of them had jobs outside the home.

"We deserve to lunch once a week. After all those hours we spend in housework! "

"And listening to all the problems there are every day at The Gulag."

This turned out to be the insurance company where all the husbands worked.

When Marian looked uneasy at this, Caroline reassured her. "It's a good enough place to work. It's just they're so cheap about time off, about going over expense accounts, about needing to meet quotas. You'll find out. But they give a good Christmas party."

The restaurant looked older than the ones in Santa Monica; it had a palm tree which went right through the roof, and a trace odor of roasting meat. The mirrored wall behind the bar went up to the ceiling with rows of all possible whiskeys and liqueurs lined up in front of the mirror which was flanked by two carved redwood pillars. Through the bottles the mirror could be seen gray and dim with age.

Instead of asking about children as her acquaintances in L.A. would have done, this group wanted to hear all about life in Santa Monica. Did she get to see movie stars very often?

"No," Marian said. "I think they mostly eat lunch at the studios. And I didn't have dinner in fancy enough places to expect them."

They were shown to a wide table while Marian looked around, and saw no other women in the restaurant. Only men in business suits. Apparently it was true—there were no other wives in Fresno who appreciated lunching.

Worries about Bro fell away while Marian wondered if the rest of Fresno dressed this well. Below their hats with big brims, Peg and Lala wore bright sundresses with full skirts and ruffles that had required a lot of ironing. They must have someone to do the ironing, a task Marian was ready to give up on. Below the sundresses, all three women had well-tanned bare legs and bright colored sandals with high heels.

"I didn't lunch with other women in L.A. very much," Marian said, meaning to excuse her ignorance but sounding maybe a little defensive. "The only women who did were those who could have a drink and stay through the afternoon."

The three looked at her carefully. Peg had seated herself next to Marian at the table. She was a tall, big-boned woman with long dark hair who, except for a big mouth outlined in the brightest possible lipstick, looked somewhat like Rita Hayworth.

"You're not a teetotaler are you?" Peg asked.

"No, but I never drank at lunchtime when I had to work in the afternoon."

"Of course."

Peg giggled. Her giggle was rather deep, almost like a purr. "We drink."

"Tom Collins all around," Caroline said to the waiter. "Is that all right with you?" She asked Marian.

"Oh yes." The undercurrent of rebellion was intoxicating. Marian was rather vague on what was in a Tom Collins. Was it lemonade?

"That is such a pretty dress," Mariam told Peg. It had big flowers in blue and orange. Their purses were glamorous too, more like beach bags, large, eccentric shapes in straw decorated with linen flowers in bright colors.

"Hawaii," Caroline responded. "Hilo Hattie. Do you go there?"

Marian confessed she hadn't been to Hawaii since high school graduation.

"Oh, you have to go if you live here," Lala said. "We spend as much time there as possible. There's nothing to do in Fresno."

"Fresno can be pretty dull. It's made up of the Mexicans— mostly farmworkers—they're very polite but they don't speak a lot of English. Then there are the 'born-agains.' You know what they're like. And then there are the ranch-owners who generally don't come downtown at all but stay on their ranches when they're not off in Beverly Hills or Acapulco."

"That is so true," Caroline said. "We're sort of marooned in the middle. It's not just Mexicans. We get immigrants from all over the world. If they come from a farming community and come to California, they head for Fresno. A lot of Armenians came in the twenties and thirties. I guess they came to buy a farm but now most of the smaller farms have been bought up. "

"The ranchers, the women, don't shop here either... no wonder... there's not much here but Sears and Penney's." Lala looked sad. "What we would do for a really good dress shop."

"I can talk about ranchers," Peg added, "Because I lived on a ranch. Till Daddy sold it. What a dusty, dull life!"

By this time, all three of Marian's new friends had whipped out their cigarettes and lighted them.

"Don't think that we don't go to church just because we talk

163

about born-agains," Caroline said. "We all do. You'll find out there's not a lot else to do in Fresno. We want you to know you are now in the middle of '*the fast crowd*'."

All three laughed and at the same time watched Marion to see how she took this. Marian joined in the laughter to prove she understood although she was not happy being so immediately and thoroughly wreathed in a cloud of tobacco. She had never wanted to start smoking but she decided to re-think that. She felt so warmly included already. Maybe she could learn to smoke just one cigarette when she was with them.

"What else makes you the fast crowd?" she wanted to ask but didn't.

Caroline asked Peg: "How was your life this week?"

Peg, in contrast to her height and move-star looks, became anxious, turning her head to look across the room toward the doorway as if afraid someone might be coming through there. "It was all right. He didn't come by all week."

"Isn't that what you wanted?"

Peg looked back at Caroline and shrugged and then turned to Marian. "Not to make a big mystery of it but I'm getting a divorce."

Lala took a deep breath. "Are you really going to go through with it?"

"Give me one good reason why I shouldn't!"

"What are you going to live on?"

"The court will have to fix that. There are the kids too."

Caroline sighed. "Have you got a lawyer yet?"

"Let him get a lawyer. If I do, I'll have to pay for it."

Lala turned to Marian. "Tell her she has to get her own lawyer."

"I don't know anything about this," Marian protested.

"You're from the big city."

Caroline interjected. "Lala, you know all about it."

Lala turned to explain to Marian. "I filed for divorce last year. He was playing around and I got mad. So he got a lawyer and the lawyer explained to me that I could get enough money for maintenance but that wasn't going to pay for trips to Hawaii and Honey's dancing and singing lessons. She's so talented, she has to have that. So I gave up and declared peace. Later on, a friend of mine from Santa Barbara told me I just needed the right lawyer. There aren't any lawyers in this town who work for women. They all represent men."

Caroline nodded and made a small moue of sympathy. "That's because the men have all the money."

"Except for Julia Jenkins, remember her," Peg said. "She's a raisin heiress," she explained to Marian. "She knows how to make things go her way. She got a lawyer from Hollywood and when he got her a good property agreement, she introduced him to every woman in Fresno, just in case. Do you have his card, Peg? I do if you don't. "

Peg sighed. "I already called him. He wants a big retainer. Also he wanted to know how much Bart makes a year. When I told him, he wasn't interested."

The drinks came. Marian was silent, tasting hers, thinking that the liquor was not that novel but she felt as if she was getting a whole semester of information here.

Lala ordered Mahi-Mahi while everyone else, including Marian, had chicken salad. They worked over the subject of divorce, and nearly succeeded in convincing Peg she needed a lawyer of her own. They wanted to hear about Marian's life in that gorgeous town of Santa Monica and Marian was comfortable enough to admit that, except for having the ocean and the cities of Beverly Hills and Westwood nearby, Santa Monica was nothing special. Fresno looked like a nice town too.

"It's just a cow town," Peg said sadly. "I'd move in a moment if I could."

When they were finished with the meal, they all perused the dessert menu, discussing the quality of the carrot cake versus the tiramisu, but then ordered only coffee. After the waiter delivered the coffee, he opened the curtains near them because the sun had shifted slightly and they looked out onto a scene of brilliant sunshine outlining the hibiscus and birds of paradise in

Technicolor.

"Perfect," Caroline sighed, waving an arm toward the air conditioner overhead because they were looking at sunshine but sat under the delightful machine which blew waves of cold air over them.

"I can almost catch a cold from it," Lala purred.

The combination of alcohol and conversation had soothed Marian enough to confess her panic about the kids and the swimming pool. All three looked at her with warm sympathy.

Peg said, "We had a swim instructor come every day for three weeks till he was sure they were okay. But they weren't babies. I don't know what you do about babies."

Caroline's cloud of crinkly white-blonde hair bounced with eagerness to solve the problem. "You need an instructor. One of the lifeguards from the college. I'll get you a name."

Caroline was emerging as their fixer, their problem solver. Both Lala and Peg had showed themselves as willing followers. Marian thought she was eager to be a follower too.

When they went out to the car, the heat was great enough to make them gasp.

"Feels like a hundred!" Peg said.

"Be sure to water your garden tonight," Caroline urged Marian.

Marian was not too worried about the garden. The few bushes that were there had been there some time. "How do you all get your legs so tan? They look really good."

There was sly smiles all around. "Don't tell anyone," Peg said. "It's our secret."

"It's leg make-up," Caroline said. "Haven't you ever worn it?"

Marian kissed each one when she was dropped off. "Thank you all so much."

"Will you come next week?"

Marian laughed. "I think if I have lunch with you once a week, I will have enough tips to get me through a lifetime."

"It's all Caroline."

Caroline protested. "Don't blame me for everything. But will you come?"

"Absolutely."

# CHAPTER SIXTEEN

"You must have liked them," Jeb said when he got home from work and saw that Marian was smiling.

"Yes. Especially Caroline. Did you think I wouldn't? What is her husband like?" She trailed him back to the bedroom where he would change his clothes.

"A good guy but he works everyone else under the table. Did you ask them about a swimming instructor?"

"She's going to try." Marian turned toward the kitchen and he followed her there. She was suddenly shy about calling Caroline. What if all that warmth she had felt, what if that had only been put upon for this one lunch? They already had a group. Why would they need anyone else?

"I'm making white bean soup."

"Oh, it's too hot for that. Can't we just have sandwiches?"

She stood in the middle of the kitchen, in confusion. What would she put in sandwiches? She had almost finished the soup. The kids had come back from the playground tired and quiet. Esperanza must have given them some magic beans. They needed to eat soon. But he was right. Sometimes it stayed over 90 degrees till ten o'clock at night. She was going to have to re-think all her meal plans.

Jeb was looking in the refrigerator for beer. "You've still got the doors locked. Can we eat outside by the pool?"

If they opened the house they would let the heat in. "You'd better go out there and decide."

"Daddy. Daddy." The kids had heard his voice and come running, in Addie's case jumping up and down while running.

"Can we go in the pool?"

"No," he said, reality catching up with him. "Let's eat in the house and have some peace and quiet."

"Agreed," Marian said. Jeb had spent the evening after he had jumped into the pool for Bro working on his best shoes—drying, stretching, and polishing them, worried that he might have to replace them. She would make the bean soup, then cool it in the freezer and put it in the blender with some sour cream.

He sat at the breakfast table to drink his beer and tell her about his day while she worked at the stove. Bro climbed into Jeb's lap and put his fingers in his mouth, listening to the adults contentedly. Addie helped set the table. Maybe their life here was possible after all.

If Caroline could just get them a swimming instructor...

Caroline made a series of calls and as a result a possible swimming instructor, a lanky high school boy named Gerald, arrived three days later. Caroline had assured Marian that he had a life-saving certificate. Marian asked that he bring it with him and sure enough he had it in an envelope in his backpack when he arrived.

Gerald was tall and awkward and looked to be in the middle of a growth spurt. His t-shirt was becoming too short to meet his swim trunks and his toes were poking through his huge sneakers. He had a badly sunburned nose, and was too shy to look at Marian directly. Studying the doorway, he told her that he was working part-time at the pool at the Y and had pulled numerous people out of it over the past six months.

Addie stood around grinning at him in a way that Marian scolded her about later.

"He's cute," said the eight year old.

"He's a teacher. Talk to him like you do to Miss Whitaker."

Gerald came back the next day for the first lesson. Marian put on her own bathing suit with a shirt over it, planning to sit by the pool to watch but be ready—even though her swimming was barely adequate—to jump in if it was necessary.

She followed Addie and Gerald out to the pool. Bro objected

to having his hand held so she let him follow behind her. When she got halfway across the yard, she turned to take his hand. But Bro was no longer behind her.

"Come down to this end," Gerald instructed Addie who was following him adoringly.

Instead there was a large splash because Bro had gotten past her and fallen into the pool immediately.

Marian yelled at Gerald, but the teenager was ahead of her. He dove for the water from several feet away, still wearing his battered gym shoes and faded shorts. In a minute he stood up in the water and lifted the baby out. Bro exploded with an indignant cry.

Gerald shook his own wet head. "He's fast."

"You're supposed to watch him," Addie instructed from the other side of the pool.

Now Bro was sobbing.

"Hey!" Gerald said loudly to Marian "Take him, will you, until he quits that."

Marian was not up to speech yet. She reached the edge of the pool and knelt down even before Gerald could meet her there. He handed her the wriggling, screaming, wet bundle.

Bro was wearing his daily outfit of training pants and life jacket, all dripping. Marian tried to hold him at arm's length so as not to get her clothes wet but he was twisting and crying out so she wrapped her arms around him to quiet him. Now she was as wet as he was.

"Shh, shh! Gerald is your teacher. You're going to have to be quiet and pay attention so you can learn to swim."

Like any two-year-old, Bro was not interested in her words but had his fingers in his mouth and his wet head against her neck trying to lock in some comfort. She had worn a freshly ironed shirt over her bathing suit in honor of Gerald's visit, and that time spent sprinkling, putting the damp shirt in the freezer and bending over a hot iron was now wasted.

Gerald peeled off his wet clothes and shoes, leaving the swim trunks underneath on, and spread them neatly on the bushes along the house wall. Then he turned his attention to Addie who had presented herself at his side. Speaking softly and ignoring Marian, he had Addie in the water on her stomach. By the time Marian looked up from Bro, Gerald had the adoring child holding onto the edge of the pool and kicking.

"Look Mom. Look."

"You could do this with him," Gerald nodded at Marian.

She was not ready to accept yet that the lesson had begun, but in a few minutes more she stood up and walked obediently down the stairs at the shallow end into the pool carrying Bro. The baby who had just gotten comfortable with his head on her shoulder now lifted it suspiciously.

Marian was soon standing in the pool and as she waded toward the wall, he looked at the alien soup and began to protest, "No, no."

The chlorine smell hung above the pool like a fog and assailed her nose. Now she was in water up to her waist. Her wet shirt clung to her body as she battled with her own fear for Bro as well as his fear. She pried him away from her body and held him at arms' length so he could reach the edge of the pool.

For a moment, Bro looked interested while she supported him above the water. Maybe when she had him in the same position as Addie, he would also begin to kick. She cautiously dipped his tummy into the pool and he wriggled in protest… a wriggle which freed him from her arms and he went under water again.

Panicked, she grabbed at him. When she lifted him up out of the water, his arms flailed angrily and he was screaming a protest.

Why not? He had trusted his mother and she had let him down.

Addie yelled in fright. "What are you doing?"

Marian wrapped her arms around the struggling Bro, and climbed the pool steps, trying to calm him. She wobbled as he threw his weight back and forth. Hadn't she known always that she would be bad at this? Wasn't that why she had wanted to hire someone?

She sat on the faded lounge chair with Bro in her lap, patting his back and murmuring to him till his sobs began to lessen. They would have to find another house, one without a pool. That was the only solution. If the company would let them. And what would Jeb say? He would blame her because she couldn't make this work.

"She's doing great," Gerald called out defensively, and Mariam obediently watched Addie kicking hard enough to keep her legs up in the water.

She wanted to scold him but he was only a kid after all. He had made no claims for himself other than presenting his certificate. Let Jeb do this; she couldn't. She longed to be back in Santa Monica.

After a while, Gerald coaxed Addie away from the pool edge and had her hold onto his arm with both hands. In that way, he walked slowly out across the pool so that Addie was now supporting her body with her kicks.

"Hey Mom. Look, I'm swimming."

"That's wonderful."

When Gerald climbed out of the pool, he was followed by an Addie who was panting at all the effort but looking pleased with herself. He dried his upper body with his t-shirt and then put it on. His blue eyes were red from the chlorine and his swim trunks were fading as they dried.

"I've got to go," he explained. "She's going to be fine at this. Should I come Monday?"

"But it's the baby I'm worried about."

"I guess he's a little young. Maybe by the end of summer, he'll be more ready."

She followed him through the house. "Should I pay you now?"

"Just by the week is enough." He was walking quickly, as if afraid that she might tell him not to come again. Outside, he got on his bicycle and was nearly to the street before she got to the door.

"Do you think you'll be able teach him? I need to know."

"They all learn eventually. We'll try again after we get her trained."

That evening when she described to Jeb what had happened, she was still angry with Gerald. He was giving up on Bro. Both children had to learn to swim and they were a long way from that.

She could feel her voice rising way above it's normal level as she followed Jeb out to his desk in the living room and pictured following Gerald out to the pool and begging him to make it work. She would emphasize that the children were very young and frightened and needed to be given confidence before they could learn.

"Not now," Jeb said. He was too tired to attack the problem now. He had to write up his sales report for the week tonight.

She woke many times in the night at the slightest sound from outside. She would sit up in bed, panicked, convinced that somehow Bro had gotten out of his locked room even though she had checked the padlocks on the outsides of their doors several times before she went to bed. When they came back from a trip to the store, she would race ahead of them into the house, even before taking her groceries out of the car, to check that the doors to the back yard were still locked.

When Gerald came on Monday, he concentrated on Addie who was doing well and ignored Bro who had a fist clenched on Marian.

That night when Jeb got home, she said: "He's just not any good. We need to get someone else."

"Maybe we can do it ourselves," Jeb offered.

But that was not a reasonable prospect. She was not much of a swimmer herself and Jeb had no spare time. He was chasing farmworkers all over the Valley to sell them insurance. Industrial insurance they called it. Farmworkers who spoke little English and worked all day. Mostly he could meet them only in the evenings, and even then they often worked till dark if the crop was nearly ready. Jeb's work day began to extend from eight in the morning till nine p.m. six days a week.

"These guys don't have much money," he told Marion. "They take a lot of convincing." And it took a lot of the small sales to make up his salary. The salary the company had decided on, they gave him every two weeks whether he had earned it or not. If he hadn't earned it, it was counted in the negative for him to earn later on. Jeb had never worked where there was a negative amount which he had been paid but had yet to earn.

"He'll never learn to swim this way," she said to Jeb another night in bed. Jeb was already half asleep. "Maybe we can get this guy to come more often."

But paying Gerald for Addie squeezed Marian's budget already. Yes, she had more money than she had ever had but she also had more household expenses. They had never had to pay a water bill when they were renters. The air conditioning was expensive and there were pool costs for chemicals and cleaning. They were buying enough paint for Marian to paint all the rooms in the afternoons when the children were down for a nap. She was planning to make some new clothes to wear lunching. At summer's end, she would need to buy school clothes for Addie.

And what would happen if the Company one day told Jeb he would get, not the amount he had been getting, but only what he earned? She had started putting a sum into a savings account against that possibility.

So she unlocked Bro's door every morning and snapped him into his life jacket and warned him about the pool, and tried keeping him in sight all day. She bought him new toys— sometimes ones he wasn't even ready for yet—on the chance that he would be fascinated by them. This was mostly an act of magic, perhaps not really effective, but it kept her panic at bay while she worried over the conundrum of teaching him to swim.

Once or twice a week she went out to the yard to sit between household chores and enjoy the sunshine taking Bro and some toys with her, scolding him in advance about the pool. She began to notice that he would walk all around to the other side of the yard to avoid going any closer to the pool than three or four feet. One day when Addie went up to the pool to look at some leaves which had fallen in, Bro started to cry.

"What's the matter?" Marian asked.

"He's afraid I'll fall in," Addie told her.

Gerald continued to come for the twice-weekly lesson. In spite of all her declarations to the contrary, Addie was learning to swim. She had days of protest and days when instead of kicking her way laboriously across the shallow end of the pool, she flirted and teased and tried to get Gerald to think she needed his attention about something other than swimming. Her tan was darkening and her dark brown hair becoming lighter in the hot Valley sun. A happier lilt came into her voice and, on the weekends when he was home, she begged Jeb to come into the pool with her.

However, when Gerald tried to speak to Bro to make friends with him again, Bro would break into tears, and run for Marian.

"Maybe we should let him alone for a while," Marian said, thinking this was all Gerald's fault. He had not convinced Bro that learning to swim was a good thing.

Gerald was clearly happy to leave the baby alone and work with Addie.

When she put Bro into the bathtub at night, she saw that his arms were tan as were his legs below the life jacket and training panties, while his back and chest were white, protected from the sun all day every day.

In spite of tears, he was growing taller, was steadier on his feet, and more interested in blocks than his pull toys. This should have pleased Marian but she thought of this as his way of distracting her from what he refused to do. He spent his days following Marian around, keeping her in sight as she vacuumed, or sewed drapes or picked up toys. Why was it that boys were so much more difficult than girls? If she had another child, she would make sure it was a girl.

Caroline laughed at this last. "Are you really going to have another? Do you really want to get back to diapers? I'm a great believer in stopping at two children."

"You're right," Marian agreed, wondering what it was that had made her think about having another baby.

There was something missing in her life right now. She knew well enough what it was. She saw so little of Jeb and he was tired and not very talkative when he was home. She remembered the closeness they had had right after Addie was born. The feeling that they were embarking on this adventure together. That comfort was no longer present in their life.

Something might be missing in her marriage, but in its place, she had Caroline. Caroline always picked Marian up first on their lunching expeditions. This gave them half an hour before they merged with the other two. In this time, they were able to talk over most of the important thoughts Marian had had in the week.

Had Caroline lost communication with her husband?

"Yes," Caroline said. "That's just as well. Bob is so intense, he wears me out."

Maybe this was just what marriage was like, and she hadn't known it because they had had that long period when Jeb was casting around for a career and she was helping him out. Probably this seldom talking was actually normal to marriage.

# CHAPTER SEVENTEEN

In August, the 'Gulag' (Caroline's favorite name for the insurance company which provided their salaries) announced a big party on the boss's ranch. Dress would be Western and children were invited too; they would be entertained at the child's pool while the adults were having a barbecue elsewhere on the ranch.

"This will be fun," The Lunch Bunch promised Marian. "The ranch is a wow, the food is always good and someone usually drinks too much and makes a scene."

Marian was not happy with this news and all their excitement did not make her happier. She did not feel at ease with this Company which held so much power in her life. She knew it mostly from Jeb's reports and having been in the lobby when picking him up because she had the car. Jeb was mistrustful of the Company, of his direct boss Tim, and the many rules which extended into their private life. Anytime Marian thought he should ask for some dispensation from these, he became anxious and usually refused.

Picking him up at work was not as interesting as she had at first expected. The building was new and very impressive; with glass walls on the inner layer while around it six feet away there was a circular curtain of concrete pierced with cutout circles to reduce the impact of the sun. That was dramatic and interesting but the receptionist, a very tall Hawaiian woman in brilliant muumuus, looked Marian over suspiciously as if she suspected there was something nefarious in the act of a wife picking up her husband instead of driving away in his own car. She let

Marian know that wives were not encouraged to come in and waste Company time.

"Western!" she protested to Jeb. "I don't want to show up as a Dale Evans wannabe."

"You'll have to. That's the dress code. Everyone will be wearing it."

"Does this idea come from the boss's wife? Because she already has a Western outfit? Therefore we all have to go out and buy one?"

He was alarmed. "Please just do it. I think they do this every year. You can wear it again next year."

This was not like the old Jeb, but she said nothing. Fresno did not normally stock women's Western outfits. By the time Marian got to the dress shop which had agreed to bring in Western costumes, everything in her size was gone.

Jeb had the answer for that. "You've been sewing. Make one for yourself."

Marian sighed and wondered, was there any such pattern? Yes, it turned out there were two in the Butterick pattern book. She bought a pattern plus fabric, plus a yard of felt to make fringe and then the matching buttons and thread, and went home in better temper, cheered by the prospect of working on a new pattern.

After her first meeting with Caroline and friends, she had set out to make a dress for lunching, one to equal their Hilo Hattie costumes. Before making up her mind, she purchased Mademoiselle and Vogue magazines, and spent two evenings studying them. She hadn't given so much time to thinking over her wardrobe since high school. For her office jobs she had always worn blouses and skirts with a dressy belt; for working at home she usually wore pedal pushers and old shirts of Jeb's. The hippie era was still in force but she had shunned granny dresses and jeans decorated with embroidery.

When her first new dress, lavender pique with tiny buttons all down the front, was finished and she wore it to one of the lunches, her new friends were impressed.

"You are really talented!" Caroline, who couldn't sew, exclaimed.

Lala, the only one who sewed, was even more admiring. "It must have taken hours to make that cording for the buttonholes. I would never have the patience."

After this success, Marian had looked for more fabric and patterns that were more difficult. She made a permanent sewing spot on a table in their bedroom. Addie was going to need dresses for school soon. Fabric was cheap and each pattern had several ways it could be used. It wasn't only the praise she liked, she also enjoyed conquering a new skill. Now she added the cowgirl pattern to the pile of projects but left it there till she could consult Caroline.

"I really don't want to go to their party," she confessed to Caroline.

"You have to go," Caroline echoed Jeb. "It's just something we have to do for the sake of the guys. Look at Peg." Peg was not getting a divorce after all. Instead she and her husband were in counseling, paid for by the 'Company' because it didn't approve of divorce.

Did counseling improve anything? Was Peg happier? Caroline reported that Peg had won a few concessions with the counselor's help and so was somewhat happier but not what Caroline would call happy. When Marian met Peg's husband Mitchell, a rawboned farm boy who insisted on telling jokes all the time and raunchy ones at that, she thought that putting up with him would take a lot of doing.

"I have to admire Peg for sticking with him," she told Caroline.

Caroline usually favored a 'wait and see' attitude. Look, the Lunch Bunch was still intact, and probably the son Michael was better off with the reconciliation. Bob thought the Company might have fired Mitchell if he and Peg had gone through with a divorce. Peg would have to decide for herself if staying married was worth it.

Marian saw she would have to accept that the Company was

a major player in her life. She cut out the Dale Evans costume and began to sew it. She didn't like the pattern much; she thought it had a lot of unnecessary features that took longer to make than they needed to—cuffs with opening plackets, a four-piece skirt with a belt and belt loops and then the fringe. But she became interested in seeing how it would look when done and finished it in a few days.

"We could have our own pool party," she said to Jeb as she tried the costume on, but he was working on his sales report. The costume looked okay on but she would have to wear it more than once to justify the time and money spent on it.

She was still resentful of the Company. "Why don't we give a party? A pool party just for five or six couples."

Jeb was not sure if it would be a good idea for his position at work as the newest salesman. "We're going to be seeing everybody at the ranch. If we give our own party we'll be leaving some people out and there might be bad feelings over that."

"I told Caroline and she thought it was a good idea. Ask her husband."

Jeb did and reported that Bob approved throwing the party. Just for the Lunch Bunch and husbands. That began to sound like fun. Marian was encouraged and began to relax about the Company party; she would work hard at making a good impression for Jeb's sake whether or not she enjoyed the event.

On the day of the party, when they went through the tall iron gates of the ranch, Marian was impressed in spite of herself. This was not a ranch like those in Western movies where the gate was of peeled logs with one log overhead and a hand-carved sign. She learned that in California a country house surrounded by fenced fields was always called a ranch because that was what the land grants from Spain had been called. From the elaborate iron gates, they could see miles of matching redwood fences across the low hills, tree lots of eucalyptus, and at least one field of horses. As they got closer to the large house on top of a hill, they could see hedges surrounding landscaped gardens and benches set out to enjoy the views.

"Oh my," Marian said.

"Aren't you glad you came?"

There was a sign with an arrow pointing to a field that was designated for parking. It had an attendant who showed them by gestures to park in a neat row. A path, outlined by red and white ribbons, led them from the parking lot to the back of the house where there was a huge pool and on the other side, a low building with one side marked by massive stone arches. The building was filled with tables decorated with white cloths and baskets of flowers. There were already about sixty guests, the women in Hollywood's version of cowgirl costumes, standing around with glasses in hand.

"Oh Mama," Addie said and pointed. There was a Mariachi band, outfitted in huge sombreros and a great deal of braid, playing and singing at top volume.

Somewhat overwhelmed, Marian and Jeb stopped soon after entering this scene and were accosted by a fat woman in a white dress. They surrendered Addie and Bro to this nanny, who was so sufficiently officious that the children went with her without protest. Several waiters whom Marian could identify as being from the Spanish restaurant in town were bringing full wine glasses to the guests as fast as they could move.

"Aren't you glad you're not missing this?" Jeb asked in a low voice as they looked around for their friends.

"Remember I told you some of them would be drunk already," Lala said in Marian's ear. "And amorous as all get-out," Caroline added in the other ear. "Watch out for that one," She pointed out a tall redhead with an angry sunburn wearing a shirt decorated with flamingos.

"That's Tim, the sales boss."

Marian turned quickly but Tim, who looked as if he had started his party at dawn, was beside her.

"Been wanting to meet the little lady!" he said to Jeb in an Australian accent. One hand was already reaching for Marian.

Jeb, who was trying to insinuate himself between his boss

and his wife, spoke up. "Tim, I promised to introduce you to my wife. This is Marian."

"Hey!" Marian exclaimed because the hand had succeeded in reaching her hip.

It was six foot Peg, whose father had raised his family on a cattle ranch, who stepped in to slap Tim's fast hand away from Marian's hip.

"How are you, Big Boy?" Peg said.

Tim grinned, pleased with the protest as much as if he had had success, while Marian made an escape surrounded by Peg and Caroline. They put their glasses down on a nearby table and adjourned to the Ladies Room to make sure Marian was all right.

The three friends stood in a row in front of the mirror in this oasis while they checked their makeup and worried if their sun block was enough.

Marian wasn't happy. "Is he going to be waiting for me out there?"

"Don't be upset," Caroline counseled. "In another half hour, he'll be too drunk to move very fast and you'll be able to get away from him with no trouble."

"Are there any more like him?"

"No others who can get away with it. Daddy Warbucks will make them stop. It's just that Tim makes a lot of money for the Company so they let him do what he wants. He's why most of the secretaries don't come to this party."

In spite of this support, when the others left, Marian stayed behind, still alarmed. She had been at the party less than half an hour. What would the next three hours be like? Was she supposed to let this drunk feel her up just because he was who he was? Was Jeb angry? Would he quarrel with his boss or, instead, be anxious that Marian would say the wrong thing?

She stayed in the restroom a long time, fooling with her hair and trying to get her nerves in hand. In a while, Caroline came back looking for her.

"He's going into the pool now. He's really swacked. If we

have any luck, he'll drown."

"Where is Jeb? I don't want him getting angry."

"I think he's okay. I talked to Bob and he's going to watch out for you. Tim won't cross Bob. Isn't the food table magnificent? At five, they will reset it with the barbecue. These people really know how to give a party."

But the small pleasure that Marian had taken in the beautiful scenery and the amazing display of food was gone. "Why does that woman with red hair keep looking daggers at me?"

"That is the big boss's wife, our hostess," was the answer. "She's probably trying to figure out how you got a dress so much better looking than hers. Don't be mad at her. I think she leads a hard life with you-know-who."

Marian was now worried on another front. Had she done the wrong thing in making the dress attractive? "I thought mine looked homemade. Doesn't it?"

"No. It looks twenty times better than any of the ones from the shop."

Uphill from the swimming pool was a copse of tall California oaks, their leaves gray-green in the brilliant sun, promising an escape from the pool and its noisy collection of adults busy proving they were having fun. Marian found a path that went upward, took a coke with her and picked a peaceful hump of dry earth to sit on. From there she could look down the other side of the hill, at the short brown grass which showed velvet waves as wind from the ocean miles away rustled through it.

All California weather came from the West because of the rotation of the earth, everyone knew that, it came day after day, now dallying, now streaking across the enormous ocean, picking up who knew what oddities on its way until it brought new and capricious atoms and dropped them on the land. Marian was convinced that was why new ideas started in California and worked their way across the country to the East Coast.

There was a low sound near her, under the trees, whether the wind or cicadas she wasn't sure. She let her mind drift until she relaxed. However much she liked Fresno which had some pluses over Santa Monica, it was also good to be away from it. She had had very few minutes of being in the natural world since she arrived in the Big Valley. This was an unexpected gift of this unpleasant day.

At six o'clock, Marian woke up from her daydream and went down the hill to look for the children on the other side of the ranch. The noise level was high and the cake was gone so they were willing to leave; with Bro on her hip and Addie trailing behind, they walked here and there to locate Jeb. There was still smoke rising from the barbecue pit and an overwhelming smell of roasting meat. The barbecue had been brought to the tables sometime earlier and had now been mostly consumed with gusto by those guests not too drunk to eat. There were fewer guests now; some must have eaten immediately or drunk their full and left. She passed the barbecue table, shaking her head at offers of any more food or drink. Jeb was sitting at one corner of the pool where there was shade, in a small group of men who were smoking and talking in low voices.

He saw her approach and stood up. He stood unsteadily and she could see his face sagging. She thought having to make conversation with his bosses and his competitors hour after hour had not been easy on him and he had drunk more than was necessary. She didn't know how much that was. Maybe he didn't know either.

"I'll drive," she said, and he nodded his agreement.

Lifting the whiny kids into the car, he admitted: "I'm glad this is over with. It was quite a party, wasn't it?"

Marian wanted to say no but didn't. She tried to sound gay. "And you tell me it happens every year. I'll warn you now I plan on being ill next year. I don't think I could go through this again."

"Don't say that. It's really important for Company morale. Earl took me inside the main house and showed me some of the art they have bought. You wouldn't believe what they have."

"I'd believe anything."

THE LIGHT IN HER WINDOW

A week after that party, they were ready for some real fun; it was time to give their own pool party, just for the Lunch Bunch and husbands.

Marian had located a recipe for Sangria and expected she would serve hamburgers and hot dogs but Caroline offered to bring all the food. She had bought a cookbook of Greek and Turkish food and had found a new Near Eastern deli where she could buy the ingredients. Peg had objected that they couldn't have a party without something on the grill. She and Howard would bring their grill and the hamburgers. Well, all right, they'd bring lamb instead of beef, if that was what Caroline wanted.

Marian and Jeb looked over their back yard, comparing it to the magnificence of the ranch, and decided improving it as much as they'd like would cost too much. They could do that next year.

Jeb dug up the plants they had put in which had died under the summer sun and stuck some Tiki torches in the holes to disguise their earlier purpose. They put a checkered tablecloth on the picnic table and draped the battered lounge chair. Lala and Howard offered to bring two other lounge chairs and an umbrella. The pool had been cleaned the day before and Marian had scrubbed the concrete apron with some bleach.

Waiting for their guests, husband and wife stood together in the shade of their open front door admitting they were a little giddy with the prospect of their own first party. Unlike the company party, this one would have only (or almost only) people they knew they liked.

Esperanza waited beside them with two shopping bags of food and toys because she was to collect all the children and take them to Peg's back yard. All the others but Bro could swim but they couldn't be rescuing him all through the party so Esperanza had been hired to take all seven children, feed them and keep them entertained. The other three couples arrived in a group.

"Hey, this is a great idea," Bob, Caroline's husband, the workaholic, said with delight. Jeb went out with him to the car and they made several trips together bringing in the food. Caroline had gone all out with new recipes.

"What a cute kitchen," Peg exclaimed when she and Mitchell hauled the yard furniture through the house. "We were here two years ago but you've done the kitchen over."

"Mostly just paint," Marian excused.

"Are we going to swim first?"

All the men had worn swim trunks under their clothes and were eager to get into the water. Howard was congratulated for bringing a volleyball.

"I don't want to have to blow-dry my hair again," Lala explained, and the other women nodded agreement. They hadn't worn bathing suits.

"We don't have to do a thing to the food but set it out," Caroline murmured.

"Howard will do the grilling," Lala said, pleased with herself. "Barbecuing is the way you get a man to cook. It's wonderful. Just have the plates ready and give lots of praise."

The women sat under the umbrella in shorts and sun hats and listened to music on the radio and smoked, and watched the men dive in the water and slam each other with the volleyball. In spite of that noise, it was very peaceful without children. They began to analyze the company party.

How many servants do you think she has on a normal day?

Someone in the kitchen and someone to do the pool and yard, and probably a housekeeper who comes out for the day.

Who else had Tim accosted?

That new secretary for sure. She was crying.

"We just have to hope he's going to be offered a better job sometime soon," Caroline suggested.

"Don't we know anyone who could invite him to another company?"

"Doesn't he have a wife?" Marian asked.

"Oh yes but she knows never to come to these things!"

In an hour the men were tired. Even Peg's husband, Mitchell, the non-stop talker, quieted down after the vigorous game of whatever it had been. They began to climb out and towel off. Howard lighted the charcoal. Jeb took charge of drinks and gave them all a choice of beer or Sangria. He was slowed down by a conversation about the Dodgers so Marian left her chair and went in to help him serve the drinks. While she was gone, Mitchell took her chair because it was under the umbrella. The other men donned baseball hats against the sun and sat outside the circle of women.

When she came back out, Marian sat on one of the lounge chairs with Bob and Jeb and noticed that instead of breaking into a men's group and a women's group as they had at the company party, they were all sitting together, talking companionably as a group.

"How do you stand that party every year?" Marian asked.

"Don't get them started," Caroline said with a laugh.

"You think that was bad?" The six old hands began to tell stories about previous company parties, stories of people who had fallen into the pool after too much alcohol and had to be rescued, stories about a new secretary whose bikini top came off and was thrown from man to man for a short time until wiser heads prevailed. Each story topped the last one.

When the coals were hot and the lamb shish kebab was sizzling, the women brought the cold food out and set it on the picnic table where everyone could serve himself. There was hummus and baba ganouch, as well as plenty of grilled sausages, fresh vegetables with dip, tortillas and beans. Caroline's food and Marian's Sangria were congratulated.

"When I hit forty, I'll have to stop eating like this," Howard said, filling his plate for the third or fourth time.

"I think you'd better stop tomorrow," he was told.

As newcomers, Jeb and Marian were regaled with stories about events when each of the couples had come to town. Peg, who had gone to high school in Fresno could tell about an even earlier time. "This used to be the nicest small town," she started. "For a couple of years, we even had a theatre series which came down from San Francisco."

When Esperanza called to say the children were also full and very tired, it was nine o'clock but finally cool. Reluctantly, Peg drove off to bring the children back to their parents after which the adults sorted out their own kids and looked at scraped knees and smears of mustard, and then packed up the uneaten food. The short, sweating Esperanza was rewarded with four times her usual pay, and the handful of money brightened her usually impassive face.

"You've been wonderful," Caroline told her, patting her back.

"We never got to swim," Caroline's tall son, the oldest boy, complained but was shushed up.

"We've got to go," the parents said, quickly herding children away from the temptation of the swimming pool.

A hand on the boy's neck to quiet him, Bob said quickly, "This was good. We have to do this again."

That night in bed, Marian and Jeb polished off the last of the Sangria and reflected happily on their success.

"They're all such nice people, aren't they?" she said. "Even Mitchell."

He agreed. "It's a good group. The best I've ever been in."

## CHAPTER EIGHTEEN

Suddenly it was the middle of September and Addie was in second grade with two new dresses that Marian had made. The days were still hot but dark was coming earlier in the evening.

Caroline was still introducing new adventures. She was a few years older than Marian, had graduated from college and had had a career as a decorator for a furniture store in Chicago before marrying. It was partly because she found Fresno so boring that she was always hunting out new activities. She was trying to start a book club though none of the Lunch Bunch was enthusiastic about this. Then Caroline announced happily that a new interior decorator had just set up shop in Fresno. The others were not terribly interested but it was not too long before the Lunch Bunch was being carried off to have iced tea with her—her name was Alicia—and seeing her 'book'.

Marian protested to Caroline in one of their every-other-day phone conversations. "Caroline, she's very nice, and I was impressed with her past work, and I would like to help her, but there is no way I can afford to hire a decorator. You're way ahead of Jed and me in income."

Caroline was instantly contrite. "I am sorry to sound like I'm pushing you into something you can't afford. I know that Jeb has just started with the company. I get carried away sometimes, and I identify with her, knowing how hard it is to start with no clients. I was thinking she might do a sketch for you for nothing so she could claim you as a client. Then she could show the sketch around as part of her portfolio."

"It never occurred to me I might get something for free. I've never used a decorator."

Caroline succeeded, as she often did. She brought Alicia to Marian's house for suggestions and Alicia produced a sketch without charging for it. After the sketch and a long discussion about furniture, Marian served a lunch of cold salmon, avocado and artichokes by the pool and the three of them—Caroline, Alicia and Marian—had a lively conversation about the possibilities for Alicia's business in Fresno.

Marian couldn't afford the elaborate flowered drapes or the overstuffed grey leather couch Alicia sketched but she did paint the walls of the living room pale teal as the sketch suggested. Instead of worrying over the furniture she couldn't buy, she framed the sketch and hung it on the wall.

Caroline gave up on finding business for Alicia but when Alaska Airlines set up a contest for tickets to Hawaii, Caroline called all three of them and told them to enter. Marian did, without telling Jeb about it. If she won, she'd tell him then.

It was sometime later that Caroline announced she had something new she wanted to talk about. "Brace yourself," Lala said to Marian.

They went to the Japanese restaurant which they seldom did because they didn't serve alcohol. Caroline insisted that they go there because she wanted a place that was quieter.

Peg, who seldom minced words, asked: "What's all this mystery?"

"I want to talk about something."

"Isn't that what we usually do?"

"No. This is different." She waited until they all had tea and had ordered food before she started in. "You know I had a job I liked in Chicago, I've told you that. I was a decorator at a furniture store. I wasn't credentialed but I had taken several courses in college and I was hired to help people who were going to buy a roomful of furniture by putting it together for them. One reason I liked this job was that, beside my salary, I got paid commissions on the furniture my clients bought. It was not a lot of money but I liked being able to make more when I did a good job."

Sounds wonderful, they all told her.

"I got the job six months after they had opened the store. Originally, they had a man in that job but he quit for a better job after only a couple of months. When they listed the job again, they couldn't get another man for it because the pay was so low so they hired me. It was my first job out of school and so I was thrilled. I was there a year and a half and I sold a lot of furniture for them, and sometimes my sketches were used in their advertising campaigns. I thought I was doing very well. Then after that year and a half, they fired me. They had found a man who would do the job for only slightly more money. What made it worse is that he had just graduated. I had a year and a half more experience than he did."

She was silent and the three looked at each other. "That was really nasty," Marian said.

There was more silence. Their food came and her friends looked at her, puzzled.

"Do you think that was fair?" Caroline prodded.

Lala looked over her shrimp salad and shook a thorough layer of salt on it. "You know they are doing that in the schools. It used to be that all teachers in the lower grades were women, right? Now they want men. They say that the men are better at keeping the kids in line, particularly the boys. Sometimes they even pay them more money. Think of all the women who will be out of work if they change to men teachers."

"I don't think I ever had a job a man would want," Marian offered. "That's why office work is so low paid. Plenty of women are willing to work at that level but most of the men won't."

Peg said: "I've always wanted to be a travel agent. I thought I might try it when the kids are grown. I hear there are women travel agents in L.A. but none in Fresno. My mother said I should wait for another war. She went to work in a factory in the Second World War. They were willing to hire women because the men were all away but when the war was over, they fired the women."

"If anyone wants to work in a factory…" Lala said.

"I know. But that's just an example. And my mother said it was good money for then. You know, just after the Depression."

"But shouldn't things be fair?" Caroline asked. "What is it about a man that makes him a better decorator than me?"

They digested this for a while.

Lala said: "In Texas you would never have gotten the job in the first place."

"In Los Angeles you would have. There are even women screenwriters now."

"Men have to support families."

"You should have gone in and flirted with the boss, and raised your skirt a little and told him a sad story." Peg.

Caroline laughed. "Not that boss. He wasn't interested. Besides, there are more and more divorced women who end up supporting their children. They need the money just as much as the men do."

"Did the new man really sell more furniture than you?" Marian asked.

"I never went back in and asked. I was so hurt I went home and lived on unemployment for a while and cried a lot. I hate that. That's what women do, isn't it?"

Peg nodded. "I know it is things like that which makes men want to hire men. Mitchell is always telling me that's what's wrong with women. Just think about it. Would you like to know that someone who works for you would burst out in tears whenever you said something they didn't agree with."

Marian was indignant. "Is that what we do? What I see is women who will take any kind of insults or mistreatment in order to keep a job. And if they have a big group of women and need a boss, they get a man who will flirt with the women, or scold them or any kind of criticism or accusations to keep them in line."

"And," Caroline said, "All the top jobs in every kind of

business go to men. Why is that?"

"Women stay home and have the children and run the household, and that's not so bad, is it?" Lala said.

"Only if you lose your husband and have to support the family yourself, then you're out of luck."

The conversation wakened a long vein of questioning in Marian. More than she could talk about at the moment. "It's the way of the world. Men run the world. Are you saying you think we should try to change that? How would we do that?" Maybe she should have been paying attention to this all along. Only thinking about it made her tired. She had enough tasks without tackling what was wrong with the way the world was already.

Caroline was silent but wearing her sweetest look which usually meant she had a lot more to say. "Let's just think about it. I'm reading this book… when I finish it, I'll lend it to you."

"Not for me," Lala said. "I don't want to see anything I'm going to have to change. I don't have enough energy for that."

That night in bed, Marian reflected first on the Lunch Bunch and how they had transformed her life. She hadn't felt so truly herself since high school. She had thought her close group of friends in college would stay with her but they had mostly left her behind in Santa Monica. Many of them were married now or else they were at UCLA. Boyfriends had taken a bigger role while the groups of girls had become more fluid. They were all moving toward the adult world of coupling, even to leaving Los Angeles, as Marian had, for the husbands' careers.

Caroline was leading her toward things she needed to think about. At the same time, Marian felt she was expanding; she could speak out in these new ways and Caroline and the others would understand her. She realized her sense of her own importance had taken a slide since high school. Then she had felt the equal of the boys; now she knew that was not true. And that hurt. She had been seeing the world in an untrue light, a rosy light fostered by the movies. She went home and looked at Addie. Addie seemed to be plenty bright but she was still playing with dolls because that was what girls should do. It was

Marian who had given them to her. But probably that was all wrong, it made girls think that was the only thing women should do.

She needed to talk this over with Addie but she didn't know for sure yet what she was thinking.

While Marian mulled over this subject, Caroline was off on another phase. She had seen a flyer for a poetry reading at City College. She had mentioned this to the librarian and the woman enthused about it. Caroline told Marian all about this. She had heard that the poets at the College were very good and many people in town had started going to hear them.

This poetry poked its head up a second time when Esperanza's sister Linda, who had agreed to babysit for them one evening, begged off because a teacher had told her she had to go to a poetry reading.

"I asked Linda to babysit so Jeb and I could go to a movie," she explained to Caroline. "And she said she couldn't do it that evening because she was going to a poetry reading at the college."

Caroline nodded. "Philip Levine. Lots of people in town are mentioning him. I think we need to go too. Why odd?"

"Caroline, she's the first generation in her family to speak English as well as the first person to attend college. What would she do with poetry? I went to college in a major city with people who had been speaking English for generations, and very few got interested in poetry. Okay, let's try it."

When Marian had quizzed Linda to explain this poetry excitement, Linda had said, "This is special poetry Mr. Levine is from Detroit. I'm not real sure where that is, but he talks different. Kids fight to get in his classes. Even the teachers in Latin American Studies are writing poetry."

Lala and Peg were not interested in trying this out, and both Jeb and Bob declined. But Caroline and Marian were intrigued and Caroline offered to drive Linda as well as Marian so they would know where to go.

In the car, Linda was shy about riding with them. "I'll have to sit with my friends when we get there," she excused.

"Of course," they said. "We just need you to get us to the right place."

Walking down a wide empty corridor, they could hear a low buzz somewhere ahead of them. It was coming, not from an auditorium, but an extra-large classroom with raked seating where there were already about thirty people gathered, half of them students but the others closer to Marian and Caroline's ages.

The buzzing ceased when the three entered the room and all heads turned their way. Linda separated herself from them quickly and left the two standing in the doorway like visitors from another planet. Marian looked around. This was not like the audiences she remembered from Santa Monica College. Here there were more men than women. Wasn't poetry usually a women's affair? The students, like students in Santa Monica, were long-haired and dressed in well-worn or embroidered jeans. Marian looked at the women to see if she and Caroline had come in the wrong clothes. But there seemed to be no standard choice.

Linda had left them to fend for themselves. Now a man who was seated nearby stood up and indicated to them that there were two seats in his row.

"Thank you," Caroline said in a low voice and moved toward the seats.

"It's Levine tonight," the man said as they squeezed past him. "If it's your first time you may be shocked at his language. But come back anyway. Some of the other people are almost as good and not so crude."

"But you like him?" Marian challenged as she sat down next to him.

The man laughed. "I'm from Detroit too. It sounds like home to me."

Marian looked over the others. Jeb had said that the people of the Valley might look as if they came from Mexico but really they came from many of the agricultural regions of the earth,

South and Central America, Asia and the Near East. What they shared was dark hair and skin and the look of people who had worked hard from childhood. The man from Detroit had dark hair but looked more like a druggist.

"Are you a teacher?" she asked.

"No, an accountant. Are you a teacher?"

She laughed. "We just like poetry. I used to go to Santa Monica City College."

Caroline had taken a seat but was not entirely comfortable. "Do you think we should stay?" she asked.

Marian nodded. Her curiosity was aroused. "Absolutely."

Caroline was shifting in her seat, uneasy about those who had turned to look at her. "Maybe I'll leave."

"Oh don't," Marian said. The buzz of low conversations had recommenced around them.

In a little while, a short man, also in jeans, came in with a rapid stride as if he thought he was late and wanted to get started. He nodded impatiently at the audience and stepped up on the platform as if he was there every day. Two men had followed him in, wearing the faculty clothing of dress shirts with jeans. They looked over the audience, waved to a few they knew and took seats in the front row. The young people who had been standing, squatting or leaning over their friends found seats and there was a general sigh of readiness.

The leader walked back and forth on the platform, punishing it, as if readying it for an ordeal. "I want to read something new I've been working on."

He began reading at first, then reciting from memory, then looking back at the page in his hand, stopping sometimes to refresh his memory, correcting some words as he went. His voice was loud, terse, his accent was rare in the valley.

The audience was rapt. He waved an impatient hand at the occasional cough. He was not asking for reactions, only giving them the gift of his work. The audience was attentive but not silent. They responded with small sounds of encouragement … indrawn breath, small laughs, murmured words of approval.

Marian found that every one of her muscles was tense as if she was afraid she would miss a word, would not be able to follow the poem to its end. When he stopped and nodded that he had reached the end, the students answered, not with clapping but with hisses and whistles of approval. The poet paused only briefly and then read two more poems. After that, one of the other men got up to read and the leader sat down, leaned back, tired.

On the way home, Marian tried to ask Linda some questions but Linda was silent and only murmured a few sounds that were not in English. After they had dropped her off, Marian couldn't quit talking excitedly, proposing ideas as if she could not stop them coming, could not shut them down while she was still listening in her head.

"Enough!" Caroline said loudly and reached out to take one hand off the steering wheel and grip Marian's arm.

"But I…"

"Okay. Enough. Quiet!"

Marian quieted finally. "Sorry."

"He really got to you."

"Yes. I feel as if I want to go home and write a response. Did you hear what Linda was saying? She was giving a response as if it had been just for her. Only she was answering in Spanish. Isn't that crazy?"

"Maybe not."

"What did you think?" Marian asked when they stopped in front of Marian's house.

"Oh my, oh my! That is some magic!" Caroline gave a little laugh. "The language… I hate all those words. It's only because I lived in Chicago I could follow it all the way. But what writing!"

"I feel as if I have to take a course in poetry. I've never done that. Would you think I was crazy?"

"No. It's very easy to do here. They encourage people from town to take courses. You should do it."

Oh yes, she would, Marian thought. At the same time she

was afraid of it. It was like a blast from a future world.

That night in bed, she was warmed by cascading emotions. The poetry had brought to the fore her awareness that she was happy here. Jeb was settled in a job that was good for him. Addy and even Bro in spite of the failure of swimming, were growing and changing in a good direction. Mariam herself, away from the constant bustle that had been their life in Santa Monica where she always had a job, had had time to sit quietly, to read or let her thoughts play through her mind. She was glad that she had shared this evening with Caroline. Caroline had transformed Marian's life. This was something she had to do again.

# CHAPTER NINETEEN

"Caroline and I are going to go again soon," Marian said, trying to tell Jeb about the power of the poetry they had heard as she cleared the dinner dishes a night later. "Linda says her whole class goes, just to hear their faculty read their new work. You might enjoy it too."

Jeb continued to sit at the table smoking a cigarette while she picked up the dishes and put away the leftover food. This was unusual. Most evenings he rushed off to his desk in the bedroom to write up his sales of the day. She was planning to make curtains for the door into the garage when he started toward the desk. The fabric was already cut and waiting on her sewing machine.

"Would you like some coffee?" she asked when, after the dishwasher was loaded and she had mopped off the table, he continued to sit, now with a second cigarette.

The smoking had only started a month ago and she disliked it a lot. It was bad enough that the Lunch Bunch lighted up as soon as they had ordered their drinks. Now Jeb smoked several times a day. The smell of smoke came with him when he entered the house and there were always full ashtrays at the end of an evening. The first few times she had mentioned it, he became irritated, so she let it alone.

"No. I want to take a walk. Let's walk down to the school and back. It's cooler now."

The curtains would have to wait. Instead of asking what was up, Marian looked him over carefully. She had few clues these days about what he was thinking. They didn't talk everything over as they had before he had this job. She had to go on observation and Jeb wasn't one who made announcements when he had reached a new thought. Now she noticed that the pinched look between his eyebrows which developed over the day at work was still there. Something was wrong and she might as well hear about it sooner rather than later. Just when things had been going so well! Wasn't that always the way? Maybe they were finally going to cut his paychecks back to what he was really earning as they had threatened.

"I don't like to leave the kids alone when they might wake up and call us. We could go out and sit by the pool. Why couldn't we do that?"

"Their doors are locked. They can't get out."

"I know. But if one of them wakes up and is frightened, I want to be here."

"Just to the school and back. That will only take fifteen minutes."

Caroline was right when she talked about how they all acted with their men, as if it was impossible to say no. "Okay. Let me take Addie's book away and make sure Bro really is asleep."

That took some time. When Addie was drifting off to sleep and Bro had not been heard from in fifteen minutes, Marian locked both doors and went in search of her husband. He was waiting out front in the yard, smoking and looking at the street trees which had developed aphids. She walked out to meet him thinking how pleasant it would be to just walk and talk with him without interference from kids or paperwork.

There was no one else in sight and few sounds from the neighborhood even though there were cars in every driveway. The neighbors were all at home but huddled indoors in their air-conditioning. Marian and Jeb turned west toward the school, walking at the same pace, quietly. Marian relaxed with the exertion. Probably it was only something normally wrong, not terrible, and they would have a quiet evening together...

But she couldn't let it entirely alone. 'what's wrong?"

He hesitated, throwing his cigarette away in the street and

keeping his eyes straight ahead instead of looking at her. Even in the dusk she could see the back of his neck was red with sunburn in spite of the straw hat he always wore. Since coming to Fresno he spent hours and hours outdoors. In spite of his dark hair he was fair and burned easily, his Irish ancestry.

"Jeb!" They had reached the scool.

"Okay." His voice was raw. "Here it is… we have to give up the house."

She stopped and turned toward him. He stopped too but wouldn't look at her.

"No." More protests rose up in her throat but she was afraid to voice them. She might make it worse, bring on whatever the catastrophe was. What could be so terrible? What had come with no warning?

"What is it? I don't understand." She put her hand out to make this go away by touching him but he stepped away from her touch.

There was just enough streetlight to see his mouth was twisted unhappily, more was coming. He turned his head toward her but didn't look in her eyes. "Okay. I quit my job today. I didn't tell you beforehand because you would try to talk me out of it."

He moved away to escape from her.

She grabbed his arm as if he was meaning to walk away and leave her standing there. Damned right she would have. "What is all this?"

He shook off her hand. Then he swallowed, accepting.

"I'm sorry, Mare. I can't do this job any longer. I made some calls. I'm going to go up to Oakland tomorrow and find another job."

"What do you mean you can't do it? You've been doing it six months." Leave not just the house but their whole new life? A broom had come down from the sky and was sweeping it all away.

She tried to keep the panic out of her voice. "I know you've been having trouble getting the sales they wanted but you said it was coming along. You told me that just the other day. That by the end of the month, you would have a full list."

"Yes. I do have it. That's not the trouble."

"Then what is?"

"Pay attention, will you?"

"I am paying attention. "

"It's hard to explain. These laborers work for very little money. You know that."

"Yes."

"They're buying insurance with everything they have above food. And they're doing it thinking... and I'm telling them... that it will keep them from starving when and if they lose the job. I believed that too. But that's not what happens. When they get fired or laid off the company immediately cancels the policy. All the money they put in just goes to the company. It's like a shell game. I'm lying to them, taking money they're going to need. They would be better off putting it in a bank but they don't know that. I can't go on doing this."

Now that they had reached the schoolyard the school itself had faded away in the dusk behind the trees and all was nearly black. The daylight was escaping, nearly gone, taking with it their life in Fresno. They stood a minute divided. Without discussing it, they turned around to walk back.

Marian was tense with the need to stop him from wrecking everything. She had to think how she to do it. "Did you talk to the company about this? Maybe it's not that bad."

Jeb laughed curtly. "It's no use talking to them. Since this Chavez guy has been trying to organize the workers, this company sees them as the enemy. They know exactly what they're doing. They think nothing's too bad for this scum. I'm just the dumb cluck they hired to do it for them."

She was too frightened to keep on talking. There must be some way to fix this, to save their life here. But if she kept arguing... she had this longstanding anxiety from her childhood. Shirley and John would argue and argue until John was near to weeping and went looking for the bourbon... this should have stopped Shirley but never seemed to… and he would drink so much he wouldn't be able to get out of bed the next morning and would have to call in sick.

When Marian and Jeb's own house loomed silently before them… with only a faint light from the kitchen shining out… the sidewalk and steps were totally in the dark and Marian stumbled and fell down.

Jeb was alarmed, reached for her but his hand groped emptiness; he couldn't see her. "What's wrong?"

"It's nothing." But as she got slowly to her feet, she could feel sharp pain in one knee and one elbow.

"How could you fall right here where you must know the sidewalk like the back of your hand?"

"I don't know. I just did." Because she had forgotten entirely what it looked like? Because she didn't want to go into the house?

The next morning Marian got up at seven as usual; she had to feed the children and get Addie off to school. A painful elbow reminded her of what had happened in the evening. As if she could forget!

"Are you going to get up?" she asked Jeb.

"Not yet."

She wanted to know if he had changed his mind but was afraid to ask. She reminded herself about the evening of poetry but it receded to some hidden place in her head and the door locked behind it. She went on to Addie and Bro and pretended that it was a normal morning, though her body was taut with the need to fight.

While the children were eating breakfast, she went back into the bedroom. Jeb was just coming out of the shower, shaved, with a clean shirt on.

"What are you doing?"

"I'm going to Oakland. Maybe you've forgotten."

She shivered. "Don't be nasty."

"All right." But his tone was still cold.

"What are you going for?"

"To look for work. Don't expect me to get it in one day. I don't know anyone who has found a job in one day."

She made the bed silently. The morning was cool. Maybe the worst of the heat was over.

When he was dressed, he said: "Have you got any cash in the house? I don't want to have to wait for the bank to be open."

"Just food money."

"Give me twenty. That will pay for gas and I may have to pay for parking. Make me a sandwich so I don't have to spend anything on lunch except for coffee."

Marian accepted that there wouldn't be a discussion now, and went to make a fried egg sandwich and also put an apple and some grapes in the sack. Jeb ate an egg and toast hurriedly and accepted the bag lunch without comment. He went to his desk in the living room and pawed through the drawers.

"I need a little notebook of some kind. Didn't you buy one for Addie?"

Marian went to her own desk and found a small book of lined pages she had bought for grocery lists and menu ideas. She followed him outside to the car parked in the driveway because the garage was still dedicated to painting and repair projects. She crossed her arms to control her nervous hands. It would be nice if he had something friendly to say.

"I'm not mad," he said, without looking at her. "When I know something I'll tell you. If anyone from work calls, just say I'm not here. Don't say where I've gone. It's none of their business."

"I don't want to move. I don't want to live in Oakland. Can't you work this out?"

He looked at her as if she was mad, got in the car, adjusted his sun visor and was gone. Their neighbor across the street was also getting into his car. He waved a friendly wave to Marian as usual though they never spoke, and got into his car. All the men in the neighborhood, though few of the wives, would leave in the next hour. Wasn't that the way it was supposed to be?

Addie was through with her cereal. She looked at Marian curiously. "Why are you crying?"

"I'm not crying. Get clean panties and put on that plaid dress."

"It has to be ironed."

"All right. Wash your face and hands and put on your shoes and panties. I'll iron the dress."

Addie was fed and dressed, and furnished with the quarter she was supposed to bring for the school picnic, and was out the door in time to join the group of children who walked to school together with one mother or another. After that, Marian had to let Bro down and dress him. It was some time before she could turn her mind to Jeb and what they were going to do. Then, at the point when she usually planned her work for the day, she sagged tiredly. What was the use of doing any cleaning or sewing or return to painting the back hall—the last room she had not painted—if they were going to uproot and leave this whole life.

She wanted to call Caroline but was afraid to. Maybe Caroline already knew? What would she say? Would Jeb have told Bob? Bro was pulling toys out of his room. She couldn't leave him loose in the house and not pay attention to him; that was dangerous with a two-year-old. She picked him up and gave him a hug but he was more interested in freedom.

She decided to take him to the library with her. He liked sitting on the floor in the children's section and pulling out books from the low shelves. There were two librarians and usually when someone came in with a child, one of them would be delegated to watch the children's area. Marian could get a couple of books for herself and then sit nearby and think while Bro worked his way through picture books one at a time. He understood that parents looked at these objects, sometimes a long time, and read from them but he couldn't quite understand how or why. Therefore he opened each one, frequently upside down, turned a page or two, then closing it up, pushing it away as if he hadn't found what he was looking for.

As she waited for Jeb through the day and then the evening, Marian marshaled all her arguments for staying in Fresno until she was worn out with them. When he was not home at dinner time she wondered if he had gone to a motel to stay overnight. If so, why hadn't he called her? She was in bed with the light out when she heard his car in the driveway. She was too tired to confront him tonight. Maybe she would pretend to be asleep.

She heard him come through the front door and turn and lock it behind him. Then he went down the hall and checked the locks on Addie and Bro's doors before he came to their bedroom.

"Marian?"

She sat up and turned the light on. It shone on a man so tired he was bent over, with the sleeves of his white shirt rolled up, carrying his jacket with one finger through the loop on the back of the collar. The protest she had been preparing was stilled.

"Did you have dinner?"

"I stopped down the highway and had a hamburger."

What took so long, she wondered. She waited some minutes, unwilling to ask what had happened and yet desperate to know what he might have committed to. Jeb hung up his jacket and pants, took off his shoes and socks and rolled his limp shirt into a ball and threw it into the corner of the room without saying anything. Marian slid down in the bed and closed her eyes against the light.

"It's hot in here," he said.

"Not as hot as it is outside."

"Hotter than the air-conditioning in the car. Goddamn this valley."

When he came to bed and turned the light out, he said: "Goodnight."

Marian felt tears come into her eyes but, all right, she would also rather wait till morning for this conversation. She had talked to no one but the kids all day. She had taken out two library books for some place to turn her mind to but they had failed to banish her anxiety.

The next morning Marian slept in because she had slept so little in the night. Jeb was already out of bed. She listened for him—had he left without speaking to her? Then she heard the front door close and, from the driveway, the car starting up. What would she do all day while she waited?

What she did was hunt out her oldest phone book, the one from college. Under McIntyre was Grandpa Frank. She didn't know exactly what she wanted to ask for, just some kind of help. Grandpa Frank was home, not always true. Almost before she said anything, he said: "You've got trouble. What is it?"

She explained, not wanting to show anger with Jeb but probably was resentful. Frank asked lots of questions and then thought over what she said. Finally he said: "Pumpkin, this is not like before. When I helped you move to Santa Monica, the guy hadn't done much but look for things he didn't like. Now is different. He's held down a couple of jobs and he says he's going to continue doing that. I don't want to come in and suggest he doesn't know what he's doing. There are always going to be some rough patches like this. I think you just have to stick it out."

Marian hung up quietly in defeat.

Jeb came in earlier this time, near seven thirty. Marian and the children were all in the front yard waiting. Marian was sitting on the steps pretending to read her new library book though the light was too low to see it. Addie had put marks on the sidewalk for Hopscotch and was complaining because Bro continued to walk his horse on wheels across them. His legs were still too short so he had to lean from side to side to push forward which made his progress very slow, but he was giggling at Addie's scolding.

When Jeb had turned the engine off, he continued to sit in the car in the driveway as if too tired to get out.

"Daddy, Daddy, look at what I got today." But Addie could not succeed in getting his attention.

Marian stood up and waited for him. "Let's not talk until the children are in bed."

He nodded, scarcely able to speak. "Okay."

"There are tacos, the meat and beans are still warm in the oven, and green salad. We've already eaten. Come on in, Bro. It's time for bed."

There was silence between husband and wife when they got in the house. Marian dished up the dinner and then went to bathe Bro and get Addie settled in bed. She was frightened by his demeanor but at the same time frantic with what she wanted to know and to say. When he had finished eating, they went back out to the backyard and sat on the old aluminum chairs. Keeping her voice low, she began…

"I'm not going to move. You will just have to work something out with the company. Tell them you've changed your mind. You'll do the job the way they want. Or offer to do a different job. Or get another job in Fresno. That's up to you but I'm not going to leave this house. It has taken all these years to get here, I'm not going to give it up." She kept her voice low in spite of her feelings. It wasn't just the children who might listen, there were neighbors on the other side of all three fences.

She had expected him to be silenced with his own distress but he wasn't. "You're out of your mind. You don't have any choice. I can't change what's happened. And I don't want to. I don't want to work for those people or accept this house, knowing how they do business."

His voice had been almost as low as hers but her next whisper was funneled with anger. "How could you quit that job and not even ask me about it? That was my job too."

"What do you mean it was your job?"

"Don't you remember I was the one who counseled you to go into insurance? And I was the one who found the job in the newspaper and told you to apply. Not to mention that it was money I earned that helped us move. Or all the shirts I've ironed and meals I've cooked so you could go to work. I earned that job too."

"Marian, you're crazy." His voice softened. "Don't be crazy now, please. We have to make this work. We have to get something else so we can survive."

This rejection of her words chilled her. Lala and Peg were right. The place of a homemaker was down there with janitors. "Well I'm not going. You can go off to Oakland but I'm going to sit right here. Addie's in school. I'm not going to take her out."

"You won't sit here long. After I'm gone and the house payments have stopped, it won't take them long to put you out."

She was shocked. "You wouldn't do that."

"I don't have any choice. I have to go someplace where I can work."

"They wouldn't do that. It takes a long time to evict homeowners."

"Of course they would. It's the company who owns the mortgage on this house. What do you think happened to the family that owned it before us? When he quit, the company had him out in less than a month, before he had another job."

Marian was beginning to lose steam. "Why did he quit?"

"I don't really know. Maybe for the same reason I did. He was Hispanic. Maybe he didn't like what he saw. So then they decided to get an Anglo who spoke Spanish but who wouldn't have any sympathy for the workers. They just got the wrong Anglo."

"What does Bob say?" She was remembering their party, all the feelings of friendship, of them all being in this together. Had all that gone away already?

Jeb's tone was more discouraged. "Bob thinks I'm crazy. He thinks you can't be worried about anyone but yourself."

Marian stood up and left him there, under the darkening sky beside the nearly useless pool. She wasn't going to give up. Something would work out.

# CHAPTER TWENTY

Jeb got up the next morning and fixed his own breakfast while Marian lay in bed listening. He came into the bedroom just before leaving. "I'll call if I'm not going to be home by dinner time. I took the money out of your purse. I'll go to the bank today and get some more but you'd better get ready to open up that savings account. We're going to need it."

She waited till he was gone and then woke the children and started her day. What could she do? Nothing except refuse everything. And what good would that do? She yearned to talk to Caroline but was afraid to call her. Did Caroline agree with Bob that Jeb was in the wrong? Then where did that leave their friendship?

It was an unusual day, overcast in town and reportedly foggy on the highway. She began to worry about his driving. This time of year, accidents were frequent because of the low-lying fog. She spent another restless day with Bro. She looked at him and decided his hair needed cutting. She cut off the baby curls and then, looking at him, cried. His hair was becoming darker. In another year, he would be no longer a blonde baby but, something strange, a dark-haired boy. He was already aping that strange phenomenon, a male.

In the middle of the day, the phone rang and Marian hesitated, full of fear. Maybe Jeb had had an accident on the highway. If it was anyone else, she didn't want to talk.

But not Jeb, instead it was Caroline. A cautious Caroline, tentative. "I don't want to interfere. I just wanted to hear you're all right."

"Caroline, what am I going to do?" Marian cried.

"Oh Sweetheart, I don't know. What is Jeb going to do?"

"Get another job. But where I don't know." She was afraid to say Oakland, not only because Jeb had told her not to but also because it made it seem more real. It mighty actually happen. How would she move to that city which was known all over America as a Negro city where there was incredible crime?

"Sweetheart, something will work out. It always does. Bob says Jeb works hard."

"He thinks there are no other jobs here. Is that right?"

"Probably. Also the company won't let him keep that house you know."

Marian began to cry in earnest. "Can you come over?"

Caroline began to hedge. "Curtis is home sick today. I can't leave him. But we can stay on the phone as long as you like."

Marian wondered if Bob had forbidden Caroline to see her. She had to excuse herself for a minute to go and get something to blow her nose on. When she came back, she was more subdued. "It's just like you said... remember? I had no say in the decision even though I do half the work."

But Caroline was not on that wavelength. "I don't know why he had to do that but you have to help him out. For the sake of your children."

"So you think I should go along with this, even though I disagree with what he did?"

Caroline's voice came over the phone full of caring and worry. "You have to. He needs your support."

"And I should support everything? Even moving away when I don't want to?"

"Yes."

But was Caroline urging support of Jeb because once they moved away, it would be easier on those left in Fresno?

This day Jeb arrived back at the house at three in the afternoon. Marian had heard the car so she went to the front door. When she opened it, she found him standing there, so limp with exhaustion, he hadn't even opened the screen door.

He looked at her almost as if he didn't know her.

"Okay, I got it."

"What?"

"A job selling auto insurance. I start right away. I found a house too. Not a house, an apartment. We have to get packed to move."

"In Oakland?"

"Yes." He walked past her and straight into the bedroom where he lay down on the bed after removing only his shoes.

"Did you eat?"

"No. But that can wait till I take a nap."

Marian went into the kitchen to cry while he slept. Addie came home from school, already cautious because something was wrong with the grownups. Her eyes looked stretched wide. She had lost a button off her dress and then buttoned it crookedly.

"Come here," Marian said. "Did you save the button? And be quiet. Your dad is asleep."

"Why is he doing that?"

"Because he's tired. Go see Bro. He should be waking up."

After Addie had left the room, Marian looked at her cupboards which had all been scrubbed and painted pale blue and had new shelf paper, and were full of dishes and pans, spaced neatly just where they would be most convenient. Would they really have to be emptied again, everything wrapped in newspaper and packed in boxes, boxes which she had just gotten rid of in the last month? The enormity of that task overwhelmed her. She stopped crying and sat down and put her head in her arms on the table.

Jeb came into the kitchen more than an hour later and found her in that position.

"What's wrong?" His voice was cranky.

"Nothing." She sat up guiltily and reached for a tissue to wipe her eyes.

Looking at her husband of more than a few years, she saw a stranger and felt a stranger. All right, she would do what she had to do since he said it was a matter of survival, but she would never say that she liked it or agreed with it.

"I have to go to the grocery store for milk and bread. You've had the car all this time and I haven't been able to."

"Take it," he said, tossing the keys.

Their plans evolved rapidly. While she was at the grocery store, she began gathering boxes from behind the market, the liquor store and the convenience store. Jeb had to go back to Oakland to his new office for two days while Marian began packing. He stayed overnight in the new apartment and talked to the utilities, old and new. When he came back from that he found a truck to rent and engaged one of the men he had sold insurance to who would help them load. Marian emptied her savings account hoping it would do more than just get them through the next couple of weeks, and went to Addie's school to get her transfer records. Jeb went to the Ford agency and traded their almost-new convertible back in for an eight-year-old sedan so they would have no car payments for the next year.

They did all these necessary tasks tiredly without communicating any affection, as if that might interfere in accomplishing this transition. Bro was silenced by the emotion in the house and went back to sucking his thumb. Marian did not call Caroline again. It seemed useless. The friendship was over, at least for now. Would she ever be able to start it again?

Then, on the morning of moving day, Caroline and Bob showed up at the front door, wearing old clothes, ready to help with the loading.

Marian began to cry and put her arms around her friend. "I'm so glad to see you again."

"It's going to be all right," Caroline murmured.

Jeb was almost as moved at the sight of Bob. "Thanks, man!"

"I think you're an idiot," Bob said, pinching Jeb's arm. He turned to Marian and explained. "Where I come from, you don't give up a job someone is paying you to do. My family came out here during the Depression, walked most of the way.

They would have done anything, short of murder, to get one of these farmworkers jobs."

"Lala and Peg?" Marian asked.

Caroline shrugged. "They said the guys won't let them come. But Peg sent cookies and asked me to get your address."

It took till mid-afternoon to get the truck loaded and the house swept clean. The ghost of their happy party with the Lunch Bunch had evaporated. There were leaves in the pool because Marian had cancelled the pool cleaner.

Leave them there, Jeb said, so she did.

He took the locks off the children's rooms and puttied in the holes. Marian wondered if the next family would wonder why there were scars there. Or would the story of their failure with the pool be told to the next family? And the story of Jeb's resignation? The failure there?

Only necessary words were exchanged between husband and wife, and few enough of those. Marian hurt too much inside.

The day was cool, a little overcast, and the town looked quiet as they drove out. The sun had receded along with their high hopes. Jeb drove the truck with Manny riding with him. After he had helped them unload, Jeb would put him on a bus back to Fresno. Marian drove the newly purchased sedan with the kids in it, plus the diaper bag, their good clothes on hangers, food for lunch, and a few precious plants, much as she had done just six months earlier to move from Santa Monica to Fresno.

As they left town, she thought : if I were a man, I would turn the other way and go back to Santa Monica with the kids and tell Grandpa Frank he had to help us. It's because I'm a woman that I'm following along, doing just what he tells me to do. Visions of what might have been rose up. The Lunch Bunch had never gotten to the discussion Caroline had promised them—about women needing to get some of the jobs that went to men, with salaries that made a family possible. But would talking about it have made any difference?

And what about the poetry they wanted to go back to hear?

The pure pleasure of it. That was another whole section of her life as it should have been that was now discarded. She had never felt as lonely as she did now. Jeb up the highway and the kids in the back seat made no difference. She had lost herself here.

"What's Oakland like?" Addie asked.

"I have no idea. Be quiet and let me concentrate."

It seemed an endlessly long way north from Fresno. The freeway pushed through bleak fenced fields of cattle, and low hills of brown grass with no towns or even farmhouses in sight. Marian felt unmoored, sent out alone into an alien world. Traffic was light, most of it going south instead of north as if to indicate that that was the rational, accepted, direction. This new old car had a noisy heater in addition to the rough thrum of tires on the blacktop so that she could hardly hear what was going on in the back seat. And then when they arrived, there would be no welcome, only the mindless work of carrying, unpacking, cooking, and then in a few days, job-hunting in a city she knew nothing about. A city about which she had heard only negatives. There would be no one to talk to but Jeb and she didn't want to talk to him. How had her life turned into this?

This voice she heard. Addie yelling over the engine noise. "Mom. You have to stop."

"I can't. There's no place to stop."

"He's crying because he wet his pants."

"Addie, I have to stay with the truck. If we stop, we'll lose Dad."

But of course, she did have to stop. She had set the kids on an old bed pad to protect the upholstery. Now it could be wet through. A short time later, when she saw a sign promising a gas station up ahead, she passed the moving truck, beeped loudly, and turned her signal on, slowing down till she made sure that Jeb got the message and turned in with her.

How would she find a job? She didn't even know if Oakland had a newspaper.

Eventually, they reached a couple of small towns and then what must be a suburban area. Marian was relieved to see white people on the sidewalks as the freeway entered Oakland, since she had always heard Oakland was a totally black city. Still concentrating on following the moving truck, she breathed a cautious sigh. Perhaps it wouldn't be as bad as she feared. They then left the freeway and were in the city and on a steep hillside which was tree-shaded. It looked peaceful enough, quiet and sunny, but the houses were tall and crowded together unlike Fresno and Los Angeles. People had been right; this was nothing like Southern California. These houses were from an earlier era, large and elaborate with fussy wood trim and small front lawns. Now the people on the sidewalks were mostly black.

## CHAPTER TWENTY-ONE

The truck slowed and suddenly drove diagonally across the street. With a grinding of gears as it went forward and then backward on the steep hill, it nosed into an empty piece of curb on the wrong side. Marian resentfully slowed the car and searched for an empty spot on her side of the street. She had to go down the hill for half a block to find one she was sure of. Now this new life was about to begin and she wanted nothing so much as to just sit in the car and let the rest of the world take care of itself.

"Why are we stopping?" Addie asked.

"I guess we're here." Marian rammed a tire into the curb so they wouldn't roll on down the hill. How could anyone live on such a hill?

By the time she got the children out, across the street and up to the truck, the men had the back open and the tail gate down at a dangerous angle.

"Go back and lock the car," Jeb said to Marian in a low voice.

Panicked, she looked around. There were no people in sight in the block but, still carrying Bro, she went back across the street, took her purse out of the car, and locked the door. This was what Oakland was going to be like. She was filled with resentment. She didn't want to be here. She could have gone alone to Santa Monica with the kids, taking the money from her savings account and started a new life in a town she knew.

"Everything is going to slide right off the truck," she warned when she got back.

"That doesn't help, Marian. But it's a nice house, isn't it?"

She hadn't even bothered to look at the house. Now she had to look up and up. There were four steps up to the small yard, then six more to the front porch and then two and a half tall stories above that. The house was enormous, once handsome but painted battleship gray as if it wanted to fade into the background, and with some scraggly vines hanging off it. There were two front doors, side by side, both with stained glass windows in them. Jeb was already on the porch, unlocking one door.

"Ours is the second floor. Go up and see the terrific view."

She set Bro down beside Addie and went up the steps to look. Inside was a long staircase up to the landing where it turned. There was gilt and white striped wallpaper all the way up, and thick maroon carpet on the steps. Arriving on the second floor slightly breathless, she saw a big sunny room with purple and gilt wallpaper and much white woodwork, plus a battered hardwood floor.

She went quickly through the apartment which was both bigger and more attractive that any of their apartments in Santa Monica. There was a big room to the front separated by French doors and to the back a bedroom, bathroom, kitchen and enclosed back porch. The bathroom had a claw-footed tub. The kitchen was painted orange. The enclosed porch was piped for a washing machine but there was no machine. She opened the door to the outdoor back stairs and looked down at a formal garden laid out with narrow sidewalks lined by boxwood shrubs. No grass. No place for children to play.

She went down the front stairs, finding her tiredness replaced with anger, and attacked Jeb. This was the last time she would let him choose an apartment. "There are only two bedrooms. How could you do that? Addie and Bro will have to share one and there will be endless trouble."

Jeb merely shrugged, seeming immune to her anger. "This was the best I could do. They shared in Santa Monica."

Short, wide-shouldered Manny was inside the truck,

marching back and forth, carrying boxes to the tailgate for Jeb to pick up and carry upstairs. He didn't seem to notice that the tailgate was getting too crowded to put more boxes down. If she didn't start carrying also, they would be here for days. What if she refused this apartment and they went to a motel while they looked at others? But probably he had already given up all their money on this place.

"Addie, take Bro and walk him around to the back yard." Impatiently, she picked up a box labeled Kitchen from the tailgate and started up the short steps to the yard. She could grow to hate this house? She could feel it starting already.

Climbing up the steeper stairs to the porch she found the box heavier than she had thought. She paused to get her strength up. Why were her legs so reluctant? She didn't have the strength to push upward. The legs didn't want to be here. She began to stagger and the weight of the box overbalanced her. One arm sagged as she tilted against the railing on the stairs. She felt a pain in her side, and then the sound of a snap, and she went through the railing and fell into the shrubs below.

Anger. Pain. Darkness everywhere because she had closed her eyes. Then slowly... voices she didn't recognize. A woman's voice. And a man's voice speaking Spanish. Manny?

Then: "Mare!"

Then the woman's voice again. "Is she unconscious?"

She woke up to that and opened her eyes on a pretty brown face.

"Can you see me? Are you hurt?"

Marian thought about that, wondering how to describe it... she hurt everywhere.

"We have to get her out of there." That was Jeb's voice, slight panicked.

"I'm no nurse," the woman said. "But we have to be very careful about moving her in case she has hurt her back."

Jeb's voice was distraught. "We need to take her to a hospital. Addie, you have to take care of Bro. Take him to the back yard and keep him there."

"All by myself? Is Mama hurt?"

"We don't know yet."

"The closest one is Highland and you don't want to go there on a Saturday, after the Friday night they've had in Emergency. Let's see what's wrong first."

Marian didn't want to know what was wrong. She wanted them to let her alone for a long while so she could rest. She resisted the hands on her.

When she opened her eyes again, she saw Manny was still moving past her, now carrying a box up to the front porch and parking it there. No matter what was wrong with her, the truck would be unloaded.

The brown woman with the soft voice was about Marian's age but smaller. "My name is Marian I'll see what I can find out. If you all need to keep working, go ahead."

Jeb gave a short laugh. "Her name is Marian too."

"We can fix that. Call me June. That's my second name. Marian, try moving this arm right here. Does that hurt?"

Marian closed her eyes and gritted her teeth, as the stranger began touching her gently, moving one joint, then another. She worked her way firmly through Marian's limbs as Marian found she could move most of them without terrible pain.

"So far, so good. Maybe we can get her up."

Her head hurt, and her neck was worse. She wanted to protest but she was dizzy and couldn't think of the words. Then the examination reached the other ankle and she let out a cry of pain.

"It's swollen already," the woman said.

"Maybe only sprained?" Jeb said hopefully. "What do you think? Do you think she's concussed?"

"I don't know how to tell. Her back seems all right, let's try sitting her up," June said.

Marian had absolutely no desire to sit up, but she was too weak to protest.

She kept her eyes closed to disassociate herself from the event while they gently sat her upright. Now she knew that the bushes she had fallen on had branches as well as leaves. Several wounds spoke of being punctured by the stalks. There was blood on her arm.

She whimpered, not wanting to use the energy it would take to protest.

"She's bleeding," Jeb said in alarm.

"Okay, here we go. Let's try this slowly."

Jeb and June put their arms around her. They raised her, ignoring Marian's sob at the pain. She sagged to one side because Jeb was both taller and stronger than June. In spite of wobbling, they carried her a few feet to sit her on the lowest step. With Marian down, June stood up, murmuring her relief and catching her breath, while Jeb knelt beside his wife, patting her for comfort.

"Do you hurt? What should we do?" he asked her, his voice ragged.

"I can't tell," was all she could offer.

June stood in front of them, arms crossed at her waist, one hip thrust out, while she considered. "Tell you what! Bring her over to my house and let's put her down in bed while you get unloaded. I'll give her an aspirin and look for some bandaids. Tell the kids to come with us. By the time you have the truck unloaded, we'll know more."

"You can't carry her that far. You're too small and not strong enough. I'll get Manny."

Marian started weeping soundlessly but Jeb and Manny ignored that and raised her onto one foot. Manny was short too but stronger than either Jeb or June. Instead of lifting her, they supported her and walked her slowly on one foot, across the yard, down the driveway and followed June into the small house next door.

"Bro?" Marian asked. Addie had not taken Bro to the back yard but stood holding his hand while she watched the grownups pass her.

June patted Addie's head as she passed her. "Honey, bring the baby along."

"This is awfully nice of you," Jeb said to June. "I hate to take advantage."

"It's not all that much," the woman protested softly.

They went through a living room and into the second room where there was a brass bed with a handmade quilt on it.

"The blood," Marian protested as they set her down. "I don't want to get blood on your good quilt."

June was not worried. "It's had blood on it before. I'll soak it in cold water tomorrow. Where's that girl?"

"Addie?"

"No. Leah!"

June took charge so Jeb and Manny eagerly left the sick room for the truck. June began to rustle around and Marian accepted an aspirin and closed her eyes grateful at being able to lie down. She felt several of her scratches being bathed. She heard Addie say: "what should I do with him" and June say: 'There's a cat here. Does he like cats?'

No, Marian said and then fell asleep so maybe the word was never spoken.

When she woke up, she was hot to one side. Lifting her head, she could see that the heat came from Bro who had taken refuge, cuddling against her hip and was also asleep. Across the room, Addie was sitting on the floor, holding a Raggedy Ann doll and conversing quietly with a taller girl whose kinky hair was in tight braids. The children were all right. Her head was reasonably all right. She fell asleep again.

"How you doing?" someone said, and Marian opened her eyes on her rescuer.

Marian-June was a very pretty pale brown woman in a tie-dyed shirt and white jeans.

"You're a Negro!" Marian said.

Marian June laughed. "That does seem to be so, doesn't it? How do you feel?"

Marian raised her head and dropped it down again. "I didn't mean to be rude. I think I hurt all over. What has happened to Jeb?"

"They finished unloading. He took the truck back and then he took the other man to the bus terminal. He isn't back yet. Are you hungry?"

"No."

"How about some chamomile tea?"

"Okay."

While the tea was being fixed, Marian considered the room. The furniture was shabby in a familiar way, much like what she and Jeb had purchased in secondhand stores in Ocean Park and Venice—two dark sturdy armchairs with cushions in Mission style, a heavy golden oak desk which had once been government issue, a glass-fronted bookcase, and an American version of an Oriental rug. On the wall was a duplicate of a print that Marian had also purchased—Van Gogh's "Starry Night." The walls were painted white and the curtains made from an Indian bedspread. Marian June belonged, not to an alien race but the familiar one of recent college student. Marian lay back in bed and gave up worrying. Somehow she had arrived in a place where she could be safely ill, at least for now.

"June," she said, sometime later when the owner of the room came back in with a small tray and a cup. "I'm sorry to give you all this trouble. You shouldn't have to put up with it. I promise to make it up to you somehow in the future… but right now, I feel really sick. I don't think I could walk across the room."

"Marian!" June corrected, and then they both laughed. "Okay, call me June. My sister does. "

"This is wonderful of you."

"It's like in the Bible. You're a stranger and you fell almost at my gate. At any rate, right next door while I was walking past. I have to take you in, don't I? My good deed for the week. At the moment, you don't have to do anything but lie still and get well. While you were asleep, Jeb and I set up the kids' beds, and we unpacked your kitchen well enough so he can get dinner tonight."

Marian was filled with guilt. "You've been working over

there too. I shouldn't even be in Oakland. I wasn't going to follow him up here—I was going to go to LA instead—but everything happened so fast, I couldn't think it out in time. He hasn't gone to the store?"

"He said you packed enough food for him and the kids for tonight."

"If a woman doesn't plan something out, nothing ever gets done."

June considered. "He doesn't seem a bad sort. Maybe just needs a lot of direction. He says he has to go to work tomorrow but I told him the kids can come over here. I'm between jobs so I can watch them a day or two. If you're not feeling better, I'll take you to Highland Hospital and have them look you over. I looked for my First Aid book but I couldn't find it. I'm better on Victorian literature."

"Thank you, a hundred times." Marian took a few sips of tea, it was Constant Comment, welcomingly familiar. "I think I need to sleep some more. Is that what a concussion does? I've never had one."

"Maybe just shock."

"After tomorrow..." she started. After tomorrow? Tomorrow she had to get up and be instantly well and start job-hunting, find childcare for Bro, and figure out how the children would manage in one bedroom.

"After tomorrow, we'll assess," June said.

Marian gave up. She didn't feel up to planning, or decisions, or work. Exhausted at the thought, she lay back and fell asleep.

When she woke up next, it felt like morning. The sun was coming through a different window and the birds were tweeting in an earnest cacophony. Bro was gone and a blanket had been thrown across her. Had she really slept through the rest of that day and then the night too? She still hurt in many places but her headache was gone. She felt better, maybe much better.

Where was June, where was Jeb and the kids, and June's daughter? It was curious but not curious enough to make her sit up. She raised her head cautiously, calling, "Hello!"

When there was no answer she let her head fall back and considered whether she felt up to sitting.

No. Not quite yet.

She dozed a while longer and then June came in wearing an old white shirt and the same jeans. "You're awake? How you feeling?"

"As if I had been run over by a truck."

"You'd better lie there quietly for a while. How's your neck?"

"It's my ribs that hurt. And I need a bathroom."

"Right there. See that door just through the arch? You've got a gash on your ribs from falling on a branch that broke. I think you may need stitches. Here take my hand."

After she had used the toilet, Marian leaned on the old marble sink and reviewed her body, testing it in small movements moving inch by inch, and finding it a little painful here and there but not terrible. She put water on her face.

"There are some clean towels over the tub." June's voice came through the door.

After finding these, Marian washed her face and hands and under her arms and carefully mopped at the bloody spots she could see.

"You okay?" June called out.

Marian opened the door, feeling much improved, and saw June tugging a large familiar suitcase across the room. "Jeb thought this might be the one you need."

Marian went to help her. June was both smaller and thinner than Marian and probably not as strong. "You shouldn't have to do that. He should have brought that in."

They dragged the suitcase to an empty space where it could be opened out on the floor. Then Marian sat down quickly on the bed to recover. She might feel a lot better but not quite as well as she had thought.

June looked her over. "You dizzy?"

"I'm getting there, but still a little weak."

"How's your headache?"

"Mostly gone."

"That's a good sign. Jeb left the suitcase on my front porch and went off to work. He left a note for you."

"Where are the kids?"

"They're in the back yard with Leah, chasing the wildlife. Probably the chameleons. You know you haven't had any food for almost a day. That might be why you feel weak."

Jeb's note included fifty dollars and the instructions that Marian was to see some kind of doctor before she did anything else. June and Marian discussed this over Corn Flakes and coffee. Marian was wondering whether she still had health insurance now that Jeb had left the job.

"Do you know a doctor who will see me?"

"Yes. No problem there. Probably better than going to Emergency. There's a good black doctor, but if you'd prefer, there's also a Chinese doctor."

Marian thought she had never had to specify the race of a doctor. "Whoever. As long as he has a degree."

"She," June said carefully.

"Okay. She. Whoever." The world was always changing, wasn't it?

"It's not too far. I've got a car. Jeb took yours. We can put all the children in the back seat and take them along and I can walk them around while you're being seen."

Marian looked at the only friendly face she had seen in Oakland and put a hand on the ragged white shirt with the warm skin underneath. "You are so amazing. You've got a friend for life." Then she was a little embarrassed. "That is, if you want one."

June gave a soft laugh. "I'll take that. Just when I could use one! My so-called husband just went off to Westwood to graduate school and left me with no income."

What Marian learned about June in the next hour was... she had grown up in a small town in Washington State, in the only black family in town, and she had come down to Berkeley to go to the University but had to work while she was there because her family could send her very little. She moved into a shared apartment and ended up in love with a man who was there, and they had gotten together. This had resulted in Leah, and in June quitting school to work and support Lionel while he finished his Bachelor's degree. Just before he left for UCLA, he had moved her over to this house in Oakland because he thought it was a nicer place and much cheaper than Berkeley.

"Did you get a degree?" Marian asked.

"An ABA," June laughed. "You know what that is... an Almost B A."

While they waited in the doctor's waiting room, Marian introduced the pressing subject of job-hunting in Oakland. Was there a newspaper with good ads or were there agencies for office work and how was the pay and how was the transportation?

June had worked in an office at the University but now that she had the house in Oakland, Berkeley was too far away and she hoped for a job here but they didn't seem to have gotten to black secretaries in Oakland yet. In which case, she might have to go back to the University.

"Well, that's ridiculous," Marian said. "Maybe I can help. When we're through here, let's pick up a newspaper and I can see what the salaries are."

Happily, it was the female doctor's opinion that Mariah did not have a concussion but that she needed stitches for the puncture wound on her ribs. She sewed that up while Marian chewed on her fingernails and wept quietly. The swelling of her ankle had lessened but it still hurt so it was wrapped with an Ace bandage after which she could walk slowly.

Marian scowled at all this delay but accepted it. Her head was still dizzy and she could tell she wasn't ready to rush into any typing tests. Besides, both Addie and Leah were sending out messages of irritation at Bro. When, after all the delays they stepped outside the doctor's office, the city was splashed with sunshine. Both women paused on the small stoop, their arms locked, and looked around suddenly happy.

"We might as well relax," Marian said. "I need another day.

We can read the ads in the paper."

"It's really not a bad town," June said, excusing the parking lot already full of older cars and the back doors of several fast food restaurants.

"The lake looked nice. Nobody told me about a big lake right in the center of town. I just have to get used to everything."

June nodded, thinking ahead. "We'll buy a newspaper and go back to my house and plan tomorrow. You'll feel better by then. After all the years you've worked, I bet you can get on at a temp agency right away."

"Thank you," Marian said, grateful for the approval. She saw no threatening figures in the immediate view of the street. Addie and Leah were whispering some secrets and Bro had put an arm around her leg while he looked around. The pain pill she had been given was taking effect. Best of all, there was the warmth of June's arm and the way she was casting an experienced eye on their day and what they needed to do. All seemed at peace for the moment and suggested life in Oakland might be manageable.

## CHAPTER TWENTY-TWO

Marian remembered that first day in Oakland when, already as depressed as she could possibly be, the air was knocked out of her and she lay on her back looking up at the sky fairly sure her neck had been broken. That had seemed like the ultimate disaster on top of losing the job and the house in Fresno. The day had been so terrible already, between driving into the unknown world, worried about the old car with its untested creaks and sighs, sure she would lose Jeb in the Rent a Truck, while distracted by Bro's peeing on the seat of the car. In fact, all that had gone on so far had been so horrible that having the wind knocked out of her was like a blessed relief. She could do nothing, therefore she didn't have to do anything. She had looked up at the sky and waited for everything to stop right there and her life to be over.

But of course her life hadn't stopped and let her alone. That never happened, although it was true that she couldn't do anything immediately. And while she waited, she had met June and it became, not just a better day, but a momentous day because she and June had formed a united front to the world before they were quite aware they were doing it.

Instead of staying with the dream of that time, of being in June's house for the first time, Marian was jerked back to her own living room in Sonoma many years later. She knew it was in Sonoma because on the wall across from her was the drawing of a New York skyline which Jeb had bought the first week they moved to Sonoma and their retirement home.

Buying the drawing had been a first in Jeb's life. Unpacking in a new house had been the usual confusing and tiring effort, and more so now that they were in their sixties and hadn't moved for ten years. Someone had suggested they take a break and visit the art and wine festival going on in the Plaza. This event had been so charming and relaxing that they had spent half the day there where there was food and music as well as wine, comfortable benches under the trees and such a convivial air that they saw their new life of retirement in a magically rosy light. Then Jeb, who rarely spent money on anything that wasn't featured in an automotive store, had come back to her at the end of the afternoon with this large bright-framed canvas.

"What is that?" Marian said, sorry she had let him wander around with a larger than usual amount of cash.

"Look, it's New York!"

That required no special intelligence. It was labeled 'New York Skyline.' "Why did you buy that?"

He had shrugged without answering, and Marian was silent remembering that he had been deeply pained at the catastrophe that became known as nine-eleven.

He said finally, "We didn't enjoy it when we were there," as if they had lost something that had almost been theirs. Marian had thought that over more than once while she wondered how many sides of Jeb remained hidden behind his laconic manner.

But now coming back from another memory, her neck was stiff and her eyes hurt because she had them tightly closed against the light. She sat up awkwardly to relieve the pain... and was filled with delight.

"When did you come?" she asked her youngest child.

It really was Lilly, lovely impossible Lilly, who managed to remain out of reach for months at a time and had not appeared in Sonoma for more five years. She was now sitting, cross-legged, across from Marian on the green leather chair under the New York skyline. Lilly, dressed as usual in jeans that were washed thin and showed holes on both knees, plus a white blouse that looked as if it had never been ironed.

Without answering, the lifelike Lilly unbent her knees, stood up and came across the room in one rapid movement to lay her cheek against Marian's and give her a kiss. Marian put out her hands and held her daughter's thin shoulders several minutes. It wasn't often she got to do that. Lilly had left home ten years ago and seldom returned.

"You look wonderful."

"Mother, why are you sleeping on the couch in the middle of the day? Are you sick?"

"No." Marian said. "I didn't get enough sleep last night."

She had been too worried to sleep. All about the party! Was anyone going to come? Wasn't she going to look foolish for having rented the historic mansion for so few guests? What had she been thinking of? Should she tell Bridget to cancel the order of wine?

Lilly stood in front of her mother, considering, examining her with the trained eye of someone who had made a career of working with the ill and impoverished all over the world. "You don't look bad," Lilly pronounced.

"Have you had anything to eat? I wasn't sure when you were coming. You were so vague about it." Now Marian could see near the front door two faded Army Surplus duffle bags and some odd-shaped parcels tied with rope. Maybe Lilly was staying longer than her usual day and a half. Marian's heart flooded hopefully. She stood up and reached for this Wanderer and gave her another hug while she could get one in.

Marian had worked at the law office for years after their move to Oakland. They were long, hard years while both worked and Bro went to childcare, and they saved every penny they could so as to buy another house. Houses in Oakland were much more expensive than Fresno and the house they bought, although it was in a better neighborhood than where they had been renting, was something of a wreck and was going to require endless weekends and evenings of repairs and painting and wallpapering.

Marian was discouraged by the thought of this next phase—

days in the law office plus evenings and weekends in renovation. She had grown to hate her life with Jeb who did nothing but work, and Bro who was weepy and demanding. So, while she typed endless letters to doctors and opposing attorneys, cajoled discouraged clients, she had yearned for some reward just for her. A reward she could give herself.

In the middle of this, she decided to have another baby, a baby that was not like Bro with his weeping, or the endlessly querulous Addie. She did not tell Jeb what she was up to when she quit taking her birth control pills and engineered more sex. In only a few months, she was pregnant again.

Jeb had been aghast. "How could you get pregnant?"

"Probably I missed some days with the pills."

"Mare, let's not do this! We're working hard enough now. I don't know how we can do any more."

"You mean get an abortion? I won't do that. I will quit working for a couple of years and stay home with the baby. That will make Bro happier too."

"Bro will be in high school soon. That will satisfy him. We can't buy a house and fix it up without your salary."

"We don't need to spend all that money on carpet and paint and new doors, and another room. We can buy it and do all the rest later on. I'll go back to work when the baby's two and we can catch up then."

"All right I'll make that deal with you if you just stay off one year and then get a better job. " She knew he was serious. Jeb had been unhappy all these years about the fact that she worked long hours for a firm which paid much less than the going rate because their clients were so poor.

Marian shook her head. "No." Her voice was firm.

Husband and wife looked at each other, measuring their resolve. "Goddammit! Why not? All those hours you work for nothing!"

"Because they can't get anyone else at that price who is any good."

"Let one of their wives do it."

"Their wives already make more money."

The argument raged up and down the room in a familiar pattern without Marian ever confessing to her reason—that she had found a place where she was needed and she wasn't going to give it up. Which Jeb guessed at but wanted her to say so he could argue her out of it. When they were both exhausted with the quarrel and repaired to the kitchen for a cup of coffee, they fell back on other things to debate. When should they buy a house? Before or after the baby came? And would they have to look for one with four bedrooms? By which time, Marian knew she had won her fight and was released to her own vision. She bought a pretty maternity dress, something she had always sewed before. She also bought a beautiful antique oak cradle, a waste as Jeb pointed out because the baby would outgrow it at four months. She warned Rodman and Rattigan that she was going to take a year off after the baby was born. There was consternation throughout the office because Marian had become the primary guerrilla in their war against the big insurance companies and the California Workers Compensation office.

To the surprise of both Marian's co-workers and even Jeb, she grew a little plump, smiled now and then, and refused to do battle over inconveniences or delays in her schedule.

June saw it. "You are positively nearly a delight to have around." Then they had laughed together because Marian's quick temper was a constant subject of teasing.

Both Marian and the baby gained weight and grew contented, auguring a new happiness. Would it be a boy or girl? Marian refused the test to find out. She would take whatever it was; secretly sure it was a girl. Which had turned out to be true. When she first saw Lilly, she fell instantly in love. She couldn't remember how the others had looked but this one seemed perfect. And that was true in its way. Lilly was always delightful, calm, interested in her surroundings but never fretful. If her diaper was wet or her gums hurt in teething, she put up with it till she was rescued and then grinned and happily kicked her legs in thanks. She accepted toys gratefully, crawled enthusiastically, and walked just at the right age. Marian wondered secretly if all this happiness was because Lilly had been a *wanted* baby. Instead of one, like both Addie and Bro, who had appeared without invitation.

Lilly was ten years younger than Bro, in her mid-thirties, and had been likened to a gazelle because of her narrow boniness and quick movements. Her ash blonde hair was wound carelessly in a topknot and was decorated with dime-store sunglasses. She wore much-washed sneakers with ties which had broken and been re-tied. She had been in the Aleutians for several years. Surely she had worn more substantial shoes there, but maybe not.

"I could eat." Lilly said cautiously.

"Well, come on then. I have some food in the house for a change. I bought some sliced ham just for you."

Lilly trailed behind her willingly enough. Her voice was soft but had a lilt in it. "I've been eating soup every day. Ham would be good, and a salad. They didn't go in for salads much."

Marian pulled things out of the refrigerator while Lilly sat at the table and watched. It was wonderful to look over and see her there in a house which had mostly been marked by her absence. "You're too thin."

"You've been saying that forever."

"You wouldn't guess what I've been dreaming about just now."

"No. What?"

Marian had brought home lettuce that was already cut and washed, a luxury. She added tiny tomatoes, ready-sliced olives and dressing. Time was when she made a salad by slicing up many vegetables. Probably Lilly wouldn't notice that she cut corners so much lately, simplifying everyday tasks because Jeb was not there to complain. But, unlike sister Addie who was a cooking fanatic, Lilly had never been terribly interested in food and probably wouldn't think to criticize.

"Do you cook for yourself up there?"

"No. No time for it. We all eat in the mess hall with the hospital staff. The only trouble with that is that they cook the same things day after day."

What she really wanted to know was how long Lilly was going to stay but she was afraid to ask. "Make a list of things you want to eat and I'll get them."

Lilly merely said 'okay' and looked around the kitchen with vague interest. This house, their retirement house, had been bought after Lilly was out of college and off on her adventures. She had visited here only a couple of times. She hadn't even come for Jeb's funeral because she had had a bronchial infection and they wouldn't let her fly. Was she picturing Jeb in the room? Marian thought of raising that subject but decided not to bring his ghost in.

She had a host of questions but was cautious about asking them. She waited till they were both seated with the food in front of them before venturing:

"Where are you going next?"

"Africa."

Marian's heart froze. "Please, not Africa."

"What do you have against Africa?"

"Everything. All those wars, all that starvation, and they have that dreaded disease." Marian's voice had risen, something she hadn't anticipated happening so soon after Lilly's arrival.

"AIDS. But I'm not going to get AIDS because I know how to avoid it." Lilly's voice had also risen. "I'm needed there."

"But you were needed in the Aleutians."

"Yes, but I've done that, and there's a doctor in Africa I've worked with before and he asked me to come."

Mariam examined her daughter's face and caught something new there. "A doctor. A man? You're going there for him?" Wouldn't it be wonderful if Lilly finally married and settled down, and maybe even had children? Why was it that Marian was seventy and still had no grandchildren? Addie had divorced after only two years and never re-married. Bro and Letitia were only now talking about starting a family. This generation was just not into marriage and families.

"Mother! Don't get that way. He's just someone I work well with. What is it you were dreaming when I woke you up?"

Mariam looked around her familiar kitchen which, truthfully, could stand a scrub and a new coat of paint, but today looked warmed and bright because Lilly was here. What would Lilly say about the party? Would she even stay for it? It was only a few days away but it had never paid to argue with Lilly. The youngest and smallest and most fragile looking was one eternally set on her own path, even at the age of twelve.

She had been twelve when Marian opened Lilly's closet one day and saw it nearly empty. Where were all the dresses bought by Marian because she loved to see them on this child, where were the wool sweaters knitted by Grandma, the good coat far better than any that had been bought for Addie, the pink raincoat with matching boots and umbrella? When questioned, Lilly had said that she had put them all in grocery bags and taken them to a clothing drive for poor people in Bangladesh because they needed them more than she did. She really preferred wearing blue jeans.

Marian had objected strenuously but Lilly had refused to tell exactly where she had taken them because she knew Marian was determined to go and get them back.

Jeb, when appealed to, had refused to demand the address. "They were her clothes. Let her do without if that's what she wants."

Which sounded as if he was punishing her, but Marian caught the hint of a smile and knew that Jeb was not immune to Lilly's charm either. Marian gave up at that and was very careful afterwards not to buy Lilly any clothes she might find 'too good.'

Why was it that this one person was surrounded with a glow that changed everything?

June had said when Lilly was only three, "She's a changeling, that one. Keep hold of her so they don't steal her back."

Lilly had been thirteen and a freshman when the herd of

boys began to congregate in their front yard ready to hang around Lilly whenever she stepped out the door. Thirteen when Jeb found she was coming home from school on the back of a motorcycle driven by someone who must be at least seventeen.

In her high school years, Lilly was invariably popular and was invited along on all sorts of excursions that were new to Marian and Jeb... camping trips in the Sierra, skiing at Yosemite, beach parties in Santa Cruz. These were often with older boys and girls so that it was hard to know what would be happening, what was safe for her. Jeb's response was usually to say no and long family controversies ensued. There were also expenses he was unwilling to pay and Marian began to take in temp work to pay for Lilly's entertainment. Through all of this turmoil, Lily had remained cheerful, unimpressed and undamaged.

When it was time for them to consider college for her, Marian and Jeb found themselves in sharp disagreement. Jeb refused to consider any more expenses for Lilly and that included college. Marian was more than surprised, also angry. It was monstrously unfair. They had squeezed out money for Addie's first two years of college and then paid for years and years for Bro. Now Jeb said he was done with all that.

"She'll just get married," he said.

So Lilly had gone to junior college—thank goodness for California junior colleges which prepared students to be upperclassmen in the state universities without charging very much—on Lilly's own money first from babysitting and then waitressing. Marian continued to pay for all the extras with money earned by typing depositions at home.

After she was through with junior college, Marian had driven Lily to the train station in Oakland and put her on a train, Marian close to weeping that her baby was off into the world but Lilly looking excited. As soon as she got to college, she got a job in the dining hall, and also acquired a mentor from the faculty who wrote to Marian several times a semester about how well Lilly was doing. Marian used some vacation time to drive down to this college in Claremont and see for herself. She reported back to Jeb that Lilly's grades were very good, and at the same time, she was well-liked. Jeb had relented and paid a share of Lilly's fees. And eventually he had even gone to her graduation with good grace.

After graduating, Lilly had embarked on a career that combined service with an interest in foreign lands and so they seldom saw her. When she did come, for a two or three day visit, she was always cheerful, contented, glad enough to see them but had little to say.

Lilly must have been hungry. She had the salad half-eaten already but paused and put down her fork

Marian silently urged her to keep on eating but knew better than to say so. The girl had always been too easily distracted from food by other ideas. That was probably the real reason she had always been thin. Marian wanted to touch her again or hug her, this child who had been like a gift in her life.

"Would you like mustard on your sandwich?"

"No thanks." Lilly looked at the sandwich and her fork but didn't pick up either. "I want to call Addie. Where will she be at this time?"

Marian was disappointed but tried not to show it. She'd rather have Lilly to herself for a little while. Once Addie arrived, the two of them might go off together. You wouldn't think they would be such great friends, being so many years apart, but they liked being together. "Well, there's no telling. Maybe in a class, maybe in the hospital. I have her cell phone number. You can reach Letty. She has a job at home now. Seems to like it though I think she doesn't want to work."

Lilly was not so interested in Letty who had only married Bro and been in the family a few years, years that Lilly had mostly been away.

"Aren't you going to eat some more?"

Lilly looked down at her plate as if she had never seen it before. Marian held her breath but in a few minutes, Lilly picked up her fork again and pushed the salad around some. Why is it she had never gotten into eating? All the rest of the family had healthy appetites.

"How is Addie? She never writes."

"Do you write to her?'

"Yes, I do. At least twice a year."

Marian was surprised. "Those must be the only letters anyone in the family writes. She's doing well I think. She really likes this job. Well, you would guess that. She has always liked telling people what to do. She is plenty able to do that now. They think well of her. She got some kind of award for her teaching. She keeps getting offers of other jobs but so far isn't interested."

Lilly was grinning. "I'll bet that's why she didn't remarry. She didn't want someone who would tell *her* what to do. If she goes on and gets a doctorate she can become the head of a nursing school. I think she'd really like that."

Marian shook her head. "Even with a doctorate she wouldn't be the equal of the MDs. That's what she says. You were just little then but her first few years were hard. Doctors aren't nice to nurses."

"Except my doctor friend. But I'm not a nurse."

She had stopped eating the salad, took one bite of the ham sandwich she had said she wanted and then put it down and pushed back her chair.

"Tell me more about him," Marian pleaded.

But Lilly shook her head. "Later. I think I need a nap. I was up all night in the car. And you never told me what you were dreaming about when I came in."

Marian had no trouble remembering this. "I was dreaming about the trip when we moved from Fresno to Oakland."

"What was that like? I wasn't there."

"I know. You weren't born for another four years."

"Or was it five?"

The memory, even after all these year, still hurt. "I was driving that old Chevrolet, not sure how bad it was because we had just bought it, and Addie and Bro were in the back seat and I was worried about them. There were no seat belts in those days. And I kept looking back to make sure they stayed seated and didn't try to stand up. I was miserable at leaving Fresno, and exhausted because we had worked madly for a few days to pack everything up that we had just unpacked six month earlier."

"And you were angry with Dad?"

"How did you know that?"

"He told me."

"Did he tell you why?"

"Yes." Lilly smiled, something she rarely did. It was a beautiful smile. "Because he quit his job on a principle. Because it was harming people instead of helping them. That's why I loved him so much after that. I keep that in my life as a sort of guide. Would I have the courage to quit a job just because it was bad for others?"

Marian was silenced. She put her hands over her face. "And did he tell you that he threw away the first good life that we had had since we married? That he did it without telling me?"

"Mother, don't do that. Don't be angry with me because I loved Dad."

Marian stood up and walked away from the table. Of course, she wouldn't do that. But Lilly, of all the children, should somehow know what Marian had gone through.

"Mother, don't be angry." Lilly's voice was ragged.

"Can't you understand what that was like for me?" Marian was amazed at the hot tears leaving her eyes, almost burning her cheeks. The last thing she wanted was to quarrel. "It's my fault because I never explained it to you. I didn't want to seem as if I was criticizing your father."

For a minute, the two of them seemed frozen in space, only a few feet away from each other. Then Lilly rescued her, coming across the kitchen, putting her arms around her mother.

"Please."

Marian took her in her arms. "I never want to quarrel with you. Let's leave this subject till we feel better. Let me tell you about my party which is why I'm all upset."

She was glad she had said this but she couldn't bring the party into this room right now. She couldn't forget this. Had Lilly turned against her? Hadn't Jeb always given Lilly a hard time, telling her that she was only interested in boys and dating, and would never be a serious person? And hadn't Marian gone out on a limb year after year for what she thought Lilly needed in spite of Jeb? It had been up to Marian to make sure Lilly got into college. The money had all been going to Bro who seemed unable to take any advantage of the gifts that were being showered on him.

And who was the serious person now? Could Lilly be any more so? While Bro was complaining about his well-paid job and making Letty work whether she wanted to or not so they could buy furniture. What was this prerogative men seemed to think they were entitled to?

"You know I nearly left him for that. Giving up the first job that gave us a decent life…"

"I know. I know." Lilly's voice was gentle. "But it must have been hard for him to do when he knew how much it meant to you. He just couldn't work that way."

"And he never even told me he was going to quit. Just did it, and didn't have another job, just told me to get ready to move." She waited for Lilly to show some sign of agreement with her mother.

"But I respect you too. All those marches and rallies you went on with June. All that picketing. When I tell people about that, they are impressed. There weren't other white people all of the time, were there? Or black people either, sometimes it was just you and June."

Marian thought back over the years in Oakland and was a little amazed now. At the time it had just seemed normal. The alliance she had formed with June their first day in Oakland had come to dominate her life when she was not at home or at work. She laughed a little at the memories.

"It was the East Bay Democratic Club behind it all. If they announced anything where people were needed—picketing or boycotting or marching, June would go, and then I would go with June. It didn't seem so dramatic at the time. We tried to keep a low profile because we had to go home to the kids and we had to work the next day."

Then memories overtook her and she began to cry and left the room, leaving Lilly with a gesture meaning it would only be a little while till she came back. She went upstairs to cry in peace.

# CHAPTER TWENTY-THREE

The first necessity for both Marian and June when they met had been to find jobs. June had some idea where to look. The first morning they put Addie and Bro and Leah all in the back of the car and started at Rodman and Rattigan, a law firm that represented people who were applying for Worker's Compensation.

At the start of Marian's first interview on that first morning, (it turned out to be her only interview), while June and the children waited in the reception room, Marian was walked past a desk that had a forlorn air. The calendar hadn't been turned for a couple of weeks, and there were so many stacks of files on the desktop it would have been impossible to spread another one out there.

"What's this?"

"That's the desk that is empty," she was told. She was slightly chilled by this view, and started the interview with pity for a law firm that was unable to find employees when they were needed. Maybe it was because they hadn't spent any money making the office look pleasant.

Certainly it was grim. The reception room had two rows of brown wooden chairs and two Early California paintings, rather dusty, plus a receptionist's desk which was adorned with many yellow sticky notices but missing a receptionist. In the secretarial room, where there were two desks but only one with a calendar, there were brown cardboard files in stacks on the floor, stacks three to four feet high, leaning precariously against walls or desks. Marian had never worked for a law firm before but she had interviewed in several and she didn't think these piles were natural to the legal business. Some of these stacks looked to have been in place for years; the floors had rims of dirt around them. They gave the impression of a creeping illness that no amount of work could dislodge. Or maybe it meant the office manager was not very good at his job.

However, it should also indicate that they really needed another secretary. This filled her with hope. But how did you find the file you were looking for? And were these files still active or were they settled and could be carted off somewhere? She was afraid to ask any of this because after their first few questions, it seemed as if they were going to hire her.

Yes. She really did have six and a half years of secretarial experience but no, none of it had been in law. "Your secretary must have left some time ago," Marian ventured at the end of these questions.

Rodman was a thin man who differed from the attorneys Marian had met in Beverly Hills. There they looked very full of their own importance and eager to encounter the world whereas Rodman looked as if he had been unhappy ever since he passed the bar.

He answered cautiously: "Two weeks." Then he looked at her as if he wanted to say more but there was too much to be explained about the nature of their business for the time they had. It would all have to wait for the next day. Shortly after that she was hired unequivocally. The salary was not what she had hoped for but never mind. Getting a job this fast, even knowing the precise date on which she would get her first pay check, gave her an enormous boost. She was satisfied they would clear up whatever these problems were. She was used to being a new broom.

They wanted her to start the next day but Marian protested. Her house was not unpacked and her wounds from the fall on the bushes still hurt. She argued for the day after and won. June, consulted in the waiting room, agreed to start the search for childcare immediately.

On the first morning, Marian packed her lunch and June gave her a ride to work with the three children in the back of the car. Jeb had offered to let her have their car but Marian didn't want to have to pay for parking. Bro rode in her lap because he was sniveling, having already guessed she was leaving for the day.

"Better put a diaper on him. His training pants are all wet."

"Don't worry about anything," June told her. "Call me and I'll pick you up."

Rodman was already in the office at eight o'clock and let Marian in with a relieved smile. Perhaps he hadn't really believed she would show up. She went immediately to her new desk and began to take the files off and stack them on the floor. She wondered if she might get a back strain before she had even cleared a space to work. She noted thankfully that the typewriter was an IBM Selectric, fairly new looking though spattered with whiteout.

She had closed the door between her office and the reception room and all was quiet for the first half hour. Then the door suddenly banged open, hitting her newest stack of files, and sending paper half across the office. The biggest man she had ever seen stood in the doorway. Not just big enough to fill the whole doorway, he was also the blackest man she had ever seen, blue-black, in a worn black wool suit and a huge pink mouth that was wide open in alarm.

Marian screamed. She jumped away from her chair and now looked around for a weapon. One came immediately to hand, the long brass letter-opener which stood in a leather cup waiting to be used. Marian brandished it with a throaty war cry.

At the sight of the weapon in her hand, the man let out another sound and his face started to crumple. His shoulders slumped and his arms lengthened helplessly.

"What the hell!" said Rodman who had come in the other door. "What happened?" he asked Marian but did not wait for a reply.

"Marcus, you know by now to wait in the waiting room till

you're called."

Marcus nodded humbly, he had his faded blue handkerchief already out, and he began to wipe his face with it. "Is it too late? My watch is broke."

"It's not late. The mail won't get here till after ten. Now apologize to our new secretary, whose name is Mary."

"Marian," Marian said. Her mistake had deeply unnerved her. What was wrong with the man? And what had she done? Threatened to stab him! The lethal spear in her grip dropped as her hand opened and it clattered back on the desk.

"I'm so sorry." She felt her face burning in embarrassment. He was still a huge pile of a man, though now brought low. With one hand still mopping his face, he was holding out the other to her.

Marian reached out tentatively for it and came within six inches of the huge paw. With the separation still between them, they both shook hands in the air. Marcus muttered something unintelligible and backed out the doorway to wait for the morning mail in the reception room.

"I'm so sorry," Marian said to Rodman. "I don't know what I was thinking."

"There are a lot of people coming in all day long," he scolded her mildly. "You'll have to get used to it."

The truth of this was demonstrated only twenty minutes later when a thin, anxious, yellowish man in a mismatched suit opened the door and peered in. "Sorry to bother you. I'm Leroy Jenks. Is the mail here yet?"

"No, " Marian said, having incorporated the party line. "Wait out front and we'll let you know."

In spite of four or five interruptions, she was able to sort out the files and ready the typewriter for its day's work by the time the morning mail arrived. All of the chairs in the reception room had filled up by then and she was tense with the anxiety she sensed from there. She took the opener to the twenty letters that had arrived, stamped them with a date stamp and carried then in to Rodman. She then learned that she needed to sort them according to whichever attorney—there were three in the office—had handled the file. As soon as she announced those people who the attorneys would see, four of those waiting in the rows of chairs went away.

Had they been confused as to when they would be seen or did they really think their turn had come? She began to worry if they had money for lunch or not? She queried Rodman.

He looked at her and shrugged. "Some of them have nothing else to do so they wait here. I can't help that."

Nevertheless the weight of their hopefulness pressed down on her shoulders. At the beginning of that day, she had been given a three-page list of the papers that were waiting to be typed, each one had added notes about its priority. There was no way she could possibly finish this list in a week. Her self-assurance fled. These expectations were totally unreasonable. This job was not going to work out. She would have to start all over somewhere else. The disappointment was keener than her worry over the men's expectations. Were all the jobs in Oakland going to be as impossible? Rather than interrupt the constant flow of Rodman's clients, she waited till lunchtime to question him.

Again he looked at her as if from far away, shaking his head slightly in confusion. "Just do what you can. Start at the top and line through what you've done. I'll add new ones at the bottom. If they've got a court date, I'll write a note on that. Otherwise don't worry about it."

She looked at him mutely.

"Well yes. We run behind a lot. That's the nature of the business. Just keep working at it."

That evening when June picked her up, Marian started immediately while taking an unhappy Bro from June's arms. "Did you have any idea how impossible that job really is?"

June nodded, guiltily. "I'd heard that. But also that they're real patient. They'll put up with a lot because nobody wants to work there."

"I can't work like that either."

Maybe it was her fault, the state she was already in. after having protested coming to Oakland at all. Now she could see there was no point in trying to change reality. According to June this type of law paid very poorly, and the firm therefore took a maximum number of cases, really more than they could handle. Some secretaries came and struggled with the workload briefly and then quickly left to work for the insurance companies that were on the side where the profit was, and who were therefore paid as much as a third more in salary. Mariam sighed and gave up thinking about escaping. Here the world was what it was.

Sad case after sad case came through Rodman & Rattigan, each man limp with fear that his livelihood was lost forever, while one attorney or another explained the small amount of money he was to get in exchange for his lost ability to support himself.

Marian was to stay for five years, bewitched by this desperate need for her.

If there was any delight in her life after her move to Oakland, it was all because of June. The two clung to each other in their twin need for comfort and understanding, and for assistance in the complex task of managing a home and children along with a fulltime job.

Communications and individuals flowed back and forth across the driveway that was two strings of concrete separated by a weedy section that produced dandelions in the spring. This strip went from the street to the back of the lot where there was a leaning garage padlocked on old tires. In the downstairs of the two-flat, a series of renters came and went—most often a husband and wife, sometimes cordial, sometimes not, who both worked and were sometimes drinking too much and or saving up to buy a house. These brief rentals had little effect on the upstairs flat and the small house next door which had become one household.

Though the bond was started by Marian and June, Jeb acquiesced, maybe because he found it easier to deal with both women than with Marian alone. Occasionally he even asked

June to interpret something Marian had said. Hardly noticed by the adults, much of the glue in the group was supplied by Leah, who had been lonely since her father left and was cheered by these new relationships. She did all the laundry in June's old washing machine. She enjoyed tending to Bro because he made it feel more like a family and was greedily happy to accept her fussing. Leah also helped Addie (who was more a playground organizer than a student) with her homework. The older girl found her own mother too unworldly a guide for the future and therefore asked Marian scores of questions both practical and far-reaching.

Marian constantly inspected June's house because nothing worked very well there, and when repairs were needed told Jeb to do them because June would read the Symbolist Poets in preference to worrying about the water flow or the heater, and her landlord seldom fixed anything. Leah appreciated this intervention and often stood beside Jeb watching him admiringly as he worked on some new repair and she could get him to explain it.

It took longer for June to find a job than Marian. As she expected, she couldn't get an office job in Oakland like the clerking she had done at the University before she moved. All those jobs were white-only.

"Sewing?" Marian said unbelievingly. In Los Angeles, sewing was the province of Mexicans and paid very poorly even when the work was beautiful.

June defended. "But this is not a sweatshop. This is the best department store in town and its 'Alterations' and the boss is very nice; she told me if I ever have a problem with Leah, I can call her and come in late. "

"But it's by the hour and no vacation or sick leave."

"The pay is good and she told me I would get a raise in three months."

Marian saw the need to stop disparaging and start appreciating. "Well, you got a job! Hooray. The hardest part is over."

"Money is coming in," June agreed. "I wasn't sure it would." She wrote to Los Angeles to tell Lionel the happy news.

Sure enough, in a little more than a year, by dint of cheerful hard work along with skill with the customers, June transformed the poor job into a good one which included sick leave. Her boss had found her two beautiful black dresses to wear to work and in them June looked very much the quality of the customers she worked with.

The two women saw each other or talked on the phone at least twice a day. They shared errands, childcare, marketing, and cooking. Addie and Leah went back and forth together willingly enough, sometimes swinging Bro between them. June and Leah took several medications for asthma and digestive trouble so Marian would add trips to the pharmacy along with her more frequent marketing because she had to feed four rather than two. In return, June would make a huge pot of chili or bean soup to feed them all. Jeb was furnished a car at work so Marian had their old car to use but she couldn't afford the daily parking so June often delivered her to work.

They talked by phone at night, the last thing before going to bed, half asleep after showering, as they analyzed their days and sorted their modest ambitions for the coming week. June missed Lionel who seldom wrote, so she called him at least once a week in spite of the cost. Marian had found it was no use to discuss long term questions with Jeb whose thoughts were taken up entirely with his efforts to sell enough insurance to meet their needs.

After they had been friends some months, June declared one day: "I can't live with myself unless I do something with the Movement."

She did not have to say what movement but Marian understood. It was the sixties and Oakland boiled with hopes, disappointments, confrontations over Civil Rights. June subscribed to the Post and began to pass on each issue to Marian.

After several weeks of this, Marian said "All right. Let's do it."

June was startled. "I didn't mean you."

"Well," Marian said. "I'm convinced." The truth of the matter was that June had begun to take part and Marian was afraid to let her go alone to these events where feelings ran so high.

Jeb did not agree. "Just because you like her doesn't mean you have to take care of her."

"You've heard her. She thinks she still lives in a small town."

"That may be true, but you don't need to be there. You have other responsibilities. She will have to look to her other friends."

June's friends from the university seldom ventured into Oakland, and almost never appeared at the times June chose to attend a march or a picketing.

"When she has another friend to go with her, I won't go," said Marian who had long experience in dealing with Jeb's doubts.

Marian and June became regulars at the meetings and events in the East side of the city. After a while, people stopped looking at them curiously.

Their neighborhood was mixed already. The large black population of West Oakland had begun to move into the white East side of town twenty years earlier, seeking the small neat houses and relative peace of the district, and a portion of the white population acquiesced. Marian was not the only white woman on the picket lines. There was a lot of 'live and let live' among people who had come across the country for a better life during the twenties and thirties, and among the large population of immigrants from Asia and South America. This did not mean that the City Fathers of Oakland were ready to give up any power.

Why were there so many black people in Oakland, Marian asked. Jeb knew. Train porters began settling there in the early part of the century because it was the Western terminal of the cross-country trains. At the onset of the Second World War, when California began building ships in a way never seen before, the word went through the rest of the country that there were good factory jobs available and a steady stream of the hungry and poorly-employed of all colors made their way West. That was good for a few years only; then the war was over, the factories shut down and there were never again enough jobs to go around.

Now, in the late 1960s when there were black riots across the country, there was a poorly paid black population in Oakland that was more than half the city but had no power. There were angry complaints that Oakland couldn't even have a good riot.

"Thank you," June said. "I like having you along."

Because it was hard and sometimes scary to get up from the dinner table and go out into the night when no one knew what was going to happen. And many evenings when they headed home late after a threatening scene, there was fear in the air.

"De nada," Marian said, imitating Bro who was learning Spanish from his babysitter. "It's very interesting."

It had become more than that. She had listened to the speeches and read the articles and looked at the poverty of the clients in her office. It was not long before she had developed an absolute certainty about the need to repair this wrong. This wasn't what they had been taught in American History. Possibly some of her family and friends far away in Los Angeles wouldn't agree but Jeb did and she thought Grandpa Frank would and she didn't need to worry about the rest of them.

When they went out at night, they wore flat shoes with laces so they could run if necessary. They carried no purses to tempt muggers, only a little change and bus tokens in case they were able to catch a bus going home. Warm sweaters and head scarves. They locked arms so neither one could be easily pushed over, and they walked quickly, energetically, looking around as they went. Also they didn't talk when they walked so they could listen for footsteps behind them. And if it was late at night with little traffic, they walked on the center stripe in the street.

"My sister Alice taught me this," Marian said. "She's a nurse and this is what the nurses do when thy have a late night shift."

"Why do they want to be in the middle of a street where they can get hit by a car?"

"Because they can be seen there instead of being grabbed from a doorway along the sidewalk or between the cars at the curb. Late at night, they can hear a car."

# CHAPTER TWENTY-FOUR

It was April 1968 when the whole world dropped out of sync. Marian was not surprised that June was not there in the alley picking her up after work. Besides it was early. Rodman and Rattigan had dismissed everyone in the middle of the day.

She wanted to groan, to proclaim heartsickness out loud along with others. Instead, she walked silently to the bus stop and waited there. The bus was late, and when she climbed in, she could tell from the atmosphere that everyone already knew. There were tears on faces, and a heaviness to the air. June would be crying, she could guess that.

There was no answer to her knock on June's door but as usual the door was unlocked.

Marian called out her name as she went through the front room, and then heard a small sound. She saw June lying on the brass bed in the second room, curled in a fetal position, her face to the wall.

"Hi there."

"He's dead," June said.

"I know. We heard it at work. They sent us home."

June turned over and raised her head. "Martin. How could someone kill him? Wasn't anyone watching out for him?"

Marian had sat down on the bed beside her, the very bed where June had placed her when she rescued her the first day. She was rubbing June's shoulder for comfort. "I guess it was a long shot from a distance. I guess if someone is determined to kill you... They even got the President when they wanted to. How did you hear?"

"It was on the radio in the car." June sat up. "That's the end of everything."

"It's really not. There are all those other people."

"They don't count."

Marian had taken June's hand and was rubbing it because it was cold. "Would you like some Constant Comment?"

June mopped her eyes. "Not yet."

"Let's turn on the radio and see what is happening. Where are the kids?"

"They're up at your house. I told them to stay off the street. There's going to be a lot of anger. I've heard a couple of guns go off already."

"Oh Jesus!"

"Don't say that," June said though she was not that religious.

"I'm sorry."

"It's okay. I'll be better in a few minutes. We knew they were going to get him, didn't we? " June raised her head as if looking around to see if the world was still there. "I have to do something."

"I'll make some tea for both of us. Is Jeb home?"

June shook her head and sat up. "He usually comes over and tells me, wants to see if I'm here before the kids are due. I have to do something."

Marian relinquished the hand. "Like what?"

June sat in the middle of the bed, her eyes puffy. The black crepe dress she wore for work was rumpled from the emotions that had felled her. "I don't know. But I can't just sit here."

There was a noise at the front door and Jeb came in, still in a suit, his face twisted with anxiety. He knew. "Where are the kids?"

"They're over at your house," June reassured him.

"I don't want them on the street," Jeb said.

"I've already told them that," June said. "And maybe we should get the cars off the street." She stood up and shook the wrinkles out of her dress. "If you would keep Leah at your house, I'm going to go."

"Go where?" Jeb demanded. ""Don't go anywhere!"

Marian was totally alarmed. "You've just said get the cars off the street and you're going to go out there?"

"I think I'll go to the market."

"The little market? Why?"

June shook her head. The little market was just around the corner, run by Chinese. For some months it had been showing signs of the racial tension in the neighborhood. The family who owned it had blocked off everything but the counter so no one could go up and down the aisles to find what they wanted but had to ask at the counter and have it brought there. "No, the supermarket."

"There's bound to be trouble there," Jeb protested. The East Bay Democratic Club had been picketing that market off and on for some months because they wouldn't hire black checkers and June and Marian had been going there on Sundays still dressed for church to march in the picket line.

"I'll go with you," Marian said. "Wait till I change my clothes."

"No," June said. "I think we should go in our office clothes. So we look like what we are."

"I don't want either one of you to go." Jeb's voice was up in a sharp tone he rarely used.

"Jeb, you stay with the kids. I don't want any white people shooting at Leah."

"Marian, I don't want you to go. You're a mother. You belong here."

Marian shook her head though she kept her voice soft. She knew better than to get in a shouting match with Jeb. "I'll watch out for her. No one will bother me. They're used to me now."

June raised her voice. Something she never did. "They're used to us both by now. It's better when they see us together. You can take good care of the kids. We won't be gone too long. But we have to show our peaceful support."

The women had their coats on in a few minutes. Their hair brushed. The lights in June's house turned off. So, as often happened, they did what the women wanted even while Jeb continued to protest. They felt the need to rush. Jeb drove the cars to the back of the driveway and locked them, then turned to go back upstairs but stopped at the bottom step.

"I'm going to call the cops," he said.

"Please don't," June said from the driveway. Then she went to him and whispered: "If anyone starts a fire in this neighborhood, get the kids into a car and drive them away. Don't worry about us. There are friends we can stay with. We'll catch up with you later."

He nodded unhappily. "You girls are out of your mind."

"Are you sure we're not?" Marian whispered to June after Jeb had gone into the house and they were half a block down the street.

"It's just something I have to do. But you don't have to come…"

Marian said nothing because she was determined June shouldn't go alone. It was only six blocks to the supermarket and they were not the only people going there. June nodded to the people they passed on the way. "Evening!"`

No one responded.

These other people were mostly black, many with tears on their faces, but grim. With no children among them, they were all marching resolutely, ignoring the two women locked arm in arm.

The supermarket had a frontage on the street of nearly a full block. Behind that was a small parking lot big enough for two rows of cars. There were already fifty or sixty people standing on the sidewalk or in the parking lot; a few words were said here and there, but primarily people seem to be waiting for something to happen.

"We were right to come," June whispered.

"I don't think so," Marian whispered back.

Scattered among the crowd there were at five pastors, some black, some white, with their collars showing. There was also a priest in a black cassock, a thin brown man who might have been Filipino. All these leaders were trying to talk with small groups of the crowd.

"It looks safe enough," Marian whispered. "Are they going to do a picket line?"

"Mmm," June responded. "But I see the cat's tail twitching."

Indeed it was. There were small erratic movements throughout the crowd, signs of emotions barely held in, of anger or fear, waiting for some spark to ignite them.

"I wish the cops would come," Marian whispered, watching this.

"No, no," June said.

After a while, they could see that the pastors were coaxing the crowd into a line across the front of the store even though the store was closed and there were twice as many people as needed to stretch along the front. June and Marian went obediently to join this line. It did not have the character of a serious picket line. No one had signs. Probably they hadn't come planning to picket. Still they consented to line up and turned to watch the robed leaders and wait to see what happened.

Now it seemed they wanted them to sing. One pastor even had a small pipe to start the song. The song they wanted to hear was "We Shall Overcome." It rose raggedly from the unhappy crowd, but it did come up, voices joining slowly but with increasing volume.

No sooner did they reach the 'overcome' than people began to sob, one after another, till it seemed as if no one could quite complete the word. June couldn't. She reached for a handkerchief, which it turned out she didn't have with her, and Marian gave her one from her pocket. This was all too much. Voice after voice wavered and stopped and was replaced by cries and whimpers.

"Oh dear," Marian said in a low voice to replace her own sobs, amazed at her sense of loss.

"Look here!" June said.

Because a new crowd was advancing on the picketers. These

were white people, eighteen or twenty well-dressed men and women, middle-aged or older, arm in arm, coming down the street, aiming at the robed figure who had been bending his head looking for them. When they reached him, he showed his approval and began to shake their hands.

"Where did they come from?"

"Maybe St. Michaels."

"Where is that?"

"Up in the hills."

The new white contingent nodded politely at the picketers and took the places in line as they were directed to, reaching for hands of those already in line, as if it was a natural thing to join hands. In a short while, the song was started again and this time continued in full force, to be replaced shortly by "The Old Rugged Cross." June reached out a hand for another hankie and Marian dug until she found one in a different pocket.

Not everyone was absorbed in the singing. Some young men who had been standing out in the street, wearing 'show me' expressions, in faded sweatshirts and black jeans, turned away impatiently as if this was not what they had come for. They moved restlessly away, their limbs showing a tendency to ripple and stretch, as if they hadn't yet found a use for them. One by one, they started down the street toward the Lake and the center of the city. The white globes of streetlights lined the avenue and showed the surrounding streets as mostly empty. There was the picket line of singers and there was the clump headed downtown, otherwise, the neighborhood was silent.

After the hymns, the assembly began to turn into a prayer meeting. There were several prayers started by different members of the clergy. The prayers brought on more sobbing and exclamations from the crowd. The picket line was no longer a picket line but a clutch of mourners. Marian took June's arm and the two of them wept together. After a while, both their handkerchiefs were soaked and they were limp from sadness.

"We'd better go," June said. "I want to see that Leah is all right."

"Jeb will take care of her."

"I know he will. Just the same…" They stepped out of the line which had never gotten to the stage of walking up and down but was only a jumbled row of grieving men and women. Disengaging from this unity was more difficult than joining it had been. It was not easy getting away. The people they were leaving hugged them before patting them goodbye, or kissed them and clutched hands in friendship though they had been friends for only half an hour.

In the distance, a car was racing into the night, squealing its brakes, speaking of other emotions, other possible events.

They walked silently arm-in-arm. Soon they were out of sight of the market and no one else was on the street. It seemed a long way home. Most of the houses they passed were not lighted but dark and looked very different in the black of night. Marian was having trouble remembering the blocks. It was cold.

June let out a small sob and then dried her eyes. "I feel better for having been there."

"Something about it helped."

When they got back to their houses, their lights were still on.

"Lock up your house and spend the night with us," Marian instructed. June nodded, too tired to protest.

When they rang to bell for the upstairs apartment, Jeb came down the steps because he had put the chains on. He opened the door hurriedly.

"Any trouble?"

Marian shook her head. "Mostly people were too upset to make any fuss. They just wanted to be together."

She leaned up against him, happy to have the warm safety of his arms. "How about here?"

"A few cars racing around blowing horns and squealing brakes."

"Did the police come by?"

"No. When I called them, they said they were all on duty and already out to the hot spots." He put his arms around her. "I'm glad you went. It was a good thing to do. You're a good lady.

You know I support you in all this."

That brought tears to Marian's eyes as she laid her face against his neck. "Thank you."

Addie and Leah were in Addie's bed nestled among various stuffed animals. When Marian opened that door, the light was out but two pairs of eyes opened wide.

"You all go to sleep now," June instructed.

They put quilts on the Hawaiian print couch from Culver City for June, and they all climbed into beds with little talking. Tired as they were, they heard but paid no attention to the constant sound of glass being broken in the school windows across the street.

The next day was treated as a holiday and turned out to be a quiet day, as they repaired their nerves. They kept the kids indoors, made hot chocolate and popcorn, and taught the kids, even Bro, how to play Go Fish.

"I can catch up on my ironing," Marian said but June sat with a quiet Leah in her lap. Now and then they turned on the radio and listened to praise for Martin Luther King coming in from all directions.

"Most of those have been wishing him dead for the last two years," June said with unexpected anger.

But change was in the air anyway. Across the country there had been too much trauma. In Oakland, the Black Panthers began their breakfast program and moved from threats to election politics. The East Bay Democratic Club began with renewed confidence to construct coalitions across the color line. Ron Dellums won his Congressional seat in 1971 and served thirteen terms before resigning. In 1977, Lionel Wilson became the first African-American Mayor of Oakland.

## CHAPTER TWENTY-FIVE

It was already the day before the day before Marian's party. Lilly had been on the phone with Addie for quite some time. Marian registered this as an interesting fact while she was trying to vacuum and anxiety kept interfering with her breathing. Which had nothing to do with the vacuuming. Nor with the phone call. She tried to distract herself with the thought that it was wonderful, more than that, maybe half way to frightening to have Addie and Lilly in constant communication. They had fought a great deal when both were at home in spite of the twelve years between them. Addie had thought Lilly was a nuisance also a spoiled brat, while Lilly, who was nice to almost everyone and a delight all around, had thought Addie was an unnecessary evil in the family's life. If an older sister had a job and had nearly finished her education what was she doing still at home occupying a whole bedroom and using too big a share of time on the family telephone? For several years Lilly drew '*Addie faces*' in chalk or crayons or dust, with downturned mouths and waves representing anger, and left them in prominent places around the house.

What Marian was wondering about was should she call off the party. After endless minutes of going back and forth and around and around over the living room carpet, she had to admit that she was still not getting up all the tiny threads or even the grit. Instead of calling off the party, she called Bridget and begged for an hour of Maria's efforts with Bridget's superior vacuum on Marian's carpet.

After Bridget had agreed, Lilly took the phone back and

continued her call, now in the kitchen, standing at the open kitchen door.

She said to her mother: "Addie's coming down this afternoon. Should she bring a sleeping bag?"

"Tell her yes," Marian picked up the purse that she wore on her back when she bicycled. "Bridget's housecleaner Marie is coming here to work on this carpet. I'm going to the library to get my check and then to the market."

"Okay. Is there anything I need to do?"

"Probably later."

Marian pedaled to the library and picked up the first of her new paychecks. When she got back outside, she couldn't resist opening the envelope and looking at the amount. It had the first week of fulltime hours and her new higher rate. It was lovely indeed.

As she went on the few blocks to Safeway, she feasted on the cool sun and the fresh breeze and thought about Lilly being there back at the house. When did it ever happen that more than one thing went right at a time? She felt like buying treats. It was too bad she hadn't brought the car, which she seldom used because of the cost of gas.

She bought round steak, plus a pound of mushrooms and a bunch of white grapes. Then she went to the liquor section and carefully picked out two bottle of inexpensive wine. That was all that would fit in her bike basket.

When she got back home, Lilly was in the back yard unpacking her duffle bags and putting piles of faded clothes through the washing machine. Marian kissed the flushed face and said: "Should I have bought more soap while I was there?"

"Addie is coming this afternoon."

"Today?"

"Yes."

"But where will I put her?"

"Oh, she can share the spare room with me."

Anything was possible if one lived long enough. "Are you sure? What are you two talking so much about?"

"She may go up to my hospital and spend a couple of weeks surveying how they treat endemic diseases. Mother, can I use your sewing machine for some mending?"

"Yes of course, but it needs to be oiled."

Addie arrived in mid--afternoon and after a late brunch of steak with browned mushrooms, the sisters sat on the loungers in the back yard and drank wine through the afternoon and way into the evening while Marian did the dishes, contented to be listening to the friendship that was blossoming.

"Bro and Letty are coming tonight. We'll have to give them the bedroom." Addie said casually, as if that was the most normal event in the world.

"Is Bro taking time off?" Bro never liked getting the twin beds. Where to put the girls?

"Oh, I don't think so. Can we go to your friend Felicia's?"

Marian thought this over. Felicia didn't like company much. Mostly because she didn't do much housecleaning. But before she could put in a call to Felicia, Addie and Lilly had decided to sleep in the back yard. Addie had brought a sleeping bag with her and they unearthed an old one from the garage. The weather was still warm enough and there was the small bathroom downstairs.

When Bro and Letty arrived after seven, all three went outside to greet them. Letty got out of the car before Bro had turned the engine off. She winked happily at Marian before hugging her. "We've got news!"

"You got a job?"

"Oh, way more than that. Think!" The look on Letty's face, a mixture of delight and teasing, was totally new.

"You're not!"

"Yes I am. How is that for news?"

Marian put her arms around her again. "Wonderful. You're sure?"

"Oh yes. Nothing else ever felt like this."

Bro had backed the car out of the driveway and drove in again, giving Addie's Lexus plenty of room. Now he came forward, puffing slightly and wearing his usual small twisted look of anxiety, to join them at the door.

"You'll never guess," he said after kissing his mother hurriedly on the cheek. "Guess!"

"It's good to see you. What is it?" Marian said, a good sport with men, even her son.

"Well what is it you've always said would be the most important news you could get?"

"But surely you're not pregnant!"

Bro grinned widely. "It's amazing, isn't it?"

"But I thought you were going to wait till you bought all that furniture." Marian drew them into the house, keeping her protective arm around Letty.

"Well yes," Bro said, smiling at his former childishness. "But we have a few months to do that. And we're not getting any younger."

"I am, but you're not," Letty teased.

Then they all stopped because Lilly had come into the room and went immediately to her brother and pecked him quickly on the cheek. "I haven't seen you two since the wedding."

She gave Letty a light kiss before standing back to look at her. "It looks as if you're still married."

"Baby Sis!" Bro said. "We can't see you if you never set foot in the U.S."

"Alaska is part of the U.S." Lilly defended.

After that, Addie joined them and everyone was talking at once. Letty had brought a roasted chicken and potato salad and apparently they expected dinner now even though it was nearly eight. With all three daughters helping, it took only a few minutes to set the table in the dining area.

Marian sat down to observe this unfamiliar mix of all her children while they picked up their forks. Addie announced that she and Lilly were going to sleep in the back yard so Bro and Letty could have the second bedroom. Not necessary said Bro. He had called the motel downtown and made a reservation for tonight.

Marian had also been working on a plan. "I can ask Bridget for tomorrow night. Are you staying through tomorrow?"

Yes, they were staying. Bro had taken some time off for Marian's party. And he wanted to crow over the sisters who were always scorning him. He was about to produce the first grandchild. He stood up to take a mock bow. He was sorry to beat out Addie, the oldest child, but she had shown no evidence of taking this duty seriously.

The women laughed. Lilly clapped and recited some Aleut poetry in its native language. Addie offered an elaborate congratulatory statement. Marian felt her tears starting. She got up and turned toward the kitchen but Addie was ahead of her and returned with the bottle of red wine she had brought and several glasses.

"This obviously calls for a number of toasts. And we have to pick a name right away while we're all together."

Bro pulled his head back. "You women are not going to name my baby."

Addie had a good laugh at that. "I work in hospitals and I see what really happens. It's the mothers who come up with the names while the fathers stew and debate and can't decide."

"You always have some statement putting down men, don't you?"

"Stop it. No quarreling."

"I know some really good Aleut names if you're having trouble deciding. You can make sure this baby has a name no one else in his class is going to have... or be able to spell." Lilly's grin was delighted.

Letty objected: "It took me two years to learn to spell Letitia. I favor a name that is real easy, four-letter names like Mary or John."

After all the glasses were filled for the second time, Marian went to the kitchen for one of the bottles of wine she had bought. She put the leftover chicken and potato salad in the refrigerator. She should have made a green salad to add to Letty's dinner. It was too late now!

When she went back to her seat in the circle, the conversation had become general. Looking at Bro, she saw how news of a baby had changed him; he was proud and at ease with his sisters. Letty too looked happy, not scared of these sisters-in-law as she had seemed in the past. Her red blonde hair was curled in a tidy pageboy and her light blue sweater and pants fitting her curves perfectly. She looked as polished as a magazine cover.

Over the second bottle of wine, Addie teased Bro about what kind of father he was going to make. Was he going to spend years leading Boy Scout troops the way Jeb had? Letty sprang to his defense.

"I know what kind of father he's going to be. He plays with my sister's children whenever we go to Orange County."

"I wouldn't call him a perfect big brother," Lilly said. "He got me blamed for a number of things he did."

"Surely not!" Marian protested. "I never punished you for anything you didn't do."

Lilly smiled. "I said blame. I didn't say punishment."

"That's true," Addie said. "You got away with so much. The Angel child."

Marian wondered if an exercise in envy was about to erupt. She turned to Letty. "But why did you decide you could go ahead before buying furniture?"

Letty nodded to Bro. "You tell them."

"Grandpa Frank," Bro said to his mother.

"What about Grandpa Frank? He's been dead more than ten years."

"He left me a pot of money. Isn't that amazing?"

Bro sat back smiling, looking adult and handsome. Maybe it was his air of success. How could it be they had never seen that look on him before? "Grandpa Frank died right around the time that Grandpa John, my Grandpa, did," he said to his sisters.

"And this was just a couple of years before Dad died, so things got confused. We didn't find this out till Letty called

Cousin Bob to ask about some of those people you wanted to invite to your party. Cousin Bob told her to tell me to call him. So I did. He still lives in Culver City, the only one who does. He was executor of Grandpa John's estate, and he asked me did I ever get the money."

"What money?"

"Exactly what I said, so he got embarrassed and said he would call me back the next day after he looked through some papers."

"There wasn't a lot of money," Marian said. "But I did get some. That was how we were able to pay off all our debts and buy this house outright."

"But it turned out he wasn't talking about Grandpa John's money, he was talking about Grandpa Frank's. Frank and John had a conversation about Dad and you just about when you moved out of Fresno."

"I called him then." Marian remembered how Grandpa Frank had rescued her marriage after they got back from New York and were stranded penniless with Jeb's mother so she had tried again when they were leaving Fresno but found him not as receptive.

"I asked him for money then." What if he had agreed? She might have left Jeb and taken the children back to Santa Monica and filed for divorce? Think what she would have missed— Oakland and the law firm, the friendship with June and their own Civil Rights campaign, the birth of Lilly. How terrible that would have been! Her eyes prickled.

She had always thought of her life as a series of scenes which she had wandered into and then had to leave before she really knew what she was doing. Now it occurred to her that they might be a series of questions posed to her by the universe and she had maybe sometimes left before fully answering them.

Bro had the floor. "They decided Dad was doing the best he could but the trouble with both families was that there were too many girls. You and Alice and then Addie, and I guess Lilly too." Bro laughed at them all. The joke was his now.

"After you had Lilly they thought that proved them right. So Frank told John he wanted to give me his money as the only male and the one who was probably having a hard time being the only male."

"And so what happened?"

"That's what he did. Frank handed it over to John who put it in a special account because I was still young. In the middle of this, before they had told anyone, they both died. Bob only found out about it because he found the account and a couple of letters between them. How about that?"

They were all silent digesting this, looking around for the now-vanished chicken and pouring some more wine. The expression on Marian's face was hard to describe.

"Why didn't we ever know about it?"

Bro went on: "If anyone knew, it would have been Dad but then he died. Cousin Bob was supposed to be in charge and he thought we had lost track till he saw the money was still sitting there in an account after all this time."

Addie was not shy about asking. "And it was still around? And how much is it?"

"That's the amazing part, isn't it? Of course Bob's a lawyer and thinks he's very well organized but I think lawyers always hate completing things, they always have these odds and ends of old cases sitting around wondering if they might revive. The money was just sitting there all this time, not earning much of anything. About eighty thousand."

"Ohhh." Loud exclamations! Everybody sat back, looking at each other while this sunk in. Marian thought about what she could have done this past five years with an extra eighty thousand dollars. Or what she and Jeb could have done. They might have gone back to New York and taken another look. Or to Hawaii. Maybe they would have had the time to get re-acquainted. She felt his loss as a sudden blow.

She got up from the table and wandered into the living room. Some of the terror of his dying, of being left with almost no money, might have been alleviated. Facing the front door, she stopped and turned around and went back to her family. She had to admit… all right, once his familiar presence was gone, everything had to change. There had been no easy way. If she had really been desperate for money, she could have gotten a job or she could have sold the house in one of these reverse mortgages.

She went back and took her chair again and looked across the table at her children.

"Somehow the men always win out!" Addie said. The air of contentment she often wore these days had left her. She turned to her mother.

"Are you going to let him have it? You should have it."

"No," Marian said. "If Grandpa Frank left it to him, that's where it goes. He wasn't one to be overruled."

"Besides," Lilly said to her sister: "You and I are doing all right, aren't we? Maybe Bro needs it more than we do, now that he's going to produce the next generation."

"I'm not interested in producing the next generation but I would like to go back for a PhD."

Lilly went on to a new subject, laughing. "Think about this! How many middle class families in this country have misplaced eighty thousand dollars… and it's still there?"

She looked at Bro. "You're sure it's still coming?"

He nodded. "I trust Bob."

Lilly finished. "It certainly proves nobody in this family knows how to handle money. And I like that. There are more important things in life. But I do think you should give Mother a small chunk so she can take a trip."

Bro had his head down, not looking at his family. "Okay."

All sorts of potential conflicts raised their heads. Lilly's eyes stayed on him thoughtfully as if considering other demands she might make. Letty looked frozen with anxiety; she had so recently become at ease in this family and now it was at risk. Addie kept her eyes on their mother as if waiting for her to declare war but Marian was shaking her head. The last thing she wanted was conflict in this newly peaceful family.

"Pie," she offered. "And coffee. You can have it either way, caffeine or not."

She kept alert expecting that there would be at least some reactions, some crankiness, and hints of childhood resentments. But all four children settled for small pieces of pie and then moved into the living room as if to spread out and get away from the dangerous subject of money. Bro became very interested in the coming party. Was Marian really going to get to see many old friends after all these years... fifty?... sixty?

Well, yes, a number of them really were coming, including June although her husband had a conflict and she might not make it till the next day.

Addie and Lilly put on their pajamas and went out to the back yard early with their sleeping bags and flashlights. They giggled at the noise of a neighbor's dog who was not accustomed to having anyone in the yard after dark and began to race back and forth along the adjoining fence.

Finally they fell asleep and woke many hours later, on the day of the party, with sun on their faces and the sound of rain. "What's that?"

"How would I know?" Then Lilly was giggling and struggling to get out of her sleeping bag.

"What is it?"

"Come on. We have to get out of here." In minutes they were out of their bags, running across the damp lawn, dragging their damp sleeping bags behind them, and being pelted on their heads and shoulders by imitation rain. Luckily, the kitchen door was unlatched and they collided as they raced through it.

"Rain!"

"It's not rain." Addie was laughing but still indignant. "It's the neighbor's sprinklers. At 7:30 in the morning! I bet he set those last night after he knew we were going to sleep out there."

"Serves us right. How did we sleep so late? Ever since I've been in Alaska, I've been up before seven."

"Proves you'll never be a nurse. That would make you late for an eight o'clock shift."

Across the room, their mother was looking pleased at the sight of them. She had the coffee perking and was reading the morning newspaper.

"What are you doing?" Lilly asked, folding the sleeping bag and looking for a coffee cup.

"I wanted to see if there is any mention of my party in what passes for a gossip column in this paper."

"Your party?"

"Yes, that's one of the delights of a small town newspaper. I made decaf. But I can make another pot."

"The trouble with you, Mother, is that you haven't worked somewhere where they leave the coffee pot plugged in all day until there's no telling what it started out as, "Addie put in.

Lilly nodded her agreement and poured herself a cup. "Do you want one too?"

"No," Addie said. "I'm going to take a shower before everyone else gets up."

"I don't know why you think that?" Marian started to say but then decided to hold her peace. There was silence in the sunny kitchen for nearly an hour while Marian finished the newspaper and started grocery and "to do" lists. Addie went off to the shower and returned fully dressed, with her hair still wet, and picked up the paper that Marian had been reading. Lilly read yesterday's Chronicle and then went and found a book she had been reading on the airplane but hadn't had time to finish.

"Is that good?" Marian asked.

"No. If you want something to read, I've got something better in my luggage."

"Thanks, but I have a whole library to choose from. I still don't know what I'm wearing to the party and we have to take the decorations over this afternoon and make sure Felicia is doing them right. Décor is not really her thing."

"Mother I wish you would wear what I brought for you. At least put it on and see how it looks."

Marian was embarrassed. "I'm sure it was very expensive but when they don't put in any darts, I never know how it's supposed to look."

There were voices from up above and doors opening and closing. Those in the kitchen looked up and waited for more definitive sounds. "They've been up for a while," Addie said. "I don't know what they're doing.

"Letty is a lot more interesting than I remember," Lilly said.

"She's a sweetheart," Marian put in. "She spent hours working on my party list and even told Bro to let me alone."

Lilly smiled at this and went back to her book after draining her coffee cup. A little while later she accepted a bowl of cereal and bananas from Marian with a nod and there was silence in the room again.

Sometime later, Addie raised her head and said: "It's really quiet here, isn't it? I like this."

But that was the moment that there were steps on the stairs and Letty and Bro came down together, damp from their showers and still yawning though they had been up more than an hour.

The companionable silence was over.

"How is it that you people want to read first thing in the morning? I like to look at the day without worrying about all the new problems in the world," Bro objected.

"I'll make waffles," Letty offered.

"She makes really good waffles," Bro supported.

There was a general discussion about waffles while Marian and Letty got out the ingredients and the waffle iron. Bro wanted sausages if they were going to have waffles; Addie and Lilly did not. Marian got out the sausages and found there were only three small ones left. How about bacon? There was half a pound of bacon left.

When the bacon discussion threatened to go on and on, she went to get her purse. "I'm going to bicycle to Safeway anyway. I'll buy some more sausages."

"Oh, don't bicycle! That takes forever. I'll drive you," Addie said.

Letty was already measuring waffle batter. "I think you need more butter too."

"Anything else?" Marian asked at the door to the garage. Where there were no immediate replies, she closed the door hurriedly and went through to the street with Addie.

"Why is it that the moment you add Bro to any group it becomes fifty percent noisier?" she asked.

"That was always true," Addie said. "Don't you remember that? What a beautiful day!"

It was. A beautiful late autumn day; Day Glo colors splashed the Valley of the Moon, the sky was poster blue, the Bottle Brush bright red, the empty fields yellow. Clear and quiet, cool with not a breeze anywhere.

"God fell asleep!" Marian said.

"What an odd thing to say."

Addie started the car while Marian began to debate whether she should cancel the party because so few people were coming? There were only twelve who had said yes, and maybe some of those might still drop out. With the children here and Felicia and Bridget and Norm, it was enough for a party. She refused to think yet about those twelve, about the excitement of seeing them after so many years… in case they didn't come.

Why had she never thought about inviting Addie and Bro and Lilly to her party?

# CHAPTER TWENTY-SIX

It seemed impossible but the party was only hours away. Marian had been full of apprehension for so many days, it was something of a relief to have it here. She had promised herself that on the night before she would go to bed early with a sleeping pill. She had even begged this sleeping pill from Addie and placed it carefully in the drawer of her medicine cabinet.

Then after the evening with all the children around the table and several glasses of wine, after the news of a baby to come and Uncle Frank's money, she forgot the pill, of course. She fell into bed after only a quick face washing, promising herself a shower in the morning, and slept like a log and didn't remember she had planned to court a drugged sleep.

Such a momentous day was not going to appear as planned. Marian had overslept and when she did wake up it was to the sound of her shower already in use. She closed her eyes against the light and lay in bed wondering who it was in the shower until she heard Letty's voice saying 'save some hot water for me'. So that would be Bro using all the water. There could be a whole morning of her children taking showers and no moment for her to get in there.

She might as well get up and lay out the rest of her day. Now she remembered the sleeping pill lying in her bathroom cabinet and thinking that was just as well—she hadn't taken one for several years and had forgotten they could produce a bad headache the first morning after. It was maybe lucky that she had forgotten.

She put on her oldest jeans and a clean shirt and went

downstairs to use the bathroom down there. Maybe she should return the sleeping pill to Addie. But then Addie had been reluctant to hand it over, so maybe Marian should keep it in care of a need later on. Just then, when her mind was beginning to focus on the duties of the day and the possibility that the party was going to be a flop, Felicia called her with an emergency.

"What's the matter?" Marian asked in a sharper than usual voice. Felicia's version of emergencies was not the same as her own.

"I'm sorry, Mare. I really am. I've been thinking about nothing but your decorations all day and I decided to cut the flowers, well not flowers of course, weeds, now and get up there to the house with them."

Marian's mind cleared immediately and focused on the items that had to be accomplished before evening. She needed for Felicia to do as planned. "That's reasonable," she said, her voice saying—'then what can be wrong?"

"I'm really sorry to bother you…"

"What is it?"

"It's my heart medicine. I can't remember if I took it or not. I don't dare take it again."

Marian tried to lower her tone of voice. "What happens if you take it again?"

Felicia's voice became alarmed. "Don't know. I suppose it might cause a heart attack No, that would be if I failed to take it. But if I took it double dose, I guess my heart might stop."

Marian sat down and took a deep breath. All she knew about Felicia's heart was, by secondhand report, that it had to be carefully monitored. "How do you usually know if you've taken it?"

"I take it right after I've had my dinner. I always do it like that. And that works. I've been taking it for three years now."

"And that works? Then why can't you remember?"

"Because I decided not to have dinner last night because I ate a lot of lunch and I'm going to eat a lot this evening at the party. So I had it all planned. I would take all my pills this morning with a glass of water and go out and cut the flowers... weeds. The ones I planned to get from here."

"And what happened?"

Felicia was getting tearful. 'Nothing happened. I went out to cut the flowers this morning and then I thought I hadn't taken the medicine so I came back in feeling faint. Then I thought, no, I did take it. Now I don't know."

"Can you tell by how many are left in the bottle?"

"No. It's a new prescription and the bottle is almost full."

Marian tried to think rationally though she was feeling very irrational. "Well, that should be better. It should say on the label how many were in the bottle when you got it. Count them and you will know."

Felicia sounded relieved. "Thank you, dearest. Thank you. I won't bother you any more now."

Marian thought about the sleeping pill. Maybe it shouldn't be left sitting around. Bro or Letty might decide it had been accidentally dropped and throw it away. Which would be a good thing, right? Then her mind switched to the clubhouse and she thought that if she got up there tonight and there were no flowers in arrangements where they were supposed to be, then flowers were not going to get to the party. Only she and Felicia would know that they should have been there. Did it matter? No. It was an extra, what Jeb used to call 'gilding the lily.' Except it would look so bare wouldn't it, not to have any flowers there? Why had she accepted Felicia's offer instead of Bridget's? Bridget never forgot whether she had done or not done something.

She was downstairs in the kitchen only minutes before Lilly and Addie came in from the back yard trailing their sleeping bags and dropping them near the washing machine. "Good morning. I wondered if you were oversleeping."

"I never oversleep," Marian declared. "Your feet are wet."

Lilly giggled but didn't protest. She poured herself some coffee and opened the refrigerator to take out the milk, waving it toward Addie. "Is there something I need to do for you today?"

The phone rang again. It could be Bridget with some last minute crisis, but usually Bridget did not have last minute crises. Instead, of course, it was Felicia, still not knowing what to do.

"Call your doctor," Marian told her.

"I hate to tell him I was that foolish."

Marian took a deep breath and reminded herself of all the times she had been foolish and Felicia had talked her out of it. She summoned her patience. "Why don't you put your pills in your pocket when you go up to the clubhouse and wait until you feel that you need them?"

Felicia's voice rose with hope. "You're so smart, dear. Why don't I think of those things?"

After she had hung up the phone, Marian said to Lilly: "When you're through with breakfast, I want you to take the garden snips and go up to Felicia's house and help her cut weeds."

"Weeds?"

"Decorative weeds. She'll tell you. She has already made a list of places to get them."

Marian did not get her shower till mid-afternoon when the hot water heater recovered from four previous showers. When Addie had arrived yesterday from Sacramento she had brought a new dress for Marian to wear to the party. Marian had objected that she had something good enough but Addie had overruled her. Now she put on the new dress—long grey and white crepe—knowing that it would not fit because it didn't have the cut she was used to. Standing on front of the mirror she had to admit that Addie had done very well for her. It even fit though it was deliberately not close-fitting. She took the tags off without looking at the price. She knew Addie would have paid way more than Marian would have.

After she had brushed out her hair and put on a little powder, she looked at her watch. There had been no word from either Lilly or Felicia. It should have been enough time now for them to get the weeds cut and arranged and to the clubhouse. It was time for Marian to go up there and see if things were getting done. She was ready to go up even though no one else was. Addie, Bro and Letty were still chatting or dressing or looking for things they couldn't find.

"I'll see all you up there!" she called out and went out the door without waiting for replies.

She had looked forward to walking even though she was wearing shoes with heels. It was only four blocks away and the end of day was beautiful, dusky, hazy, the wind still and a glow in the sky left from the sun which had been ripening the grapes. She was glad to be alone and catch her breath. It was three weeks past her birthday; the harvest had been late this year and the cast of the sky and the land were in tune, as she would have asked them to be if she had had time to think about it.

When she was born, in the thirties, Los Angeles had probably been hot and still but without a harvest because it was nearly a desert filled only with empty acres of grazing land, small orchards, and tiny new homes awaiting the promise of scant winter rains and the new industry of movie making. A hopeful time her father had told her. The Depression had been ending. He had gotten a loan to open a hardware store and that had been enough encouragement for them to marry and start a family. The town had filled up with refugees from the Dust Bowl and the reports of war in Europe had been promising enough for the building of a new factory near the port of San Pedro.

The Clubhouse was a three-story Colonial mansion, built with cattle money in another hopeful time, shortly after gold had been discovered in Sutter's Creek. Now it's columns and balconies gleamed whitely through the evening from its setting of magnolias and roses. Marian smiled at it, grateful for this anachronism. She was glad the descendants had decided to opt for a large gift tax deduction and the community was happy to have been given the elegant space in spite of the repair bills that came with it.

A few lights were on in the house already, if not because of Felicia then probably Bridget and her winery friend. Marian went through the screen door and turned up the lights on the wide porch and the large two front rooms one on each side of the staircase and center hall.

She was greeted from a narrow table beside the stairs by the huge bouquet of dried herbs and weeds that Felicia had promised. Set in an aluminum milk pail, they extended four feet in the air and three feet to each side, a truly stunning study in tans and browns. They were not as lovely as the bundles of roses would have been a few months earlier but they were dramatic and had that dramatic Felicia design.

If Felicia had since taken a heart pill and was now lying down somewhere, at least she had done come through with this arrangement.

The party was nearly about to start, after all these months of hopefulness. Whatever may happen now was in the laps of the gods. Marian caught a glimpse in a mirror of the matching spell of her new dress in white and grey selected by Addie. Would it have been better to buy her something that matched her purple hair? She went through to the kitchen.

Here there was another light on and two stacks of trays of wine glasses, probably left by Augusto. Also here was Bridget's Maria laying out canapés.

"She's coming," the housekeeper promised.

"I always trust her," Marian smiled, "and you're wonderful to be working this late. Thank you.""

Her heart jumped. She heard the front screen door opening and hurried back to the hall. Someone was here already. She told herself that she would not be disappointed, however few people came. If no one else, Addie and Bro and Letty and, best of all, Lilly would be here soon and they would all drink wine and joke with each other, a party in themselves.

Just inside the front door, waiting by the magnificent bowl of weeds was a tall, buxom woman of her own age.

"I'm sorry," Marian said. "It's a private party!"

"Mir! You don't recognize me. I don't blame you. It's all this weight. But I do what I can!"

Marian felt faint. "Peggy?"

"No, it's Laura. It's been so long. But I would know you anywhere."

"Laura?" Marian could feel herself turning red. This was a woman she had last seen when they were nineteen. She put her arms around the stranger. "I'm so sorry."

Laura gave her a tight hug. "I told Rod you wouldn't recognize me. I was in an auto accident a few years ago and when they began to put my face together I told them they might as well improve it. Here's Rod, you will remember him."

Hugged before she was ready for it, Marian did remember him—the high school football hero, bigger and more battered but recognizable. Trying to breathe, she managed to squeeze back.

"I'm so glad you could come. I didn't see your name on the list of those who were coming. But you look great, both of you."

"Hell of a thing Jeb not being here. I thought he was the kind would go on forever." That was Rod of course. They had come to the wedding, probably the only time he had met Jeb.

"The reason I wasn't on the list," Laura said happily, "I said we couldn't come because we always go to Michigan and see Rod's dad this time of year. But he died, so here we are. Peggy thought she would come but she's ill. I tell you, if they're not dying in car crashes, they're just keeling over. Good thing you had the party this year, not next."

Marian was awash in emotions, not knowing whether to laugh or cry. Even though she hadn't been close to either of these in high school, she remembered a million small things about the two of them because that was the way of high schools—the people you knew then you remembered as if they had been part of your whole life. She remembered that Rod had gotten onto the varsity team because a guy named Falkhousen had broken his leg in the first practice of the season and Laura had been very upset because she was sure Rod would be injured and they wouldn't be able to go to the Prom together. Fifty years had fallen away in these few minutes since these two came through the door.

"I'm so glad you came," she said, and meant it, though she couldn't think anything she wanted to say to them. "Look, here is the server with the wine. Have some while I see who else has come in."

While she had been talking, Bridget had come through the door, signaled hello and gone back to the kitchen to move things along. Bridget, a bit overweight herself, but handsome in a pale blue silk Chinese robe, embroidered with scarlet and silver.

She had been followed by Bro, Letty and Lilly but not Addie for some reason.

"Oh, I like the flowers," Letty said to Marian.

"Really weeds, not dried flowers," Marian grinned. "Much cheaper. Also it's too late in the season for the wonderful roses that grow in this garden."

"It's my fault," Letty murmured. "I should have found the names sooner. We could have had the party last month."

Marian gave her a hug. "You were wonderful. Without you, no one would be coming."

Someone else from high school came and was re-introduced by Laura and Rod. Sam remembered Jeb from all those years ago and still wanted to talk about him. For some reason, she shouldn't have, but Marian was upset at his presence. After a few minutes of this, she introduced him to Lilly so they could have a Jeb-approval fest.

Bridget came back to admire Marian's dress. If you thought about it, that was somewhat ludicrous because Bridget's embroidered robe had probably cost twenty times more than Marian's. But she didn't blame Bridget for these extravagances. Ever since her second husband had returned and moved in with the fortune he had made in Silicon Valley, Bridget had treated herself to a twice a year Hong Kong shopping trip.

"You must have taken my advice and gone to the Church Mouse," Bridget said, with a grin.

Marian laughed. "You're telling me it looks secondhand. No. Addie brought it. It was from the outlet stores."

Bridget flushed at this faux pas. "I'm sorry. It looks more expensive than the outlets and we know that things in the Church Mouse were originally quite expensive."

Marian hugged her. "I know, I know. Nothing could upset me when you're furnishing all this wine. Addie picked this out and she has better taste than I do. If she chooses it, I know it will be all right. "

Her head came up. "Where did the music come from? Did you bring music as well as the wine, and the hors d'oeuvres which smell wonderful?"

"That's all because of Mario. He thinks you can't have a party without music so he brought his own player."

Marian blinked with pleasure. She would never get anything done without Bridget's friends. "He's a wonder. You're a wonder. What would I do without your help?"

Then someone came through the door that Marian knew she knew but couldn't place. Age was like a mask covering over a familiar shape with a new layer that was strange. But this was a man and there weren't many men she had invited.

She went across the room to greet the new guest, trying to guess. "You must be Phil Lucas." Someone she had been looking forward to seeing after so many years. She had to admit disappointment. Of course men of seventy were more disappointing than the women. He was as tall as she remembered, still straight and strong looking but his new layer was plump, sunburned red and with a very thin layer of hair. A small paunch came over his belt which strained to hold it in.

He blinked at her in embarrassment. "Marian, good to see you. I hope you don't mind that I came. I was coming to California anyway. I'm just sorry I never made it when Jeb was still with us. No, I'm Bill from New York."

Jeb's friend Bill who had put them up at his apartment in

New York. Who had had a girl friend named Bonnie that Marian wanted for all these years to see again. The first person she had thought about when the idea for the party came. Only she had waited too long.

She took his hand, grateful that he was there. "I'm glad you came. I'm just so sorry I didn't try to see both of you sooner. Come and meet my children."

Among the people in the front room who were now being served wine in proper wineglasses by Bridget's friend Mario, Bill's eyes fell on Letty who was looking extremely pretty and of course thirty years younger than most of the others. "Who's that?" Bill asked.

"My daughter in law." She introduced Letty and Bill.

Bill's eyes began to sparkle. Marian squeezed Letty's hand in sympathy because Letty was getting less of a good deal. But Letty was beginning to sparkle at the obvious admiration showered on her. Let Bro pay attention to his pretty wife instead of thinking of her as an addition to his income!

Marian left them to go to the front porch and look out at the lights coming through the tall trees, hearing the sounds of voices of guests walking up from the parking lot, and thinking that she was having fun. She should throw one of these every six months. Why had she waited all these years?

While she stood there wondering if she wanted a glass of wine or rather just to wait there and see who was still coming, someone came out of the dark with the familiar noise of high heels crushing the gravel of the path from the parking lot. It was a woman and as she came into the light from the front porch, Marian thought here was someone else who was so familiar and yet she was sure she hadn't seen her for many years.

"Patsy Plum from London," Marian exclaimed. "You had no trouble getting here?"

Patsy Plum would always be recognizable. It wasn't that she hadn't grown older, she had, was very thin and a little bent, but had kept her black hair color and still wore her clothes with the same panache.

"Marian!" Patsy said in triumph as she reached the steps. "You can't lose me in the wine country. I've been in this building plenty of times." She came up the wide wooden steps and kissed Marian on the cheek probably leaving a trail of fuchsia lipstick.

"I really didn't think you would come this far just for a single party." Actually Marian felt gratified. You had to do something dramatic to bring Patsy Plum all the way from London. And it was dramatic, wasn't it?

Because Patsy was looking up at the mansion and the mansion built in the 1850s but designed to look like Virginia in the 1750s with its shutters and deep porches had a *Gone With The Wind* glamour. Music came from the open doors, something that might be a Mexican version of jazz aided by guitars as was most California music. She might be seventy and close to broke but she had finally done something dramatic.

Patsy, of course, would not let her have all if it. "There's a party in Beverly Hills on Wednesday. It's political and I'm getting interested in those. But of course they cost so much. I must say Marian, you look good. I like the hair. I bet Jeb would not have approved of that when he was alive."

"You're right there." Marian said, smiling, and took in Patsy's costume which was always worth looking at. "You have to tell me why you are still living there, even part-time, in Culver City."

Patsy's conversations had always been sprinkled with little references to her superior knowledge of celebrities. Hopefully she had spent last evening with someone worth mentioning.

"You haven't met my daughter!"

Because here came Lilly dressed in a floaty white lace thing, which Marian knew had a seam coming apart down near the hem, but looking wonderful as she always did. "Lilly, here, meet someone who went to high school with me."

Lilly blinked but smiled pleasantly.

As might be expected, Patsy took in Lilly with only a glance, because lovely as she was Lilly was only a young woman not someone who was likely to invite Patsy somewhere new and exciting. While holding out a limp hand, she extended her gaze to the rest of the porch and the other people who were beginning to fill it. Here was Addie in a black knit sheath and Bro with a Western shirt and a Texas string tie. Marian didn't think she had ever had such a first-rate opportunity to spread her family out for someone from Beverly Hills.

"Addie, Bro, meet an old friend of mine from Culver City, Patsy Plum."

Like the well brought up children they were, they surrounded this odd creature who was wearing tons of make-up and midnight blue satin with a décolletage that opened to her waist.

"Pleased to meet you..." And so forth.

"Get her a glass of wine," Marian said to Bro who went inside to obey her.

But Patsy's gaze had fastened on Bill from New York. Perhaps he didn't look much like London but he was male of a reasonable age. She put on a big smile for him, waiting for an introduction from Marian.

"This is an old friend of mine from New York," Marian said.

But Bill had gotten a frightening glance of the décolletage and stepped quickly away.

Patsy was now facing the front hall with its huge bouquet of weeds, the dill waving its wands at her from between the spears of rosemary. She stepped back nervously but she was not to be distracted by any other than live bodies. "Is there anyone else here from Culver High?"

"You won't believe who is here!"

Bro had returned with a glass of red wine

"Not red!" Patsy told him. "It stains. But thanks anyway. I'm terribly tired of Scotch. Are these really your children? How did you have three?"

"It's a long story," Marian said. She felt Patsy's eyes on her as a dead weight, and wanted to sigh. Back all those years ago, Patsy could hardly be bothered to talk to Marian. Now, for some reason, she was interested and Marian didn't have any shorthand versions of the story of her life. She wanted to remember who else was coming. There were people who counted. People she had been yearning to talk to for many years when she had been buried in the law office in Oakland. Patsy was not one of those.

Caroline! Where was Caroline? If nobody else, she deserved to see Caroline. Only a year or so after she and Jeb left Fresno, Caroline and Bob had moved to Orange County where he got a much better job and then divorced her. Marian had heard all this by mail but with one problem and another, they had only seen each other one weekend in all those years.

"Addie!" She pleaded. "Maybe you can find Laura!"

Addie nodded and took Patsy's arm. "I know just the person," she said, and steered Patsy indoors. Laura had also been at high school in Culver City and maybe she would even be pleased to see Patsy, or amazed, or even just willing.

"Here's someone looking for you," Mario said beside Marian, His tray of glasses was empty and he was probably headed back to the kitchen for more but he politely pivoted the woman in front of him so that she was facing Marian.

"Caroline!" Marian said thankfully, giving her a kiss on the cheek. She needn't have worried that she wouldn't recognize her friend from Fresno. Something had kept Caroline looking exactly the same. Maybe that was the wonder of plastic surgery, or maybe just Caroline's genes.

"I would recognize you anywhere," Caroline said and gave Marian a hug. "How do you do it?"

"Me? I know I don't look the same, but you do."

"Well, not the same," Caroline said. "Your hair is definitely new, as is my face. But you look just like yourself."

"Whereas you look like a successful interior decorator. Patsy Plum would have picked you out immediately."

"Who's Patsy Plum?"

"No use worrying about her. I think she's got someone else to talk to by now. I was so afraid you wouldn't make it."

Caroline laughed. "I drove the whole way. I had no time to

get plane tickets and then call for a car rental in Sacramento or SF, so I just hopped in the car. I drive half of my life as it is. Orange County is like that, not to mention clients all the way to San Diego."

If Marian was seventy, Caroline was a few years older. She looked it but healthy and fashionable and well able to handle a successful business while charming everyone. "Your life must agree with you."

"Does it ever! I knew I was going to be happier once I got over being divorced and seeing my house and all its furniture go to someone my son's age."

"Did Bob really do that? The louse. Have you told him he was?"

Caroline grinned. "I don't have to. He's not enjoying the marriage. He likes the job and he's making scads of money but he can't deal with getting older and she's being a brat."

"Where is Curtis?"

"When he saw there was going to be a lot of money, he decided to stay with Bob. He's trying to be a musician and still needs someone to support him."

"Does he come see you?"

"Yes, and tries to find another man for me. It's all right. He's still growing up."

Marian squeezed her shoulder. "It's hard to know about kids, isn't it? I just decided Bro is going to make it. He finally got a nice wife. You need to see Addie. Can you stay over a few days? I will get my friend Bridget to put you up. You might even be able to sell her a re-decorating. She can afford it."

Caroline nodded. "I planned to stay if it was possible. It's been so long. We deserve it. So how do you like being single?"

"Better and better. If I look good it's because I spend a lot of time riding my bicycle to save money."

"If you don't have the money thing figured out yet, I'll help you."

"It's all right. I think I've got it worked out now. You will definitely stay?"

Caroline nodded.

"Then come meet Addie and Bro grown up, and then Bridget."

The ice in Marian's heart had melted. She felt it moving with the music. How hadn't she known that a party was what she needed? She looked around at the crowd. She didn't even need to talk to them... just seeing them here was enough, knowing that they were still in the world and would still like to know her and be friends.

"Mother, guess what?"

And there behind her was Lilly with—unmistakably—June.

"Oh June." They embraced.

"This is the changeling, isn't it?" June gestured toward Lilly.

Marian looked June over and noticed her tired look. She was thinner than ever with a few lines in her face. "Is he treating you well?"

"Oh yes. But not as well as you and Jeb did. He's a department head now and I have a lot of duties that go with that."

After Marian gave birth to Lilly, she had had that year of delight, and had returned to work, though not at B& B because she had promised Jeb. That year, June's husband, Lionel had received his degree in Clinical Psychology and invited June to come down and watch him be awarded the degree.

"Are you really going to go?" Marian had been indignant. "After he walked off and left you?"

"Maybe. I'll see."

June had then gone home and had a long telephone talk with Lionel. After that, Lionel had sent her a plane ticket and she had taken the plane to Westwood to see the ceremonies. Lionel was being interviewed for several possible University jobs and was about to take one. He wanted to know where June would prefer to live.

"You mean you're going to go live with him?" But don't we have a good life, Marian thought.

But June was ready to go back. She explained it would be

good for Leah to have a father on the faculty of a university, to have a father at all. She accepted and he took a job in Claremont out east of Los Angeles. Marian cried for several days, out of sight of June and Jeb. After June left, Marian was buoyed by Lilly who was turning out to be the delight that Marian had promised herself. Lonely, she made friends again with Jeb and Jeb was contented with this new version of his family.

Since then, she and June had visited only once. "Can you stay? At least a few days?"

June shook her head. "But," she said with a grin. "In December, he's going to a big conference back East, and I thought I would come up and stay for a week or you can come down."

"Yes. Absolutely, you come up. I have two bedrooms, and there are loads of small trips to make—to the ocean and the mountains and all the wineries. All those trips we talked about and never had the time or the money for."

Their hands came together and they laughed, the long friendship restored. Marian went on: "Addie was hoping to see Leah. Did she come?"

June shook her head. "That girl started a catering business. She almost never takes a day off. She's making so much money that everything we used to earn looks like nothing at all."

"And," Marian laughed. "I hear she's got a daughter who's a ballet dancer."

"Artemis! She's only in ballet school but she's cute as a bug. We'll have to wait and see how far it goes."

Marian took June's hand. "This was what I needed. Thank you for coming."

"I'm sorry about Jeb. He was a very good man."

"He was, wasn't he?' She looked around the room and felt the light that Jeb had brought to her life. It was near her even now. Sensing it, looking around at her family and friends, she felt the tears she hadn't shed for him finally start.

IF YOU ENJOYED

**THE LIGHT IN HER WINDOW**

LOOK ON AMAZON FOR THESE OTHER BOOKS BY

**Mary Lou Peters Schram**


*KLIK*
a San Francisco radio station in the '70s.


*Taddy and Her Husbands\**
an impoverished runaway to San Francisco in the sixties
marries a succession of wealthy men


*Pursuing Happiness . . . One More Time\**
four friends in an adult community look for love


*Molly's Leap\**
the daughter of Phyllis from *Pursuing Happiness*
fighting the real estate wars


*\*available on Kindle*

www.ingramcontent.com/pod-product-compliance
Lightning Source LLC
Chambersburg PA
CBHW062127170626
46813CB00002B/598